The Peveretts of Haberstock Hall

Meet the philanthropic Peverett siblings: unconventional, resourceful and determined to make a difference in the world.

Raised at Haberstock Hall, Anne, Thea, Thomasia and Rebecca know that they have the means and the knowledge to help those less fortunate than themselves. Each with their own mission, they won't be dictated by the patriarchal confines placed on them. But is the world ready for the sisters to make their mark?

Generous in spirit and heart, can these women find men who will be their advocates rather than adversaries?

Meet the men worthy of these kindhearted women in:

Anne and Ferris's story
Lord Tresham's Tempting Rival

Thea and Edward's story
Saving Her Mysterious Soldier

Both available now

And in Thomasia's and Rebecca's stories

Coming soon!

Author Note

For this note, I wanted to focus on the backdrop of the Crimean War from the British perspective. First, this is the first war captured in photographic images by Roger Fenton. Second, the telegraph made it possible for reporters, like William Howard Russell of the *London Times*, to give the public a real-time look at events. It also exposed the military's incompetent managing of British troops. About two hundred and fifty thousand allied troops were lost due to illness and sanitation problems, and 25 percent of British soldiers who left to fight in the Crimea never came home. The Scutari hosptial, where our heroine works, became the reform project of Florence Nightingale, who cleaned the place up using her own funds to buy food and cleaning supplies. Mary Seacole, who was a Jamaican British nurse, established the British Hotel (hospital) in Balaclava. Readers can learn more about Mary and the British Hotel in William Peverett's story.

Meanwhile, at home, public discontent with British handling of the war led to the January 1855 snowball riot and severe upheaval in Parliament. You can read more about these developments over on my blog, bronwynswriting.blogspot.com.

The Scutari hospital was located in Turkey, across the Black Sea from Sevastopol. British ships would ferry soldiers over from battle, sometimes taking as long as thirteen days to make a crossing. Before Florence's arrival, the hospital was a death trap full of Crimean fever and dysentery. Florence and her nurses battled with British military daily to improve those conditions.

BRONWYN SCOTT

Saving Her Mysterious Soldier

HARLEQUIN®
HISTORICAL™

Recycling programs
for this product may
not exist in your area.

ISBN-13: 978-1-335-40755-9

Saving Her Mysterious Soldier

Copyright © 2021 by Nikki Poppen

This edition published by arrangement with Harlequin Books S.A.

For questions and comments about the quality of this book,
please contact us at CustomerService@Harlequin.com.

Harlequin Enterprises ULC
22 Adelaide St. West, 41st Floor
Toronto, Ontario M5H 4E3, Canada
www.Harlequin.com

Printed in U.S.A.

Bronwyn Scott is a communications instructor at Pierce College and the proud mother of three wonderful children—one boy and two girls. When she's not teaching or writing, she enjoys playing the piano, traveling—especially to Florence, Italy—and studying history and foreign languages. Readers can stay in touch via Facebook at Facebook.com/bronwynwrites, or on her blog, bronwynswriting.blogspot.com. She loves to hear from readers.

Books by Bronwyn Scott

Harlequin Historical

Scandal at the Midsummer Ball
"The Debutante's Awakening"
Scandal at the Christmas Ball
"Dancing with the Duke's Heir"

The Peveretts of Haberstock Hall

Lord Tresham's Tempting Rival
Saving Her Mysterious Soldier

The Rebellious Sisterhood

Portrait of a Forbidden Love
Revealing the True Miss Stansfield
A Wager to Tempt the Runaway

The Cornish Dukes

The Secrets of Lord Lynford
The Passions of Lord Trevethow
The Temptations of Lord Tintagel
The Confessions of the Duke of Newlyn

Visit the Author Profile page
at Harlequin.com for more titles.

For health care workers everywhere who stand on the front lines of unseen battles. Thank you for standing in the breach for us.

Prologue

British Barrack Hospital, Scutari, Turkey
March 10th, 1855

We're going home. The words drew Edward to the surface of his fever dreams, towards the pain that awaited him upon waking. It was not a journey he cared to make often but he did it to hear the mellifluous alto tones that heralded the return of his angel. He would be hard-pressed to classify her as an angel of mercy. Not when she scolded him when he resisted his medicine and crossly cajoled him into eating his food when he'd prefer to starve himself into oblivion or badgered him into living when he'd prefer to do otherwise. But she was an angel, nonetheless. *His* angel.

He'd come to depend on the touch of her cool hand on his brow, the competent fingers that soothed the burns on his chest with aloe and kneaded the wrecked muscle of his thigh where the Minie ball had pierced it. Those hands, that voice, were the sum of his world. That and the pain. Those had become his constants the moment the Minie ball had hit him, shattering his leg, shattering his memories.

If there'd been life before that moment, he didn't know what it was or who he'd been in it. He only knew who he was now: Edward, she called him, and he was to call her Thea. His angel. Edward and Thea, the only two people in his little world of hands and voices.

'Major Lithgow is arranging everything. We leave tomorrow,' his angel explained as she massaged his ruined leg, strong fingers digging into the tissue. 'We'll take a ship to Marseilles, then go overland to Boulogne and sail to England from there. It's the route I took upon arrival here in the autumn. We will take it slowly, you needn't worry. The nursing corps did the journey in two weeks coming out, but I think Major Lithgow has arranged for us to do it in three. There will be a chance for you to rest between stages.'

She was giving him plans and details, rebuilding his world by offering him things to remember in that no-nonsense tone of hers that dared him to summon his own seldom used voice to disagree with her. It made him feel less alone and more connected; it made dying harder. His angel was counting on him, fighting for him whether he wanted her to or not. 'I will be with you every step of the journey,' she assured him.

He found his voice, raspy and unused; so little these days was worth the effort it took to speak, but she was. He would find his voice for her. 'They can spare you?' He knew they couldn't, not for the effort of sending one man home. His angel ran this ward. She was everywhere. When he couldn't keep his eyes open to watch her, his ears strained for the sound of her stride, fast and staccato, to hear her voice as she gave orders.

'Florence needs me in England. She absolutely insists that I am more valuable to her there than I am here.' Her reply was brisk, almost as if she were trying to convince herself it was true. She moved around the bed to his other leg, massaging it even though it had not been wounded. Massaging kept his muscle healthy, she'd told him. He didn't care what the reason was. He liked her touch. It made her the tiniest bit more human, not a dream that would disappear. 'The Sanitary Movement needs me to make the case in England now that the war's mismanagement has made the Movement's platform about health and hygiene of paramount importance. I am to share first-hand, through letter writing and lobbying the papers, the experience we're having here with those in London who have influence, although I dare say I can write letters from here. Florence insists it's not the same as being in England, where I might be available to give talks if needed.'

He heard the reluctance in her voice. She didn't want to leave, although it was beyond him why anyone would choose to stay here. This was a place where men came to die, which made it all the more fantastical that he was being allowed to leave. People had been expecting him to die for months now, all except his angel.

'Why am I coming?'

'Because England will do you good.' She gave him a smile, still trying to reassure them both the return home was for the best.

Because if he stayed here without her, he would die.

His angel understood it was the force of her will that

had kept him here this long. She let another smile gloss over that fact. 'When we get home, you'll get well; we'll make your leg strong again. When it is, we'll walk in summer meadows beneath blue skies, we'll pick strawberries from the fields and feast on their sweetness until our hands are sticky from their juice.'

She was a poet with her words and the picture she painted of strawberry meadows and blue skies sounded like heaven, smelled like it too, a place so far removed from the stinking hell of pain and fever he currently lived in. He managed a grunt. She was teasing him, of course, dangling a carrot in front of him so that he didn't decide to die tonight. It wasn't so much that he *wanted* to die. What man did? It was just that he wasn't sure he wanted to live. What was there to look forward to in this misery where he found himself? A man whose world was defined by his pain. A man who had no notion of who he was or where he was from, only what his angel told him.

She pressed a cool kiss to his brow. 'Sleep well, Edward. I'll see you in the morning.'

He managed the same one word reply he gave her each night. 'Maybe.' He breathed her in, all clean herbs and lavender, a moment of escape from the foul smells of the hospital. In that brief space, he was sure he felt her smile against his brow. One more day, he thought as he sank back into the fever and the nightmares that waited, his strength spent. For that smile he'd give her one more day.

Chapter One

Three weeks later, Hertfordshire, England
April 2nd, 1855

Thea had forgotten how quiet Hertfordshire was. It grew quieter still, the farther they got from the train station, until the only sounds were the snorts of the horses in their harnesses and the muffled rumble of the wagon wheels rattling in the ruts of the country lane as it made its jouncing way towards Haberstock Hall. It was quiet enough to hear a man breathe. That was what worried her. The man on the stretcher beneath the canvas-covered wagon wasn't so much breathing as moaning.

The rough ruts of the road had taxed the last of his strength, whatever had remained after three weeks of travel by every type of conveyance and route imaginable: overland, over sea, by ship, by train, by wagon. The man was pale, his breathing sharp and rapid against the pain of the enforced movement of the road. She did not like the look or sound of him.

Thea tucked a blanket about him. 'It's just a little farther, and we'll be home.' Well, *she'd* be home. She had no idea where his home was, other than somewhere in England. She knew little about him, only that she had to save him. Something deep within her required it, just as she knew if she'd left him behind he would have died. He might die anyway.

He coughed, a rattly, worrisome sound that had her checking his forehead for signs of recurrent fever. He'd not had one since Marseilles and she'd hoped perhaps it was gone for good. Apparently, that was too much to hope for. He was hot to the touch. She reached for her valise and took out the bottle of poppy syrup, debating another dose. He'd have to be moved from the wagon and taken upstairs once they arrived. It would not be an easy or comfortable move for him, and she hated subjecting him to more pain. 'This will help.' She hoped. She'd hoped bringing him home to Haberstock would help too.

Uncharacteristic doubt swamped Thea. Perhaps she'd been wrong to risk the journey. The barracks hospital at Scutari, the medical headquarters of the British military presence in the war-torn Crimea, with its fevers and disease, was a decidedly *long* way from the cool, clean peace of the English countryside. It was not a journey to be undertaken lightly with a sick man. But to remain at Scutari for a spring and summer punctuated by bouts of dysentery and cholera would have been a certain death sentence for him. Such a fate was unacceptable to her.

He'd not survived a winter of fevers simply to succumb to a summer of cholera, not when she could save him. *If* she could get him home: home to Haberstock Hall, a healthy, bright place full of healing; to her father, Dr Alfred Peverett, who'd been saving lives in Hertfordshire for years, and who was a renowned proponent of the Sanitary Movement. Surely, he could save the life of a soldier whose worst enemies seemed to be the ravages of dirt and filth and his own mind.

She'd felt certain, when the idea had first come to bring Edward home with her, that if she could get him home to an English spring, all would be well. But, looking at him now, lying on the stretcher, pale and shivering, his face taut with pain, she was no longer so certain.

'You *cannot* die on me, not when we have come so far—' she whispered the admonishment, a cross scolding, daring him to thwart her plans '—not now, when help is on the way.'

Not before you tell me your name, your people. You will not die alone and forgotten.

She'd made that vow before, at the bedsides of far too many men who would not see English shores again. She had a satchel at her feet full of letters and tokens she'd promised to see delivered to loved ones in their stead: letters and tokens they would not live to deliver themselves. Her promises were assurances that they would not be forgotten, that their families would have something to recall them by.

'We're nearly there,' the driver called to her, and Thea moved forward to peer over his shoulder at familiar surroundings: the turn towards Haberstock Hall, the tall brick chimneys coming into view over the last rise just before the whole house was revealed. Home. Hope.

Her heart gave a kick as the house appeared, a rambling, comfortable country estate at the end of the drive, a brick Elizabethan manor. There'd been a healer at Haberstock Hall for centuries. She'd once thought that healer could be her, back when she'd not understood the limitations society placed on gender. But the next healer would be William, her twin. William, who was still away, doctoring on the front lines of the Crimea in Sevastopol.

It wouldn't be the same being here without him. Without any of them. After years of living daily with her siblings, the Peveretts were now flung far and wide into new places, new lives: her sister, Anne, was in London, married with a new infant boy Thea had yet to see. Her youngest sister, Thomasia, was up north with their aunt, expecting a child at any moment by Thea's calculations. Her other sister, Rebecca, was there as well, to be on hand to help out with the newborn. Becca would likely stay the summer.

Only her parents remained at home. Like the rest of Hertfordshire, Haberstock Hall would be quiet. Just what her patient needed—a quiet, clean place where he might recover his health, his mind, where he might find his place in the world once more. Not unlike herself.

Thea settled beside Edward, checking his heated brow and noting the sweat that stood out on his skin. From fever or pain? Both? She murmured soothing words in the hope of offering a promise of comfort. 'It won't be long now; one more move and you'll be settled.' That made one of them at least. For her, being home threw into sharp relief the question of who she would be now that she'd been to war, had stood on the front lines of death and battled for men's lives. She'd had a place in Scutari, a sense of who she was. She didn't have that here. Here, she only knew what she wasn't, what she couldn't be.

The wagon halted and Edward coughed, growing agitated despite the dose of poppy syrup. His demands on her attentions pushed aside more existential concerns. He needed her in the here and now. She made to move towards the back of the wagon but his grip on her hand wouldn't let her leave.

'Where are we?' he rasped, putting a whole three words together. It was a veritable oratory coming from him.

Thea bent near, smoothing damp, dark blond hair back from his face. 'Home, just as I promised.' She gently disengaged and this time he let her go, perhaps placated by her words or the effects of the syrup.

At the back of the wagon, one of her father's grooms waited to help her down. 'Welcome back, miss.'

The words were hardly out, his greeting barely acknowledged before she began issuing orders. There was no time for formalities. 'Simms, there's a man inside who needs our attention. Get a few others to help you move him upstairs.' She glanced at the steps where her parents waited, the staff assembled to welcome her home, and marshalled her troops, starting with the housekeeper. 'Mrs Newsome, we need a room readied, and have Cook heat water for washing.' The words galvanised the staff into action, Mrs Newsome directing the two maids while her parents raced forward. Homecomings might be rare occurrences at Haberstock Hall, but emergencies were not.

Thea offered her assessment in rapid tones as her father joined her. 'He has recurring fever, intestinal pain, a cough—brucellosis, I think.' The men lowered the stretcher from the wagon and protectiveness surged.

'Carefully now, watch his head.' Edward groaned and she was beside him in an instant, murmuring her soothing litany. 'You're going to be fine. These men are helping you. I'm here.'

She directed the stretcher into the front hall, up the oak staircase and down the long corridor to the room Mrs Newsome and the maids were hurriedly preparing. It wouldn't take much. A room was always at the ready at Haberstock Hall. Her father was beside her. Someone ran up with his bag from the surgery, no doubt sent by her mother, who would be overseeing things from downstairs. Peveretts were good in a crisis.

'How long has he been this way?' Her father reached into his bag, pulling out his stethoscope as the men settled Edward on the bed. Edward shivered and she pulled the covers up to his waist.

'Since he was brought in after the Battle of Inkerman in November. He was wounded by a Minie ball in the thigh.' Thea gently lifted his nightshirt, revealing the burns on the right side of his chest. Even with her care, he inhaled sharply. 'He got the burns perhaps from a torch at Inkerman after the fog rolled in or from trying to fire a cannon. We aren't sure,' she explained, stepping towards Edward's head as her father placed the stethoscope to his chest. He moved to Edward's clavicle, all the better to listen to his lungs, Thea knew. She knew, too, what her father would hear there: the sharp, rattling inhalations that caused his cough.

Her father stepped back, thoughtful, as he stroked his chin. He watched her with grey eyes. 'What do you believe causes the cough, daughter?' This was the old ritual, the one he'd used to train her and William, making them think instead of handing them an answer on a silver plate. It had done more than make them think; it had made them defend their convictions, taught them not to doubt. She'd relied on that confidence countless times in the Crimea to stare down military doctors who thought they knew better. She called on that confidence now.

'I think it's damage from smoke inhalation, perhaps an impaired respiratory tract, but I can't be sure. I *hope* it's not the latter.' That would be more difficult to mend. 'I hope a cooler, cleaner climate will help his lungs heal in ways they could not in Scutari.'

'He is not coughing up blood?' her father asked, making a short examination of the thigh wound.

'No.' It was one thing to be thankful for: no signs of consumption. She pulled Edward's shirt down and drew the covers up.

'Then your assessment is as good as mine. Time will tell about his lungs. His burns are healing. You've been using your mother's aloe and honey on them,' her father noted appreciatively. 'His leg is mending, although the muscle will need significant exercise if he's to walk again. But these are not the things that cause him to suffer as he is now. He's thin—too thin,' her father mused. 'That would be the fault of the brucellosis and whatever other bacteria he's encountered, his diet is at fault as well.'

He fixed her with a penetrating stare as he delivered his diagnosis. 'We can cure him, Thea. There's nothing wrong that time and good care can't fix.' Those were the words she'd travelled a continent to hear and yet there was none of the expected relief. The unspoken 'but' hung between them as her father steered her out into the hallway. 'He has to want it, Thea. He has to *want* to get better.'

'He does,' Thea insisted. 'He's fought for months against enormous odds; the conditions at Scutari alone were enough to kill a man when the nursing corps arrived.'

Her father arched a greying brow. 'Be sure you're not confusing who did the fighting.' He lowered his voice. 'It's not enough for you to want it for him, daughter. *He* has to fight for himself. *He* has to have a reason of his very own.'

Thea met her father's stare with a steady gaze. 'That's rather difficult, given that he doesn't even know who he is.' This was the mystery she'd brought him home to solve. Why did a man with no head wound or brain trauma not remember who he was, or where he was from? A look of understanding passed between them, one healer to another. 'I couldn't leave him, Father. How terrible it must be to be trapped in an injured body, unable to do anything for oneself, to be so alone and imprisoned in a living, waking nothingness without even a name to call his own.' And so, against the advice of the doctors who'd taken a single look at him and consigned him to death, she'd given him one: a name, a single word to hold onto in the darkness, something from which he might fashion a new self, should the old self remain elusive. Today she'd given him something else to go with that name: a home. If she couldn't give him his memories, she'd build him a new world.

Home. Edward shivered beneath the blankets, wanting desperately to feel warm, to stop his teeth from chattering, his head from pounding, his gut from roiling. Home was supposed to be a refuge, a safe haven. But he was not safe from his ailments. Perhaps that was because being home should mean something to him, something significant, and it didn't. Like his name, home felt empty, borrowed.

Perhaps he'd been expecting a miracle, that being home would cure his ailments, restore his memories. Angels performed miracles, didn't they? Why should his angel be any different? She'd brought him to this place of fresh linen and clean smells, this place of quiet and peace where men didn't cough and moan day and night. That should be miracle enough, but it wasn't. This wasn't his home. He felt he should know if it was. A man would intuitively know his home.

Frustration surged with fever. Why did nothing make sense? Why wouldn't the memories come? Surely, he was more than aches and pains and brokenness? A man's hand touched him gently on the shoulder. 'I'll help you wash.'

Edward stiffened at the contact. He'd been touched and prodded too often by strangers in the past months. He wanted no one's hands but hers. Where was his angel? She'd promised to stay with him. She would *not* leave him in a strange place with strange people. He knew nothing, not where he was or who he was, but he knew her, and she would not abandon him.

With fever strength, he gripped the man's hand, stalling him. 'Where is she? Where's my angel? I want her. Only her.'

Chapter Two

She was beside him in minutes. He had only to summon her and she appeared. It was rather impressive really, although in hindsight he felt a bit of a cad for having done it. He'd pulled her away from her family and her homecoming because he was jealous that she *had* a homecoming. This wasn't his home; these weren't his people. Did he have them? People? A home? He'd been selfish. He didn't want to share her. Perhaps he'd never been good at sharing, not like she was. She shared effortlessly and gave selflessly.

'Are you well?' Her cool hand was at his brow. 'You feel better.' She confronted him, hands on hips. 'You'd best have a good reason for interrupting my supper.' Oh, how he loved that acerbic, clipped tone of hers, always scolding and never meaning it.

'I missed you,' he managed to rasp out. He could only manage so many words. He saved them all for her, each one hoarded like miser's gold so that he might have the treasure of her conversation.

She smiled and pulled over a chair to sit beside the

bed. The loneliness in him eased. She was going to stay. She wasn't going to desert him and rush back out. She poured him a cup of water and helped him to drink, their hands curling together around the cup. He swallowed and willed his throat to work. 'Is this place your home? Haberstock Hall?'

'Yes.' A soft smile took her face, softening its sharp planes. She was pleased to be home, to be in the place she loved so much. 'You remembered.' He pretended some of that smile was for him as well, that his remembering had also pleased her. Of course, there'd never been anything wrong with his memory since he'd been brought in from the battlefield. It was everything in the past that he couldn't remember. He had no difficulty with the present. That day at Inkerman had divided his life into two eras: the remembered days after the battle and the unknown that preceded it.

'You told me about your home on Christmas Eve. There was a plum pudding for supper that night at the hospital and I managed to keep it down.' He continued to attempt to dazzle her with his memory. She might be surprised to know all the details he remembered: how her voice sounded, how she smelled, what she looked like, her dark hair coiled in a neat bun at her neck, a few curls escaping from her carefully tied kerchief, her dark gown, her white apron, her eyes the colour of fine cognac with their amber lights.

'You fed me stories of holidays at Haberstock, of banisters draped in evergreens, wreaths with red bows and mischievous mistletoe balls hung throughout, of tables groaning with homemade delicacies, puddings and pies, of Christmas geese stuffed with chestnuts, candied fruits, marzipan and oranges.' What he would have given for just a slice of a Christmas orange. He'd enjoyed her tales that night as much as he'd enjoyed his plum pudding.

Now he was here in the bosom of her home and family, a family, who'd not forgotten her even when she was a continent away. 'Do you know what else I remember about Christmas?' he asked, desperate to keep the conversation going, to keep her beside him. 'You opened your box of gifts with me.'

'Yes, I did.' She gave a little laugh and reached over to turn up the light. 'Do you remember who gave me what?' she quizzed. She did it for him, he realised, these little prompts that proved he was capable of remembering, that were meant to provide him with hope that other memories would return in time. But it had been five months. He was starting to wonder if they would return.

He cleared his throat. 'Rebecca sent you the little watercolour of flowers in a glass jar that she painted all in purple, because that's your favourite colour.'

'Blue-violet, actually,' she corrected, and he gave a hoarse chuckle.

'Yes, blue-violet, not purple,' he amended with mock seriousness. 'How silly of me to not note the difference.' They laughed together. He liked that—the two of them laughing together in the lamplit darkness. How many times had she made him laugh in the dark at the hospital? How often had that laughter eased him to sleep?

'Your mother and sister Anne, the one in London with the new baby, sent lavender and honey, and more aloe.' He went on with his recitation of gifts—gifts that were meant for her but had been used on him: the aloe for his burns, the honey for his throat, the lavender for his solace. 'Your sister Thomasia knitted you a scarf. It was blue-violet, I believe,' he was careful to point out with dry wit.

The herbs and aloe had been wrapped in the scarf and they'd left their scent behind on the soft wool. He'd been too tired to keep his eyes open. His angel had placed his hand on the yarn, on all that softness. She'd held it to his nose, letting him breathe it in. The joy of that must have shown on his face. She'd whispered to him, 'Raise your head just a little and I'll wrap it about you.' He'd found the strength for that. What a gift it had been to lie there, listening to his angel read the London papers sent from her father while he breathed in hope and peace.

'You've forgotten William,' she teased him, calling him back to the present.

'William sent the lemons. Three of them, in a netted bag. You squeezed them into my water and made me drink it,' he groused but they both knew it had been the most delicious thing he'd drunk in months. She'd shared every gift she'd received. He often wondered how many other men she'd made lemon water for. How many others had she shared her gifts with? Had she read the London papers to the other men? Probably. But he was certain no one else had worn the scarf. He sighed. 'All the men loved you, our Lady of the Night.' She'd fought for them against the hospital director, Menzies, by day over food, over medicine, blankets and baths, and comforted them by night. How many more would have died if not for her? Him, certainly.

He shifted on the clean sheets, his body still marvelling at the feel of fresh linen against his skin. He was getting sleepy and his throat hurt from so much use, but he wasn't ready for her to go. 'Now it's your turn. Tell me the story about how you knew I was going to live.'

She blushed in the lamplight. 'Are you sure you want that one? It's a little morbid.'

'I'm sure,' he croaked, managing a smile. 'It has a good ending.'

The day hadn't started well. A ship had arrived at dawn, carrying more wounded from Inkerman, although heaven only knew where they'd put them. The hospital was at capacity. It was mid-morning and the wounded were still being carried off the ship and sorted into piles: the living and the dead—those who'd died in transit before they could get off the ship. If the voyage didn't finish them off, Scutari would. She'd been at the hospital for two weeks, long enough to know it was more of a fever ward than a place of healing. Scutari was used to do nothing more than segregate the infectious from those who might survive their battle wounds. Of course, the nursing corps was working on changing that, one day, one ward, one man at a time. At times, like today, it seemed an impossible battle.

'Living to the right. Dead to the left.' The order was given ad nauseam in the monotonous tones of Menzies' second-in-command, Lieutenant Stewart, as if he were sorting bags of flour instead of men, lives, just feet from where Thea oversaw the washtubs. The man was utterly without compassion or regard. Men were merely another commodity to him. Thea had gone toe to toe with him before. It had not been a pleasant experience.

'What about this one, Lieutenant?' He's nearly gone. Didn't think he'd last the night. Lost five quid on it.' Two men laid a stretcher down for the lieutenant's inspection. *'Dead by noon, for sure.'*

'To the left, then. He'll be dead before the burial detail gets to him.' Stewart dismissed them with a wave. *'Next—dead to the left, living to the right.'*

That was beyond the pale. Anger surged through Thea at the callous dismissal of a wounded, living man. She could do little for the dignity of the dead in this place, but she would not stand for disregard of the living.

'Jane, take over for me.' She wiped her hands on her apron and strode forward, her voice raised with all the authority she could summon as one of Florence's lead nurses. This was her ward. She was the nurse in charge in here, not that it meant much to Menzies' men. *'What's going on, Lieutenant? Is this man alive?'* Others stopped working to stare.

Stewart gave her a sneer. *'Just doing my job, Miss Peverett, sorting the living and the dead. Do you have an issue with that?'*

'I do when the living are consigned to death prematurely.' Thea held his gaze for a long moment before she knelt to the stretcher. The man was pale, lifeless already, his breathing barely perceptible. She didn't want to admit it, but Stewart might be right. This man was beyond them, somewhere between life and death. Still, he deserved better.

Thea glared up at Stewart. They'd drawn a crowd now and she wasn't going to back down. *'Living men get a bed. As long as he breathes, he is to be treated as such. Menzies' own orders. I'd hate to report that his lieutenant almost buried a man alive. There are words for that 'mistake'. Incompetence. Murder. Court martial. None of them would look good in your file.'*

Stewart blanched but he was conscious that the last time they'd gone toe to toe he'd not come out on top. He had to save face. 'He'll be dead within the hour.'

'I don't think so.' She was about to rise when she saw it, the droplet glistening at the corner of the man's eye as it hovered on dark lashes, a single tear beginning its slow descent down a pale cheek. A man who could still conjure a tear hadn't given up all hope of life, not yet. She would fight for that man. Thea gently touched her finger to it and stood, brandishing her wet fingertip with its glistening tear. 'Do you know what this is, Lieutenant? Proof of life. Dead men don't cry.' She didn't wait for a response. She pushed past Stewart. 'Gentlemen, bring the stretcher. Let's find this man a bed.'

'And so you did. The end. But to *what* end?' Edward finished for her in hoarse, weary tones. He needed to sleep.

She fixed his evening draught for him. 'To be here, to be home in England. To get your memories back. You *will* get them back,' she assured him as he drank. 'And when you do, we'll sort it all out. But first you have to get better.' She took the cup before giving his hand a final squeeze and leaned over to turn down the lamp. 'I'll see you in the morning.'

'Maybe.'

She smiled in the dark at the words.

* * *

She smiled all the way back to her room, three doors down the hall. It did her good to see Edward in better spirits and showing some early resilience from the travel. It was proof that, despite today's setback, he was getting stronger. That smile lasted until she shut the bedroom door behind her and reality was finally allowed to sink in. She was *home* at Haberstock Hall, in the bedroom of her girlhood—a room she didn't have to share with anyone.

Someone had thoughtfully laid out her nightgown and unpacked her things. A lamp had been left burning; Rebecca's painting of blue-violets was propped up on her writing desk. Each of these were luxurious little acts of consideration, done by people who knew her, people to whom she didn't have to prove herself anew every day, who accepted her as she was.

That acceptance had been in evidence from the moment she'd stepped down from the wagon this afternoon, giving orders. It was, no doubt, not the homecoming her parents had envisioned, but they and the staff had been more than adequate to the tasks at hand without questioning her or scolding her. But that was where the acceptance ended—at the borders of her family. Haberstock village had made it plain years ago that she was an odd duck, a woman wanting to study medicine, to follow in her father's footsteps instead of her mother's. She might be allowed to accompany her father on his medical visits, but she'd not be allowed to practise medicine on her own. Things changed slowly in small villages and sometimes not at all.

The window was open to let in the breeze of a spring

evening and Thea glanced towards the window seat, half expecting to find her mother awaiting her despite the hour, curled up on the seat, her latest herbal tract in hand. But only half expected.

Her mother was wiser than that. As much as her mother might have wished for a cosy conversation with her newly returned daughter, she had understood the import of her daughter facing this moment of home-coming on her own: that it was time for her daughter to recognise what this meant for her—she was home alone, without her siblings. But for how long? What would her path be next?

Thea strode to the window and let the cool air wash over her. She closed her eyes to better take in the sounds of the evening, but there was scarce little to hear, only the croak and ribbit of the frogs, the chirp of the crickets, and in between them just silence. Just stillness. There was no stillness in Scutari. There was only constant movement, constant sound. Even at night. There were the moans from the sick, the rustle of her room-mate, Jane, as she prepared for bed, the rap on the door as a nurse stopped by to double check instructions, an urgent summons from Florence to discuss the latest crisis. There was always something that commanded her attention.

Thea could not recall the last time she'd slept an entire night. She was always up, always making rounds, snatching sleep in naps. But here there was nothing, no demands on her night. No one needed her.

Except Edward.

For now.

He wouldn't need her for ever. One day he'd be well,

his mysteries solved. He would go back to his family, whoever they were, wherever they were. He'd return to his old life, and she would go on with hers. She leaned on the windowsill and looked out. Would it make her happy to go back to being her father's assistant again? The one people asked for only after ascertaining her father or William were unavailable? It was a far cry from being in charge of a ward, from issuing orders and arguing with officers, from saving lives on a daily basis. Would she return to London and the Harley Street Establishment for Gentlewomen During Illness where she and Florence had worked? Or back to London to champion the cause of the Sanitary Movement? Tonight, she missed Scutari.

Thea turned from the window, pushing the thought away. What was wrong with her that she *preferred* a battlefield hospital to being home? She still had battles to fight, she reminded herself. She'd come to wage a political battle for the soldiers suffering in the Crimea from a lack of decent care. She'd promised soldiers to deliver their final tokens. There was Edward to mend. He was counting on her to have a battle plan for him. Now that he was here, it was time to contemplate what came next, how to cure him, how to get his memories back. Oh, yes, there were plenty of battles to fight right here.

She took a seat at her writing desk and pulled a sheet of paper from the drawer, a ritual reminiscent of her nights in Scutari when she'd write out the next day's schedules by lamplight.

She made a list of tasks for the morning. She'd write to the local MP about the Crimean situation. She'd sort through the articles and letters from the soldiers and organise them. This list was followed by another list, this one of medicines and treatments, a list of foods to eat, a regimen for exercise that would strengthen Edward's muscles and his leg. She paused. That reminded her. Rebecca had built a walking contraption to help old Mr Flaherty when he'd broken his hip. It was more supportive than a cane, while enabling the user to get around. She wondered if it was still among Rebecca's things in the cottage she used as a workshop. Thea made a note to look for it tomorrow. It would be useful for Edward in a couple of weeks, once they got that far. Before then, they had to work on building his stamina. They'd start with sitting up in bed, then move to spending time sitting up in a chair before they ventured to taking steps. He was still weak, and she didn't want to risk a fall.

Chapter Three

Three weeks later, the end of April

He hadn't fallen once. As a prize, he was being allowed to try out a cane today, and to attempt a journey downstairs after weeks of travelling up and down the long upstairs corridor with the three-sided walking contraption his angel had dug up for him. He'd felt like an old man, tottering along the corridor in his nightshirt, sweating from the mere effort of going at a snail's pace. But he'd mastered the hallway, practising until he collapsed from exhaustion, his leg screaming from the exertion, a pain that was only relieved by his angel's hands and the opium draught.

He was sweating already this morning as he waited for Simms to escort him downstairs. In part from the excitement of something new to explore today—a new room, a new task. He *was* growing exceedingly bored—which Thea said was a good sign, as apparently cantankerousness grew apace with one's recovery—and he was sweating from clothes. Yes, *clothes*. He'd dressed for the momentous occasion of going downstairs: trousers, shirt, waistcoat, jacket and a forest-green cravat, all courtesy of Thea's absent brother William's wardrobe.

He'd be dressing from now on, he decided. No more ambling about in nightshirts. The nightshirts were definitely more comfortable, but it was the principle of the matter. If he wanted to be treated as a hale man, he had to act like one. And he did want to be a hale man, although he knew he was still far from it: still walking with aid, unable to run, unable to ride, unable to endure a day without a nap or two, unable to reclaim the memories that hung just out of reach or to get through a day without the opium draught that eased his pain. Still, a façade was better than nothing, and he was honest with himself as Simms rapped on the door and came to help him downstairs, a façade was all he had—a flimsy house of cards that would collapse the moment his leg gave out. Perhaps that was why he worked so hard to ensure that it didn't.

With Simms on one side, a thick hawthorn cane on the other, Edward began the slow trek to the staircase, where he handed the cane to Simms and opted to grip the smooth oak banister—the one the Peveretts draped with evergreen boughs at Christmas—as they made their descent one torturous step at a time. The lifting movement required of his leg was agonising.

If he'd been unobserved, he would have stopped at each step and gathered himself until the pain passed. He'd not have cared if it took half an hour to navigate the twenty-three leg-throbbing stairs to the bottom, but he was not alone. His angel was there at the base of the staircase, looking up at him, and he dare not fall, dare not fail, dare not stop until he reached her. From the shining look on her face, she wanted this victory for him as much as he wanted it for himself.

Thea had dressed for the occasion too. Gone was her usual dark work gown and in its place was a feminine dress of green lawn printed with delicate twining leaves and trimmed in a fresh white lace at the square neck. Her hair was done differently today as well. Her serviceable bun was gathered into a loose chignon and she'd left a few soft curls free about her face, all of it serving to remind him that his angel was a woman, a pretty woman, who often shrouded that prettiness in plain gowns and aprons, although an observant man would not be fooled by the disguise. He hadn't been. Real beauty was not obscured by clothes, nor was it something that thrived only on the surface of a person's character.

He was breathing hard by the time he reached her but, to her credit, she didn't mother him. He was tired of being cossetted. She said only, 'I thought we'd sit in the music room; it gets the morning sun.'

The music room might have been heaven. Golden morning light flooded the blue and cream room through the long windows—the *open* long windows, he noted, letting in a wondrously fresh breeze, gentle enough not to chill. The scents of spring were on that breeze, the scents of *life*. A vase of daffodils stood on a table, a polished Broadwood piano was placed against one wall, a sofa and chairs were clustered about the unlit fireplace. But it was the cellos that caught his eye—both of them—anchored in their stands, waiting. For whom?

'Do you play?' He nodded towards the instruments as they took up seats in the wing-backed chairs.

'Yes, the cellos are mine and William's. All of us play something,' Thea explained. 'My younger sisters and my father play the piano. Anne sings. My parents believe that music is good for the soul, that it has healing properties. It certainly lifts one's spirits, if nothing else.'

'Would you play for me?' Edward asked. He suddenly wanted nothing more than to hear music, to watch those competent hands of hers on the strings, on the bow. How long had it been since he'd *heard* music?

She retrieved the cello and experimentally plucked at the strings, tuning it. 'I haven't played in over a year,' she warned. But he would not have known or cared after the first notes, low and mellifluous like her voice. He closed his eyes and let it flow over him. The piece was a Vivaldi *Adagio* as soothing as the morning, the *arco* of her bowing as light as the birdsong beyond the window, and yet there was a stately solemnity, a certain yearning to the piece. He could have listened to her play all day and the instincts of his soul knew he'd *missed* this, missed *music*, in the months between Inkerman and now.

He opened his eyes slowly when she finished, ready to ask her for another piece, ready to beg her not to stop, when a maid appeared in the doorway. 'Miss, Cook has a question about the menu for supper and your mother is in the village today, tending to a new baby.'

Thea glanced at him, torn for a moment between answering the summons and leaving him.

'Go on, I'll be fine by myself for a while.' He reached for his cane and held it aloft with a reassuring grin. 'I have my hawthorn stick and I won't go far.' The pain in his leg still persisted from the trek downstairs. He wouldn't manage much more beyond a journey to the window.

'If you're sure? I'll only be a few minutes.' Thea rose and he felt a moment's pleasure in having eased this small decision for her, followed by a healthy pinch of guilt in knowing that he took up more than his fair share of her hours. In the weeks since he'd arrived here, she'd sat with him, read to him, played cards with him, brought her correspondence to his bedside so that she might do her work near him in case he needed her. He'd kept her tethered to the Hall. Perhaps she might be with her mother now, out of doors, tramping through the country lanes of Haberstock if not for him.

He would try to be more independent, he vowed. Now that he could dress and make his way downstairs, he could entertain himself in the library or sit on the terrace and she could carry on with her normal duties. *Without him.* He didn't like the thought of that, of Thea moving beyond him, going where he couldn't go. She'd been his anchor—all he'd known and still all he knew. Without her, he was among strangers and in a strange world with nothing to call his own. But he couldn't rely on her for ever.

As if in defiance of the idea of being left behind, he braced his cane and pushed awkwardly to his feet, his thigh muscle rebelling. He wasn't going to chase anyone down soon. He made his way inelegantly over to the piano and managed to lift the lid. A surge of pride went through him at accomplishing the task. Three weeks ago, he wouldn't have had the strength to do it.

Or the desire. But this morning had awakened something in him.

He peered inside. It was a well-made instrument, and well-kept from the look of the strings. He shuffled to the bench and managed to sit down, his thigh aching. His muscles were at the point where it didn't matter if he stood or sat; they were simply just going to hurt. He picked at the keys, his fingers running a scale as he tested the action: very good, not too quick. He struck a chord, followed by a progression and then he was playing. His eyes shut, the *Adagio* came from somewhere deep within him, flowing through his fingertips as they moved across the keys, louder here, softer there, slower here, until the pain in him eased and all was forgotten except the music. He did not question it, did not want to. It didn't matter where it came from or how it got there. He only wanted to play.

Someone was playing the piano, although playing seemed too limiting of a word. Caressing it, coaxing the most beautiful sounds from it, was more accurate. Those sounds halted Thea as she made her way back towards the music room. It was the *Adagio* she'd played earlier. For a long moment, all she could do was listen, captured by the beautiful, aching quality of the music. It seemed everyone in the house had stopped to listen as well. Which posed the question, if everyone was listening, who was playing? It was a testament to the music that the thought hadn't occurred to her before, so entranced was she in the sound. Was it her father? But no, he was working in his surgery. There was no one else who played. Except…

It couldn't be. But who else *would* it be? Thea began to run and then thought better of it. She slowed as she approached the music room. If Edward was playing, she didn't want to disturb him, didn't want to disrupt whatever magic was occurring…whatever he might be remembering. At the door, she stood stock still, mesmerised by the sound but more so by the sight.

Edward sat at the bench, his back to her, the newly fed breadth of his shoulders starting to fill out the dark blue coat. He'd stolen her breath this morning. She'd focused so long on the patient that she'd not been prepared for the man who'd come down the stairs in jacket and trousers, hair combed, jaw freshly shaven, hazel eyes alert. The transformation had been quite astounding. Now, he was transformed once more, his dark blond head bent forward. Perhaps his hazel eyes were closed, as they had been when she'd played, his mind somewhere far off, transported by the music. What did he see in that far off space? What had he discovered?

At last, the final note fell and the music stopped. Thea held her breath, waiting for more, willing him to start again. But he only sat, head bowed in the quiet that followed.

'That was stunning.' Thea broke the silence softly, approaching the piano, a hundred questions thundering through her mind.

He turned and she saw his face, a study in consternation and shock, his eyes focusing on her as if she were his anchor in an unsettling world. She offered a smile. 'Did you know you could play like that?'

'Yes. No. I must have known it, though.' He flexed his hands and looked at them as if they were strangers.

He reached for his cane and Thea moved to help him back to the chairs. 'No—' he waved her off, prickly at the suggestion '—I can walk on my own. I walked all the way over here. I can walk back.'

He sighed into the chair and she could see the visible signs of pain etched about the tight brackets at his mouth. She should offer to call Simms and see him upstairs, but her curiosity was rampant. What had prompted this revelation? Had a memory shaken loose? She feared if they left the site of the 'miracle' they'd lose their momentum.

'What happened? Did you remember something?' Thea reached out, soothing him with a stroke of her thumb over the back of his hand, noting the long, elegant fingers with renewed interest. A musician's hands.

He shook his head. The aftermath had left him jarred. 'I just sat down and began to play. It was not intentional. I didn't know I could do it. I just did it.' He furrowed his brow. 'I don't know how or if I could do it again.'

'There's one way to find out.' Thea rose and quickly retrieved a sheaf of sheet music from the bookshelves. 'Here, look at these—do you recognise the titles? The notes? The markings?'

He pushed the portfolio away. 'No, I don't want to look.'

'Don't want to look or don't want to *know*?' Thea accused sharply, confused by his rebuff. His reaction was baffling. Why was he not ecstatic? Why didn't he see this as a breakthrough after months of a stone wall built up in front of his memories, after months of not knowing?

He set his mouth in a grim, obstinate line she recognised too well. He was intractable when he was like that. She'd not let him get away with it when he'd been on death's doorstep and refusing his medicine, and she could not let him get away with it, not now, when they were close to something. She set the portfolio aside and knelt before him, taking his hands, her tone softer. 'What is bothering you, Edward?'

'I'm not Edward,' he snapped at her. Another might be turned away by the surly tone, but Thea had endured worse and he didn't mean it. He was frustrated, frightened, and he was lashing out. 'Why would I remember I could play the piano and yet I cannot remember the most basic of facts about myself—my own name?'

Ah, there it was. The real crux of the matter. 'That will come too. Perhaps remembering the music is the first step towards remembering more,' Thea encouraged. She smiled, teasing him. 'Until then, I think Edward is a perfectly good name for you.'

He harrumphed with distaste. 'You could have picked any name and you picked Edward.'

'For Edward Jenner, the inventor of the smallpox vaccine,' Thea replied in laughing defence of her choice. 'What grander name is there? Especially here at Haberstock Hall, where we're all named after physicians.' She recognised that the conversation was moving away from the piano performance, but the tension was leaving him and that might be for the better.

He harrumphed again. 'Thea is not a doctor's name.'

'It's short for Dorothea. I was named for Dorothea Erxleben, the first female to be awarded a medical degree from a university,' she answered smartly, running through her siblings. 'William is for the English anatomist, William Harvey. Rebecca is named for Rebecca Guarna, one of the Ladies of Salerno, who actually practised medicine for women, and Thomasia is named for a female physician from Italy during the time of Pope Sixtus in the fourteen-hundreds.' She ended her recitation of the name stories she'd been told through childhood with feigned smugness. 'See, Edward fits right in.'

'Would you like that, Thea? For me to fit in at Haberstock Hall? I might never leave,' he teased, but only with his voice, *not* with his eyes. She'd seen the seriousness that had flickered there, however briefly. It was a dangerous question. What if he never went 'home'? What if he never remembered? What if he stayed for ever? What if this *was* his new reality? If so, it would tie them together for always. She could not decipher if it was wistfulness or fear regarding such a reality that prompted his words. Perhaps neither. Perhaps he was merely getting even with her for accusing him of not wanting to know the truth.

'There are worse places to fit in.' She shrugged it off with a smile and rose, shaking out her skirts. She would envy him the fitting in. She'd never quite mastered it. 'I'll have Simms help you upstairs. I'm sure you're tired.' She'd not meant to keep him up this long on his first outing downstairs, but it did please her that he'd done so well. Progress would come quickly now. 'We might try the terrace tomorrow,' she suggested. 'Unless you'd like to come back here? You can visit the music room any time; the house is yours to explore.'

Who knew what other hidden talents he might unlock

here or in other rooms if left on his own? She should want that for him, this first step of independence, this first step back towards remembering and reclaiming who he was, and yet it was quite likely his first step away from her as well. While he needed her, she had a purpose. She could put off making decisions about where she went next.

'What will you do with your day?' He pushed to his feet, stubbornly struggling to rise without help.

'I have letters to write and packages to send to some of the Scutari families.' This, too, was a temporary purpose. At some point the letters would be written, the tokens delivered. With them settled and Edward healed, her sense of purpose would grow smaller still. There was an irony in knowing that the better she did her tasks, the faster she'd lose her purpose.

'It's good of you to do that,' he offered. Beneath the gruff compliment, she heard the apology: *I am sorry I snapped at you earlier. It wasn't you I was angry with.*

Simms slipped into the room, ready to assist him upstairs. There was little time and no privacy to offer a response other than, 'I'll see you for tea, Edward.'

He would know from her tone what she really meant: *I did not intend to push you so hard in a direction you were not ready to go.*

She was always counselling him to patience. She needed to take her own advice. His memories would come in time. And yet, she thought as he exited the room with Simms, there might be something more she could do to expedite that.

Experiences like today might provide the keys in the most unexpected ways and in unexpected places.

Who would have thought the music room would have triggered such a response? What other responses might be garnered from a trip to the stables, or a walk in the gardens? Or a picnic by the pond? The healer in her, who wanted to cure him, wanted to see this human being restored to full health, was eager to arrange such outings as he could handle. But the woman in her, the woman who'd seen him come down the stairs today fully dressed, who'd been by his side for six months without ceasing, who understood he was her last tie to the war, to the place where she'd felt useful, harboured the worry: what happened when he remembered? What happened when he found his family and went home? The woman in her was less eager than the nurse to find out. Thea wondered, did that make her a coward?

Chapter Four

He was a coward. Edward studied the face that met him in the mirror over the washstand. He leaned against the basin, careful of his aching leg. Simms would have stayed to help him, but he'd wanted to be alone with his thoughts. He was all Thea accused him of being. He hadn't wanted to know what was inside him. He hadn't consciously thought to play the piano, hadn't consciously remembered knowing how to play. He couldn't explain why he'd been drawn to the piano or how he'd played it, only that once he'd started, he hadn't wanted to stop. The piano, the music, was part of him.

That had been glorious, but what else was part of him? What else might emerge at any given time? Would it be less glorious? Was the reason he couldn't remember because his mind was protecting him from something darker? Something that he'd done? Something that he was? Why couldn't he remember Inkerman? Had he done something despicable on the battlefield? Led his men into danger? Wait. Why did he think he'd *led* men? Was that his pride talking? A pride that wasn't satisfied in having been a foot soldier?

Edward splashed cool water on his face, willing the questions and the doubt away. Not knowing was the coward's way out. He had to do better next time, *if* there was a next time. Yet 'doing better' came with a cost. Would Thea like the man he discovered? Would she regret having saved him? *That* was not a reason to stall. She was his nurse, his angel. She'd brought him back from death, saved him when others would have seen him buried alive. She owed him nothing more.

He owed it to her to move on with his life, to discover what that life was, although it seemed strange to contemplate a life without her. She'd become intrinsic to him, to Edward. Edward belonged to Thea. But that wasn't who he really was. That other person inside him owed others, just as Edward owed Thea—others who had no names as of yet. If for no other reason than for the sake of a family who might even now be struggling in the wake of his supposed death or disappearance. Who knew what they might have been told? Had the military written to say he'd been missing in action or, after months of no further report, had someone written to say he was dead, his body lost in a foreign land? Were they reeling? Had his 'death' caused them hardship on top of grief?

Do you think you even have a family?

Surely, he did. Surely, he wasn't alone in the world. Everyone belonged somewhere. Even him, a man with no name to call his own. Even Edward had a place— Haberstock Hall—and even Edward belonged to someone. Edward belonged to an angel.

'There's a special place I want to show you.' Thea kept her hand at his elbow for support as they carefully traversed the garden flagstones at the back of the house. The day was fine and she had a destination in mind, although it would not be attained without some worry on her part: worry that he might trip over the pavers, worry that he might fall and injure his leg, worry that the outing might tire him too much, although the last was not likely to happen. Edward had demonstrated a rapid return to good health in the time he'd been at Haberstock, his stamina increasing daily. 'We are celebrating today.'

'What are we celebrating?' Edward slanted her one of his cynical hazel glances as they made their slow progress.

'Your one-month anniversary here. It's the second of May today.' It was hard to believe that thirty days ago he'd been feverish and too weak to do more than groan, let alone get out of bed. Now, he played the piano daily, filling the large, quiet halls of Haberstock with exquisite sound, although he'd not remembered any more about himself, as a musician or otherwise. She found him quite often in the library, perusing books of an afternoon instead of napping, another sure sign that his strength was returning in full.

'And how are we celebrating? Are we going somewhere or are we just exercising my leg because you're a martinet?' He gave her one of his wry smiles that hinted at his dry, sometimes irascible humour.

'*We* have a destination in mind,' Thea said smugly, pointing to an arch in the wall just up ahead. 'I've been saving it for when you were well enough to see it for yourself.' There were other signs too, that he was indeed returned to health and well enough for ventures out of doors, signs she noticed, she told herself, because she was a healer, because she was intimately acquainted with his body after six months of constant care—all reasons that were strictly professional and nothing else. His appearance was less haggard, his colour good, his eyes sharp when the pain of his leg didn't ride him hard. Her brother's clothes were growing tight. Very soon, Edward would need clothes of his own. His beard grew quickly, requiring a regular shave, and his dark blond hair had taken on a healthy sheen that turned its length a glossy bronze, a length, it had occurred to her, that he might like cut. It was long enough now to be clubbed back in an old-fashioned queue.

'An arch?' he replied, trying to appear unimpressed, but she could see his curiosity was piqued.

'Not any arch—a doorway to a walled garden,' Thea scolded. 'You mustn't be disrespectful, Edward, it's my favourite place at Haberstock.'

Mrs Newsome appeared in the archway, a basket in hand. 'There you are! What a beautiful day to be out, Mr Edward.' She bustled forward. 'Are you taking in the garden today? Miss Thea has been busy getting it into fine form.'

'Has she, Mrs Newsome?' Edward slanted a look in Thea's direction, nascent curiosity burgeoning into genuine interest. 'Is this where you've been disappearing to of an afternoon?'

She felt her cheeks flush at his question and she silently chided Mrs Newsome for calling attention to the act. She'd not wanted to make a show of it. She did poorly with direct praise.

'The garden needed taking care of, so I did.' Thea

made light of it as Mrs Newsome headed back to the kitchen. 'I'm the only one that uses the space and it hadn't been looked after since I left.' Which had resulted in a year and a half of neglect. She'd been busy clearing weeds and pruning back bushes that had run amok but the result was worth it to see the look on Edward's face when he stepped through the arch and took it all in.

Edward turned in a slow circle, leaning heavily on the hawthorn cane. 'This is marvellous, Thea.' He breathed in deeply, wholly, fully. What a different breath he took now, compared to the rattling breaths he'd arrived with. The brucellosis was gone; whatever he'd suffered from the smoke inhalation was gone as well, his voice no longer raspy. 'I think I will always recall our Christmas in Scutari when I smell lavender.' He gave her one of his rare warm smiles. 'It's not just lavender I smell here, though, is it?' He gestured to the lilac bushes trained to climb up trellises and across the wall. 'There's honeysuckle.' He nodded to the pink and yellow flowers growing in the beds. 'Roses too. It's quite the whimsical fairy garden, a garden of scents and colours.' He paused, his brow furrowing, and she knew he'd heard it. 'Where's the water coming from?' He made another slow circle, cocking his head, determined to find the source.

'There's a bower behind the lilac trellis. I'll show you.' Thea led him the short distance to the little paradise within the garden, to the whitewashed gliding swing that rocked back and forth, skimming the ground, to the fountain, whose trickling sounds had the ability to block out the world and create a new one, one that was comprised only of flowers and scents and the sound of water. This place had worked its soothing magic for her many times. She wanted it to work magic for Edward too.

They settled in the glider. 'This is one of Rebecca's creations.' Thea set the swing into perpetual motion with a gentle push of her foot.

'But the garden is yours.' Edward's gaze was on her, and she felt his mind working to place her in this space, to understand what it meant to her.

'Yes, it's mine. Anne and my mother have the herb garden, Rebecca has her workshop. I wanted a place of my own where I could sort out my thoughts, some place private.'

'And quiet, I'd wager,' Edward offered thoughtfully. 'With so many siblings, privacy was bound to be at a premium, even in a house this large.' He cocked his head. 'Is that why we're here? To sort me out?' He gave a self-deprecating chuckle. 'Is this your way of suggesting I've outstayed my welcome?'

'No, never think such a thing!' Thea protested. She was in no hurry to have him leave. She was bungling this horribly. 'I believed it would help if you had a place to go where you could be private too, alone with your thoughts, with yourself, so that…'

'So that I might remember?' Edward finished her sentence with a sigh. 'I know you're disappointed. I've remembered nothing since the piano.'

'Disappointed?' Was that what he thought? 'I am thrilled beyond measure at your progress, Edward. You can walk, you can breathe again without that awful rattling cough, your lungs are recovered, your fever has not returned. We're going to need to call the local tailor for you because you're about to split the seams on my brother's wardrobe. You are going to live! That does not disappoint me in the least and it should not disappoint you.' But it did raise other questions about the future and what it might look like.

'In need of a tailor, am I?' He plucked at his lapels, pretending to preen.

'Yes, tomorrow, in fact, my father has arranged for him to come up and take your measurements. We can't have you looking second-hand when the vicar comes to dine at the end of the week,' Thea teased with a cheerfulness she didn't entirely feel. Today was indeed a watershed day—the day Edward took another step towards leaving his reclusive existence behind, memories or not.

People were curious about the stranger at Haberstock Hall and in a small community there was no ignoring it. Now that he was sufficiently recovered, it was time to introduce him to the village. It would start slowly. The tailor would meet him. The vicar would meet him. Her father and mother had discussed having him join them in the Peverett pew at church on Sundays. She was going to have to share him with all of Haberstock.

'I am grateful, Thea, for everything you and your family have done—but mostly for what *you've* done, what you've sacrificed. All of your time.' He gave her a careful look. 'Your career. I'm not sure you'd be home right now if not for me. You'd be with the nursing corps doing battle with Menzies, no matter what Miss Nightingale asked of you. I don't think anyone makes you do anything you don't want to do. You came home because your loyalty to Miss Nightingale and to me demanded it.'

Had she been that transparent? 'Because the cause demands it,' she corrected. She didn't want him feeling guilty. 'The battle needs me here.' It was the same litany she used to assure herself that she still had purpose, that people still needed her. 'There are MPs to lobby about the military's outright negligence in conducting this war, from managing their supply lines to keeping track of their men and caring for them. The press has exposed to the public that which has long been the hidden purvey of the military and now the military must be accountable. There is plenty of work to do here so that others aren't lost. There's a lot of different ways to save lives.'

'And yet you wish you were back there,' he concluded softly, his words barely audible above the burble of the fountain. 'Sometimes I wish I was too. Not that I want to be hurt or ill again, but I knew that world.' They were exchanging secrets, words only meant to be heard by the other, secrets only the other would understand—secrets that would never leave the sanctuary of the bower, secrets the world beyond the bower would think were sacrilege.

'Does that make us bad people? Ungrateful?' she asked quietly, aware that a certain trickle of relief flooded through her at his confession—the relief of not being alone, of having someone to talk to who understood.

'I think it makes us honest. At least I understood that world. Live or die, that was all there was. But here, each day is full of the unknown in both frightening and glorious ways. Am I making any sense?'

Yes. Entirely too much sense. Thea nodded. 'I was a doctor there. I understood my role, my duties. I'm not sure who I am here.'

'Doctor?' His attention shifted at the words. 'But only men...' he began and then thought better of it.

'Yes, only men can be doctors.' She shot him a sly look to let him know she'd caught his incredulity. 'But in an emergency, a woman can be too. I was a doctor there, even if not in name. It's all I ever wanted to be.' How many afternoons had she come to this very spot to grapple with that same reality—that her life, her ambitions, were limited by her gender? 'A man can be a doctor, even if he's a very bad doctor, but a woman who would be an excellent doctor cannot even attempt it.' Except in the Crimea, except when there was no one else to stand between men and death. She'd taken advantage of that and had revelled in it.

'And you wanted it badly enough that you were willing to go to a war zone to have it. You're quite a woman, Thea Peverett.' He gave her an appreciative smile and then cocked his head to study her. 'I'd say you'd given it all up to go to war and pursue your dream, but I realise I don't know what exactly you'd given up. What did you do, Thea, before haring off to war?' He smiled, the action crinkling the corners of his eyes.

'I worked with Florence at the Harley Street Hospital for gentlewomen. It is noble to be able to serve anyone, especially to serve other women. Women should have their own access to health care from other women, not men who pretend to understand.'

'But it wasn't enough?' he prompted when she'd hoped to get away with the short version of the story.

'It should have been. I got to come to London, one of the biggest cities in the world. I took a flat with my sister, Anne, and worked in the hospital. I even went to a duchess's ball for a fundraiser. It should have been adventure and satisfaction enough.' Thea looked down at her hands. 'My brother got to go to war, to do something useful, and I was jealous, so when the opportunity to be part of Florence's nursing corps came up, I took it.'

'And did you feel useful?' Edward's voice was soft in the quiet of the garden.

She nodded. 'Very much so. I felt useful for the first time. I was using all of my skills, making decisions, directing change, saving people. I felt so useful, Edward, that I would have rather stayed at war than come home and not be useful anymore, to have no direction, no purpose.' She had not confessed that out loud to anyone.

'You fear that,' Edward said. 'You fear having no purpose, being useless, although I doubt you're ever truly useless.' He laughed. 'It's not in you to sit still. I know, I used to watch you from my bed in Scutari. You moved enough for both of us.' He paused, gathering his thoughts. 'I would wonder how it was that some man hadn't already snatched you up. Did you have a swain at home? And, if so, how had he let you go off to war? I didn't wonder that last very long, though. No one stops you.'

She'd been comfortable talking about the war, comfortable exchanging dark truths, but not with all this talk about herself. The question caught her entirely off-guard and it was not comfortable in the least. She whispered one last dark secret beneath the fountain's burble. 'I'm not good with men.'

'Not good with men? Who the hell ever told you that?' Edward gave a derisive laugh. 'Surely you jest. All the men in Scutari adored you. I believe I've mentioned that before.'

'Not all men, not Menzies or Lieutenant Stewart,' Thea corrected. There were other men too that she hadn't been good with. 'I'm too managing.' And at one point she'd been too naïve and had overestimated her appeal. That was years ago. She'd moved on from that lesson. She put out her foot to stop the swing and got up, putting an end to the discussion.

Edward concentrated on setting the cane right and pushing to his feet. 'What's beyond the garden, Thea?'

How did he mean that? Literally? Figuratively?

'The stables.' She opted for literal. 'See that door on the other side of the garden? It lets out into the stable yard.'

'Shall we visit the stables?'

'Tomorrow, perhaps. I'm behind on my letter writing. I am working on a piece for *The Times* about the Sanitary Movement,' Thea improvised hastily. It was true; she was working on a piece. She needed some distance from Edward and his probing questions. There were some truths she'd prefer not to be reminded of. She'd brought him out to the garden to help him sort through his thoughts, not hers.

She felt Edward's hand on her arm, warm and firm. 'I've upset you. I did not mean to. Thank you, Thea, for this afternoon, for the garden, for making this beautiful space for me. I will be sure to enjoy it.'

I am sorry I probed too deeply. Thank you for taking me into your confidence.

Would that she could understand another human being the way she understood Edward, a man with no name. How ironic that the one man she felt a connection with was a fiction, a man she'd made up out of whole cloth. Although there were some who'd say that was the only kind of man she'd ever have.

Chapter Five

She'd fixed the garden. *For him.* It was a gesture of extreme kindness, the kind of gesture Thea made so effortlessly, from sharing Christmas gifts to sharing her home, and her family, with a man who had neither. The generosity of the garden was not lost on Edward each time he visited, which was often over the next few days. He enjoyed the sanctuary it provided, although he'd have enjoyed it more if Thea was with him.

Thea had made herself scarce in the intervening days. All because he'd said too much. In his eagerness to know her, he'd asked for more than she was willing to give and she'd retreated, just as he had over the memories in the music room. They both had their vulnerabilities, it seemed. He feared the past that was as of yet unacknowledged, while she feared the past she knew. What was in that past? The desire to know swelled with the urge to protect. He wanted to know, wanted to avenge her for any slight done. His angel deserved a champion, someone to protect her after she'd done so much to protect others. Thea would never admit it, because she didn't like to admit to weakness, but he'd touched a nerve there.

Edward lowered himself into the swing and closed his eyes, breathing in the lilac. He should have kept his mouth shut—he should not have spoken his thoughts: *I would wonder how it was that some man hadn't already snatched you up.* For it was clear she hadn't been. No men had called in the month he'd been here, no suitor who'd waited at home while his beloved had gone off to war. It *did* mystify him, though. His angel was a paragon of generosity and caring. He was curious how such a woman went unnoticed or, based on her comment, perhaps unappreciated.

I'm too managing, she'd said just before she'd ended their conversation. Not for him, though. To him, his angel was intriguing, interesting for just those reasons—because she didn't fit the mould.

His thoughts wandered down a side path in his mind. Had he known boring women? Was that why he saw Thea for the rare jewel she was? If circumstances were different, perhaps he'd be the one doing the snatching up. If he were a man with something to offer a woman: a name, some position in the world, a home, he might find himself calling on Haberstock Hall. But he had none of those things, not even the memory of what those things might be, and if it weren't for the war, how might he and Thea have ever met? Perhaps it only mattered that they *had* met and now he had the chance to be in the orbit of this incredible woman.

For what purpose?

What would happen to them once his memories returned, once his old life returned? It was a burning question, although it burned a little less brightly with each day that passed with no further memories. Perhaps there would be no old life to return to. But that prompted its own set of questions. How might he build a life here, from the ground up? What might he offer Thea, then? Would she even be interested in him as more than a patient?

They had started their association as patient and healer, but they'd moved beyond that. There were moments, like in the bower, when they flirted with true friendship, and with each other, trading stories and secrets, moments when it seemed they were both in accord, pursuing that friendship together, and then there were moments of retreat, moments when she would ask about his leg or if he was too tired and they would both remember their roles.

He'd like to stop being her patient and start being her friend in truth. She seemed to lack them here in Haberstock. Perhaps her friends were in London or in the Crimea.

For a woman who gave so much of herself, it appeared to him that, outside of her family, she received little in return. Perhaps that was of her own making. He'd got too close in the bower and she'd fled. For a woman who knew how to fight for what she wanted, it was a curious tactic indeed to choose flight. It posed the question: what had happened to her to cause such a contrary reaction? Had someone once been allowed to get too close and it had gone sour?

He hadn't seen her for more than a few minutes alone in the days since. If asked, she'd say it was because they'd been busy. It wasn't untrue, but neither was it

the real reason. She'd been avoiding him. Still, he was
here in the garden because he hoped she'd come and because he was indeed seeking solitude, a respite from the
house. Over the last several days he'd acquired a sched
ule: breakfast in the parlour with the family, a morning
spent at the piano with his music or appointments with
the tailor who came to the house to take his measurements, or to do fittings and alterations. Then luncheon,
followed by an afternoon spent in the library, a walk in
the garden or an appointment with Dr Peverett to as-
sess his improving condition. That last was part of her
scheme to avoid him or perhaps an admission that their
relationship *was* changing as he changed, as his health
improved, and his independence grew.

The man who'd lain in bed unable to do anything
was gone. Edward rejoiced in that even as he recognised the incompleteness of the accomplishments. His
was a modest schedule, the sort kept by an idle country
gentleman, and even in his joy at being ambulatory and
out of bed he felt the emptiness in it. If this was to be
his new life, he needed to find a cause, something beyond himself to devote his time to. He laughed softly,
thinking of Thea and her fear of being purposeless.
Perhaps he feared that too—one more thing they had
in common. Perhaps neither of them was the sort who
could just drift through life.

'I thought I would find you here.' Thea stood framed
in the archway as if his thoughts had conjured her there.
He would see her like this in his mind for ever—the
way he knew her best, dressed for work in a dark blue
dress, white apron, silky dark tresses tucked beneath a
kerchief. 'Father and I are done with calls for the day. I

saw that the tailor had left an order of clothes. Are you ready for tonight?'

Tonight was dinner with the vicar and the newly elected MP for the district, a man Thea had engaged in active correspondence leading up to this evening's gathering. Edward gave a wry smile. It would be his first official outing. But it was more than that. It was his debut.

'Ah, yes, my entry into Haberstock society.'

'Well, we can't keep you under wraps indefinitely.' Thea laughed but he noted she didn't deny it. If this was to be his life now, he had to meet people and build new connections, new memories to replace the old. He knew too that Thea was right. He couldn't skulk around the Hall and become a secret, something the Peveretts were perceived as hiding. It would only add to the odd-ity of him. Frankly, he was odd enough without the extra drama of being hidden away: a man home from war with no recollection of what happened before a ball had torn through him.

Thea extracted a pair of scissors from her apron pocket and held them up, clicking the blades together. 'Would you like a haircut before the big night?'

His body reacted instantly, another piece of evidence that he was nearing full recovery, and that his awareness of her as more than his healer had grown exponentially with that recovery.

Yes, if it means your hands on me.

Once, her touch had been a source of comfort and connection, now it had become something more. He was no helpless, sexless patient lying in a bed any longer, something Dr and Mrs Peverett had likely taken into account even if their daughter appeared to be oblivious to the evolution. In deference to that shift, Simms had gradually taken over shaving him and Dr Peverett had taken on the task of massaging his leg. The massage was still effective, just not as enjoyable.

'Do *you* want me to cut my hair?' Edward sensed a certain reticence hovering beneath her question. That reticence was his own as well. His hair had become long and shaggy, but it had also become a souvenir of sorts, a reminder of what he'd been through, a testimony to his strength, like Samson. And yet to cut it, well, wouldn't that also be a sort of victory? A sign that he was stepping ever closer towards a return to normalcy, to reclaiming himself, even if he didn't know who that person was?

Thea gave an experimental click of the scissors. 'It's not my hair.'

Sometimes, to move forward one had to let go. Edward ran a hand through the thick length of it. 'You'd best cut it. We don't want the vicar to think you're housing a barbarian,' he joked, coming to sit on a stone bench before her. 'Do your worst,' he chuckled. 'You should cut it before I become any more attached to it.'

She moved behind him, her fingers threading through his hair as she took its measure. He closed his eyes, letting his mind and his body revel in the moment. It felt so damn good to have her touch him again. He heard her exhale, steeling herself for the task. 'All right, let's turn you into a proper gentleman.'

Thea was surprisingly—or perhaps not so surprisingly—good at hair-cutting. She was a healer, after all. Scissors, stitching, sewing were all second nature to her. Her touch was competent and sure as she settled into the rhythm of barbering him: comb, cut, snip, trim, comb, cut, as the lengths of his hair fell to the ground. He'd have gladly been Rapunzel with miles of tresses to cut if it would have prolonged her hands on him. Good Lord, that bordered on the pathetic, saved only from desperation by knowing that it was not just any human touch he craved but hers alone. He could connect in body and in mind with Thea, the only person with whom he could do such a thing. He would want to connect with her even if he had five hundred friends.

Thea moved to stand in front of him, bending down so that their eyes met, hazel stare to whisky gaze. He could see yellow flecks in those amber depths. He wanted to see her soul there too but, as hard as he searched, that piece of her remained elusive, perhaps more closely guarded after the lapse in the bower. Still, it leaked out in other ways: in her actions, in the stories she told. Did she know she gave a part of herself away even as she tried to protect it?

Thea ran the comb through his hair, drawing it forward to check the symmetry of its length. 'Hold still; I want to make sure it's even.' He would be as immovable as stone for this woman who'd brought him back to life, a reminder his body was more acutely aware of each day. This *woman*. This woman who'd defied an army for him, who'd defied death itself for a man who did not even know who he was. Some might attribute his feelings to gratitude but what he felt for her was more than that. Gratitude did not rouse a man. Spirit and passion did. Thea burned with them.

She stepped back and studied him in considering si-

lence and he could not quite read her gaze. What he saw
in it was incongruent with the simple satisfaction of a
job well done. 'There, you're completely transformed
now.' Was that regret he heard lingering in her tone?
Did she not want him transformed? He reached for her
hand out of a need to reassure her, comfort her.

'It's still me, Thea.' Was she, too, aware of him as
more than a patient, as he was aware of her as more
than a healer? Did that awareness make her uncomfortable? Uncertain?

'But vastly improved.' She sheathed the scissors in
her apron pocket and looked away.

I'm not good with men, she'd said. Did she prefer
him as a patient, a role she understood? She was good
with patients.

'Not so much improved.' He gave her a wry grin. He
might look different on the outside, but on the inside he
was still Edward, a man with no memories, no name to
call his own, a man who still needed her. Was that it?
Did she worry over losing him? That in transforming
him she would transform *them*? What would they be if
they were not patient and healer? But surely she knew
that transformation was inevitable whether she cut his
hair or not. They'd been transforming ever since she'd
decided he was going to live.

'The local ladies will get a look at you and swoon.
You'll have invitations to teas and picnics; you'll be fed
until you burst,' she warned. 'You'll need another new
suit of clothes for all those calls.' She made a playful
frown of disapproval, but he heard the concern beneath
the teasing: he wouldn't want her company any longer
when offered other companionable fare. That was not

the only concern, though, merely the tip. He saw the larger concern immediately. She thought if he didn't require her assistance he would no longer find her company desirous on its own. It was astonishing to think a woman of her confidence could have such a low opinion of her own company. He would have to disabuse her of such notions.

He rose and brushed at his trousers. 'I shall endeavour not to make an ass of myself at dinner then.'

Thea cocked her head, teasing him with the dry wit he'd come to rely on in the Crimea. 'That might be difficult. It takes more than a haircut to make a gentleman.'

They laughed together, easy and companionable, but his mind had latched onto the last of her comment. 'Do you think I might be a gentleman, Thea?' He crooked his free arm and they made a slow tour of the walled garden.

'I think there are hints. There are your manners at table, your manners when we walk about, always offering your arm, always holding open a door, always allowing me to pass through first.'

She'd been watching him eat.

He barely heard the rest, so intent was he on those words, his response torn between being flattered—she'd been watching him—and the idea that she was a scientist studying a specimen, objectively and ruthlessly gleaning every hint of truth from the observation. She did not regard him in the way a woman might regard a man: the way he often watched her.

'Then there's your appreciation for our library and your musical skill,' she continued, 'both of which mark you as someone who likely came from a background of education and means. Conservatoires are not accessible to all and sundry, neither are they affordable.'

Edward nodded. Between the piano and the things he'd discovered in the library, some affluence in his past seemed likely. It needn't be extensive wealth. 'The wealth of gentry would be enough to have sent a son to a conservatoire and to have bought a commission,' he offered his thoughts out loud. 'I'd been thinking on it, puzzling it out, working the equation backwards, if you will. If I don't have the specifics of who I am, I can start more broadly and work towards those specifics through a process of elimination and reasoning.' And, in doing so, he hoped to trigger more memories. It had not triggered anything significant, nothing that was of use to him. He'd not mentioned it to Thea, wanting to wait until he had something more meaningful to report. He was no closer to knowing his name than he had been.

Thea favoured him with a smile and squeezed his arm. 'That is an admirable method. I've written to Ferris, my sister's husband, to see if he has any suggestions as well. He works with soldiers at the Chelsea Soldiers' Home.' Her smile widened and her whisky eyes softened. 'We won't give up, Edward. We *will* figure out who you are.'

Thea *would* figure it out. He believed that. She was tenacious and he found himself clinging to that tenacity when the enormity of not knowing threatened to swamp him. He was not alone in the fight. A formidable soldier fought beside him, fought *for* him. That was what Thea did best—fight for others. But right now he didn't want to be the patient, he wanted to be the man, so he changed the conversation as they headed to the house to dress and prepare for the evening. 'Tell me who is coming to dinner. I assume the vicar doesn't come alone? And the MP? Is he bringing a guest?'

Thea made a face. 'The vicar will bring his wife and his nephew, who is quite odious. The MP is Shaw Rawdon and he's sent word that he's bringing his sister. Rawdon seems congenial enough, based on his correspondence.' But not the nephew, Edward noted. She'd not offered the nephew's name, neither had she offered any reason for the nephew's odiousness. He'd like to have asked but they'd arrived at the back terrace. It was time to let her go.

Edward raised her hand to his lips for a gallant kiss that was only half a mocking parody. 'A gentleman, am I? Well, I suppose that's all the more reason not to make an ass of myself tonight in front of the vicar's wife and the MP's sister.' He grinned while she laughingly extricated her hand and slipped inside, leaving him to his thoughts.

He was a gentleman, or he *might* be. For the first time something akin to hope began to unfurl, slow and tentative, when he thought about his past—the hope that came with being able to look ahead and lay plans for the future. Under the right conditions, a country gentleman had something to offer a doctor's daughter. What would Thea think of that? She deserved to be courted by a man who could offer her the world, a man who understood her and who wouldn't seek to change her. She was pretty but she should not be reduced to the sum of her looks.

Edward began the slow climb up the stairs, leaning heavily on his cane, the ache in his leg offset as he was buoyed up by a sense of hope. That hope seemed fantastical even to him. In practical terms, the idea of courting Thea was only a daydream. He had nothing to offer her *yet*, not even the truth of who he was. A man should at least be able to offer his name and a home.

The rebuttal to that common sense came swift and sure. How long did a man who'd had a brush with death wait to fully start living again? It had been six months. The memories might not come back. If they didn't, he'd have wasted time and he knew now that he did not have an infinity of days before him. War had taught him that. A young man's life might be cut down at any moment by a bullet. Patience was not a virtue—it was a prison. He was determined to break out, starting tonight.

Chapter Six

Edward was a marvel. Thea studied him over the rim of her wine glass. Tonight, in the candlelight of the Peverett dining room, he looked the consummate gentleman in his clothes: a dark blue jacket cut close to his body, a pewter silk waistcoat embroidered in blue vines beneath. The ensemble revealed the newly restored breadth of his shoulders and the trim line of his waist, emphasising an athletic physique. His freshly cut hair was brushed into glossy waves of dark blond perfection and either he or Simms had rendered him with a clean-shaven jaw, all efforts which served as poignant reminders that he was a man of some bearing and no small amount of attractiveness—an attractiveness Thea was acutely aware of each day that passed.

Edward was no longer a sick man who hovered at death's door, but a man who walked with her in the garden, who talked with her, shared his thoughts and listened to hers. His attraction went far beyond a suit of clothes. It made him dangerous to her in a way patients weren't. Thea glanced down the table to where the vicar's nephew, Clive Donnatt, sat, a passably attractive man attempting to enhance that attraction with bright, expensive clothes in the hope of detracting from the small bump on the bridge of his nose. She'd been taken in by a handsome face before, thanks to Donnatt, who'd introduced her to a man whom she'd thought had cared for her opinions. The betrayal had stung mightily. She'd not let a man get near enough to fool her again. Not even Edward, although that became more difficult by the day.

Anyone from Scutari seeing him now would be hard pressed to recognise the man at the table. He certainly had more innate elan than any other male there, outshining the soberly dressed vicar and the flamboyant Donnatt, who fashioned himself a man about town although he was currently rusticating in the country. Even the handsome russet-haired MP, Shaw Rawdon, seemed to fall short in comparison to Edward. One could argue she was biased but Thea didn't think so. She'd seen the glances Rawdon's sister, Susan, had cast in Edward's direction and the discreet perusal given to him by the vicar's wife, who wasn't supposed to notice such worldly things.

'I say, let the military do its job. Reporters and that uppity Miss Nightingale are out of line with their interference. It's a national security issue, if you ask me.' Donnatt held forth to the table at large. 'The military needn't answer to the general populace, who haven't any idea how to run a war. It follows that the same populace is not entitled to have an opinion about such things.'

What a little fool, Thea steamed. How dare he condescend with the 'great' wisdom of his mid-twenties and his limited life experience? She was about to respond, to give him the tongue-lashing he deserved and to defend her dear friend, but Edward was faster, and more efficient.

'Are you a soldier yourself then, Mr Donnatt? And as such have an expert military opinion to contribute?' With a single question Edward silenced the popinjay. He followed it with a slow swallow of wine, challenging the vicar's nephew with his gaze. 'I *am* a soldier who saw first-hand the mismanagement in the Crimea. I suffered from it first-hand as well. If not for Miss Peverett—' his gaze moved from Donnatt to her, a little smile flickering on his lips '—I would have died. Without her and the efforts of Miss Nightingale's nursing corps, I assure you several did. I do not think reporting the truth equates with interference.' Edward's eyes moved to Rawdon. 'Miss Peverett has an incredible and different view of the war from her position. I think you will find her perspective enlightening.' His gaze flickered towards her. 'Would you please, Miss Peverett, tell us about Scutari?'

'I would be delighted to hear of your experience,' Rawdon echoed. 'It would be most helpful for me as I prepare to return to London.'

Another woman might demur, but Thea did not dare, nor was she inclined to do so. She was cognizant of the honour Edward orchestrated for her. In a few sentences he'd shut down Donnatt and elevated her from a bluestocking shrew to a subject matter expert. He'd given her her moment to educate Rawdon, to secure an ally in Parliament. She would have to remember to thank him for this. Had anyone ever so deftly championed her?

She took a small sip of wine and began. 'When we

arrived, there were two thousand men boarded at the hospital in Scutari and only fourteen baths. The hospital lacked the most basic of supplies, ranging from towels to shirts to kitchen utensils. Aside from supplies, our largest problems were what I like to call the three Ds: dirt, drains and diet. After only a day's work it was obvious to me why this hospital had the highest death count.' Her gaze flashed briefly to Edward. 'Men did not come to Scutari to be healed—they came to die.'

'One cannot make a single hospital the representative example of what is occurring in a region as large as the Crimea,' Donnatt scoffed. 'It's just like a woman to make drama out of nothing more than a little housekeeping. Now there's all this to-do over one crowded hospital and all because a few women had to wash some floors.'

'It was not and *is* not the case of one crowded hospital,' Thea snapped at Donnatt. 'Men were and are dying across the Crimea from typhus and cholera at rates that are ten times higher than deaths from war injuries.' She fixed her attention on Rawdon. 'I have letters from my brother, William, who is a doctor serving in Sevastopol. It's the same there. The harbour is filled with the carcasses of dead animals and sewage. The lack of sanitation is at the heart of these death rates. It's no wonder that British troops' deaths are higher even than our allies, the French. These are wasteful deaths, Mr Rawdon, not patriotic ones. The military, and the government that allows the military to behave in such a fashion, must be held accountable for the lives they deploy.' She studied Rawdon closely for a reaction, aware that even as she watched the MP, Edward was watching her.

Rawdon leaned forward with sincere interest. 'Hear,

hear. I must say I am in complete agreement, Miss Peverett. Nicely said. Let's hope you never want to stand for Parliament, or my seat is in danger. I have appreciated your correspondence these past weeks and now that I've met you in person, I see that appreciation is well warranted. You are a force to be reckoned with. I only hope I can do your cause as much justice as you do.' He raised his glass. 'A toast to you, Miss Peverett, for your service and to you, sir—' he nodded to Edward '—as well as to your recovery.'

After the toast, Rawdon leaned back in his chair. 'I am pleased to have met you, Miss Peverett, and you, sir. I regret that Susan and I will be leaving soon for London, next week in fact, now that the Easter break is over and the Season begins in full. I would have liked more opportunities to discuss the Crimean situation with you, but I trust I might have the privilege of your correspondence and we can continue the discussion in that manner?'

Mr Donnatt slid a sly glance at Edward, bent on revenge, before turning his gaze on Rawdon. Thea braced herself. She and Clive Donnatt were of an age and she'd been the recipient of his incivility on many an occasion. 'Taking advice from a man with no memories, Rawdon? I'd be more concerned about losing my seat over *that* than the fantasy of a woman ever sitting in Parliament. Perhaps you were unaware of Edward's disabilities?' He turned deceptively guileless blue eyes on Edward. 'I *do* understand that correctly, sir? You have no recollection of who you are? That's mighty convenient, I think.' He chuckled. 'Who among us hasn't wanted a clean slate at one time or another? Hmm? And what a lovely fresh start you have at Haberstock Hall. You've been taken in, housed and clothed in style. I'd say you landed on your feet or, in your case, your one good leg,' he made an inelegant reference to Edward's injury before casting a cold smile in Thea's direction. 'You can't ask for a better advocate than Miss Peverett, of course, Rawdon. She's quite keen to protect the weak.'

Thea wanted to slide under the table. Her ten-year-old self might have. She was made of sterner stuff now, although she still hated the way Donnatt could reduce her efforts to something that appeared nobly but naively misguided. They might as well be ten again, the robin's nest between them, depending on her to save it. She was just as unable to defend herself now with words as she had been then and he knew it. She didn't dare rip into him at the supper table in front of guests and resorting to her fists as she had then was out of the question here. At the table, she could only concede with Rawdon watching. It was so easy to corner a woman.

'She's quite keen to champion *justice*, not weakness,' Edward corrected, his tone making it clear that he disagreed with every implied sentiment in Donnatt's remark. 'There *is* a difference. I find her determination admirable and inspirational.' He'd championed her again, the second time that night he'd come to her rescue, not to protect her but to elevate her. She flashed him a smile.

'Such motivations are certainly the key foundations of the current reform movement,' Rawdon put in diplomatically, moving the conversation to less personal territory.

Her mother rose, taking the opening to remove the

ladies. 'We will leave you to your port and politics, gentlemen. When you've finished you can join us in the music room for some entertainment.' It was a welcome removal, although Thea cast a questioning look at Edward, her healer's worry surging. Would he be all right? She didn't like the idea of leaving him on his own among strangers and an enemy. He and Donnatt were not going to be friends, something that did give her a sense of satisfaction. But Edward gave no indication that he minded staying at the table. He seemed entirely at home as he leaned forward to listen to something her father said and the sight of it warmed her insides.

She missed him though when the four women gathered in the music room. Miss Rawdon proved to be excellent company, expressing an interest in the Sanitary Movement. But Thea could only muster a portion of her usual enthusiasm to discuss the cause. Her thoughts were back in the dining room with Edward. Was her father watching out for him? She should have warned him better about Clive Donnatt this afternoon. Were they still sparring over her under the guise of politics?

Donnatt's behaviour tonight was nothing new. He'd been trying to cut her down to size since they were children. Tonight, though, she'd had a champion, someone who was willing to stand up to the bullying grandson of a baron. *That* was different and it was a wonderful, novel feeling that left her giddy in a dangerous, swept-off-her-feet kind of way. It was not a feeling she was used to, nor one she could allow herself to become used to. She took care of herself. She relied on no one. It was better that way.

When the men entered the music room a half hour

later, her eyes went straight to Edward, searching for signs of distress. Was his leg paining him? Had the evening been too much? It was his first outing among others, after all. It was bound to take a toll on a man who'd been bedridden a month ago. But Edward appeared to be in good spirits, enjoying himself even as Rawdon slapped him on the back, laughing at a joke she couldn't hear. Their friendship was well on its way to being established. For a moment, an uncharacteristic stab of envy poked at her, that Edward had fitted in so effortlessly in one night when she never had in a lifetime of trying.

Be fair, Thea, you never tried, her conscience prodded.

She hadn't wanted to fit in, not at the expense of compromising her dreams. She could have conformed—she could have not practised medicine; she could not have thought herself the equal of a man. In exchange, she might have been the village darling. But she'd not wanted to fit in, not at that price. She'd simply wanted to be accepted the way she was. That had been too much to ask for, as Donnatt had made painfully clear with his pranks. No man would choose a wife who managed him as if she were his equal.

Edward's gaze moved around the room. Was he looking for her? Her pulse leapt irrationally at the thought. Of course, he was looking for her; she was the only one he knew. But others were looking at him. She saw his gaze pass over Miss Rawdon, and Miss Rawdon's welcoming eyes beckon for him to join her at the settee, a natural enough choice given that her brother and he were getting on famously.

The warrior in Thea bowed to the inevitable. Edward would not choose her; men who had a choice never did, not when they were healthy and the pretty blonde Miss Rawdons of the world awaited them. But then a miracle happened. Edward crossed the room and took up his place at her side, smiling that wry grin meant just for her as if they shared a secret as everyone settled into clusters about the room and Donnatt glared from the fireplace, where he posed at the mantel.

'You seem to have made an enemy,' Thea murmured as Edward settled on the sofa and set aside the hawthorn cane. He stretched out his leg with a relieved sigh.

'I'm in good company then. He doesn't like you much either. You might have warned me.' He slid her a questioning look that asked for details but there was no time to answer. Her mother invited Miss Rawdon to begin the entertainment. The pretty girl rose and stood before the piano. She began to sing, a performance as pretty as she was, not unpredictably. Why hide *behind* an instrument when one was as lovely as Miss Rawdon? She could just stand there and open her cupid's bow mouth and men would fall over themselves. And she was nice, genuinely nice, Thea thought. It was hard not to like her. She sang two old folk songs and then concluded with a duet, joined by her brother. The MP had a passably good tenor, not that anyone noticed. Miss Rawdon would have offers galore from London's marriage minded men before the Season was out.

The vicar's wife was asked to play next and then Thea's mother performed on the flute. It would be her turn next. Thea felt her hands grow clammy. She'd not be able to hold a bow at this rate. Her music was for herself, her family. She didn't enjoy performing in front of others, especially when the audience included Clive Donnatt. He would be sure to point out her mistakes, even in a flawless performance. She searched for an excuse, a way to beg off as her mother's flute solo ended.

'Thea, my dear,' her mother began, and Thea wiped her palms surreptitiously in the folds of her skirt. 'Would you honour us with a cello piece before the tea arrives?'

She hesitated for a moment, long enough to give herself away, apparently. She felt Edward move beside her, reaching for his cane and pushing up to his feet. 'Why don't we both play, Thea?' Thea. Not Miss Peverett, as he'd called her at dinner. His gaze held hers in a long silent message. He'd seen her discomfort when others—not even her own mother—had not. He had read her need without words and put himself at her disposal so that she would not face the room alone. He offered his hand, championing her again. 'We'll play the Vivaldi *Adagio in G.*'

We. A small word that connoted so much about their journey from Scutari to Haberstock. They *were* something of a 'we' now, weren't they? He'd called her 'Thea' in front of everyone, he'd championed her *three* times this evening. *We* was a warm word, but also a frightening word. She wasn't used to 'we', only 'me'.

'We haven't practised together,' Thea whispered sotto voce to him as they settled with their instruments.

He smiled and whispered back, 'It will be fine. Trust me.' That was something else she wasn't used to. Trusting others, trusting men.

It's just a song, Thea, don't be such a goose! she scolded herself, making a last adjustment to her cello.

She shot a final glance at Edward.

There was a spark of mischief in his eyes as he smiled back with his secret message: *Let's show off. I want us to succeed. Let's put Donnatt in his place.* She could do that. This wasn't so much a performance as it was a bit of revenge for the attempted insult at the dinner table.

Thea bowed the opening measures, crisp and clean. The piano joined her cello in the third measure and all thoughts of revenge fell away with the room. There was only her and Edward and the music. His timing was exquisite, his expression of the music divine. They might have practised endlessly together for this moment, so effortlessly did they complement one another. He caught her gaze and held it as the last notes faded, his hazel eyes wide open gates to his soul.

This is a piece of me, the real me.

The only piece of his real self that he had. And he'd given all of it to *her*.

Thea was breathless as she lifted her bow. She didn't want to give him back to the guests, but a return was inevitable. Miss Rawdon was on her feet, claiming Edward's attention with her praise, the vicar close behind her, wondering if Edward would be interested in helping out with music lessons at the vicarage school. He was swamped, leaving her alone to put her cello back on its stand, but not quite as alone as she wished.

Donnatt was at her back. She felt him before she turned. Perhaps if she didn't turn, he'd go away, but he only stepped closer until he needn't raise his voice to be heard. 'Do you think to humble me by flaunting your walking wounded in front of me? Do you think the attentions of a soldier with no memory proves anything?'

There it was—the ultimate humiliation he'd served to her years ago when he'd quite publicly declared she was unworthy of marriage. She did turn then, in a sharp whirl that forced him to step back. 'Such a comment suggests I think about you at all. I don't.' Even in a room full of people where he could do no more than insult her, he made her skin crawl, made her feel in danger.

He let out a long-suffering sigh. 'You just don't want to admit that I'm right. You are unnatural, you and the Nightingale woman. Women your age should be married, not trotting off to war. They acquire a certain reputation.'

'For what? Independence? Self-reliance?' Thea glared at him.

'A woman of loose morals who shares her favours indiscriminately. Even sick men have a penis,' he snarled.

Thea bristled, anger riding her hard. 'You are beyond the pale with your baseless accusations.'

'Baseless? I saw the way Edward of the no last name looked at you tonight. Don't be so quick to discredit me, Thea. I have eyes. You can't get a decent offer of marriage, so you opt for the indecent.'

'Decent? What do you know of decency? You, who slanders a woman in her own home, at her own dinner table?' Thea seethed, ready to give him the tongue lashing he deserved, company be hanged.

There was movement over Donnatt's shoulder and relief filled her as Edward approached, his expression grim. 'Your uncle needs you,' he dismissed Donnatt curtly and took up his place at her side. 'I am sorry I couldn't get here sooner. Miss Rawdon was difficult to evade.'

'Not at all. She's very pretty,' Thea snapped, still bristling with anger.

Edward shrugged and gave a grin. 'Perhaps. I prefer brunettes, though. Especially if they play the cello.'

Thea laughed and elbowed him discreetly in the ribs. 'Stop it, Edward. A girl might think you're serious.'

His smile broadened. 'Maybe I am. We make a good team.'

As friends, perhaps. She could allow nothing more for her own well-being and Edward was being generous. He'd discover soon enough he didn't need her. In the span of an evening, he'd charmed the MP's sister, he'd become his correspondent and endeared himself to the vicar by accepting the request to help with music lessons. He had ingratiated himself into the community while she had nearly started a fight by arguing with a guest.

Chapter Seven

The guests departed shortly after the tea was served. The Rawdons were the last to leave. Thea shut the door behind them and sighed. 'You did well tonight. Are you tired?' She turned to face Edward, who was leaning heavily on his cane. They were alone in the foyer; her parents had drifted back to the music room. 'I can mix you a draught.'

'I'm fine,' Edward assured her. 'I thought I might sit up in the library and read a while. Care to join me? I would like company.'

'Yes, I'll come and sit for a spell.' As she climbed the stairs beside him, the healer in her tried to justify it as a means of looking after her patient, but the woman in her knew it was a weak answer. There was none of the patient about him tonight. He'd been all gallant man. She ought not to join him. She ought to go straight to bed, to forget how handsome Edward had looked tonight, how loyal he'd been, how he'd championed her and chosen her. Remembering those things conjured up dangerous fantasies of what life could be like if Edward stayed, if he made a life here, with her, at Haberstock

Hall. The fantasies birthed questions that brought her up short in their demand for examination.

Who would he be to her in that life? A husband? What did he give her beyond friendship? A family of her own? Regardless of his ability to offer those things, did she even want them? She'd not thought of such things for a very long time. Life was too short to spend time thinking on the impossible, not when there was so much to do and so many others to save. That was where she invested her hopes. She saved no such hopes for herself.

Edward ushered her into the library, allowing her to pass before him, and it was immediately obvious that he'd made the library his. Thea noted the indelible mark he'd put on it as soon as she stepped inside. It might be her house, but she was in *his* territory now. A chair and hassock had been repositioned near the fire to accommodate his leg, books lay on the small round table beside the chair and on the long study table that dominated the centre of the room.

The subtle changes in the room, this once non-specific space used as a schoolroom for the Peverett children, made it definitively masculine now, and the knowledge of that masculinity imbued this late-night visit to the library with the same discernment she'd experienced at the supper table when he'd looked at her, when he'd championed her.

There were the beginnings of something more brewing between them, perhaps more than the beginnings. It would be up to her to embrace those things.

Thea trailed her fingers over the long table's polished surface. 'William and I spent hours in here doing our lessons, learning our medicine.' She tossed him a little smile with the memory, trying to lessen the sense that she was the intruder here, a guest in his space.

He stumped over to the sideboard and poured a brandy. He raised a second glass in question. Did she want any? 'No, thank you.' She moved to take the chair across from the one that was clearly his and waited for him to join her. 'You're sure your leg doesn't hurt too much? You've been on it a long time today.' She fussed with the hassock when he sat and stretched his leg out, his free hand absently reaching to massage the thigh muscle.

'Thea, I'm fine.' There was a touch of finality to his words, a gentle insistence that said her fussing wasn't welcome. 'I want your company, not your nursing, not tonight.'

The words unnerved her. When had a man ever *wanted* her company? She sat back in her chair, her hands quiet in her lap, with nothing to do. What was she if she wasn't a nurse? What use could she have to a man like Edward, who was so self-sufficient, if it wasn't care-giving?

This is how he leaves you. He starts to realise he doesn't need you anymore. You knew this was coming.

And yet he'd chosen her tonight—chosen to stand up for her, chosen to literally stand beside her when he could have gone to Miss Rawdon.

She didn't dare put too much stock in those gestures, no matter how they quickened her heart. A gentleman was loyal, that was all. It was a simple explanation. Perhaps he felt he owed her his allegiance for the time being, nothing more.

'Thank you for what you did tonight,' she began,

wanting him to know she'd been aware of his efforts and they had been appreciated.

The praise made Edward uncomfortable. He shifted in the chair. 'The man is a bully and he was trying to bully *you*, of all people, something he should realise is impossible. You hardly needed me.' He winked and took a swallow of his brandy. 'The likes of Clive Donnatt are child's play compared to your usual. You've handled Menzies, after all.' There it was. The Crimea, the one thing they always went back to, the one thing that drew them together, the one thing they shared with each other and no one else. It had found its way into a simple conversation as they dissected a supper party, something that couldn't be further from their life at Scutari. Was that all they had to bind them together? What happened when those remembrances weren't enough?

He'll leave. You know that, Thea.

'Still, I couldn't help myself from jumping in.' Edward swirled his brandy and looked at her. His gaze changed the tenor of the room to something potent and serious. 'You don't deserve to be spoken to that way. You are all that is good and kind and strong.'

She let herself pretend for a moment that he meant those words, that they weren't driven by duty or a gentleman's code. It was a dangerous pretence. The longer she indulged, the more tempted she was to forget that she was the sum of his remembered world. Of course, she meant something to him; he had nothing else that did. She was his lifeline, his way back. She reached for the poker beside the fireplace and stirred up the fire, desperate for distraction. She had a poor record with men; she knew better than that.

'Thea, tell me about Donnatt. What did he do?' Edward's gaze was still upon her as she sat back down, obstinate and probing. She knew him well enough to know he wasn't going to let the subject go.

She met his gaze squarely, more in control of her own stare this time as she formulated a two-sentence summary of her humiliation at the hands of Donnatt. 'He dared a man to pretend to fall in love with me. When I was convinced, he exposed the prank.' That had been years ago; she'd been eighteen, barely out in any type of society. Since then, she'd reduced the episode to twenty words and not very long or descriptive words at that. There was no emotion hidden in them, just the facts.

'What a dastardly thing to do.' Edward didn't shy away from subjective language. 'It must have hurt, very much.'

'It did, at the time. Not anymore, though, and not in the way you might expect. It was a stupid prank by stupid, small-minded men who were intimidated by a smart woman, a woman who didn't have any use for them. They could not fathom such a thing.' There was venom behind her words despite her attempt to cultivate a nonchalance about it. 'It wasn't my pride that lay trampled on the ground but my naiveté, that someone so smart had been so thoroughly duped. What did that say about the quality of my intelligence? I vowed no one would get past my guard again in such a way, and they haven't.'

She smiled a little. She *did* take pride in that, in being the equal of any man, and even their superior. 'His prank also did me a favour, although I'm sure he'd be wroth to know it.' She gave a wry smile. 'He prepared me for the world of men. My parents took Anne and me to London when she turned eighteen to meet the sons of doctors, sons of friends of my father. But not one of them saw me, just a moderately pretty face that became less attractive to them as soon as I opened my mouth.'

Not to me. Edward looked up from his brandy. *I see you*, he wanted to cry out. *I see your beautiful, powerful mouth, I hear your words. You are so much more than you think, than what others think.*

He wanted to challenge Donnatt on her behalf. 'Why would he do such a thing out of the blue?' he probed.

'We'd been adversaries since childhood. He spent summers here with his uncle. He and some other boys spent their days roaming the fields and getting up to mischief, bothering the little animals. It all started over a robin's nest. He'd been smashing eggs. I'd seen the broken shells all week when I went out for walks. I caught him in the act and confronted him.'

Edward sensed there was more to it than that. 'He relinquished the nest just because you asked?' That seemed unlikely.

Thea shook her head. 'No, he relinquished it because I punched him in the nose in front of his friends.'

'Ouch.' Edward rubbed the bridge of his nose. 'That bump he has; was that you?'

'I'm afraid so. I did try to persuade with words first,' she said. 'Do no harm, and all that. Violence is always a last resort.' That she had used it at all spoke of the desperation she must have felt. It spoke also of the fierceness of her desire to protect the helpless even at a young age.

'What happened after that?' Edward tried imagining a ten-year-old Thea punching Donnatt and found it wasn't hard.

'He dropped the nest, I picked it up and I ran for dear life. The boys were on my heels, but I was fast and I was clever.' She still was. She'd been one step ahead of Menzies at the hospital, always ready with a quick argument or answer when her practices had been questioned.

'And the eggs?' Edward feared the story ended poorly despite her best efforts. Sometimes things were beyond saving, but he couldn't stand the thought of his Thea being disappointed. A little rill of tension went through him as he waited, quite invested in the outcome.

She smiled softly. 'I put the nest in my father's surgery and kept the eggs warm. They hatched and the birds lived in the walled garden for a while before they flew away. I like to think their relatives are in the Haberstock woods and meadows.'

A happy ending, then. He was glad. A little wave of relief eased through him. 'It was an expensive battle, though,' he commented. It had made her an enemy for life in Clive Donnatt, an enemy who'd exacted his revenge years later. Whether she admitted it or not, that battle had scarred her and, like all scars, it had reshaped how she saw herself. She believed her power, her strength, was possible only at the cost of being undesirable, unmarriageable. A younger Thea had once desired those things otherwise the prank wouldn't have had any teeth, otherwise her parents would not have taken her to London. Perhaps she still did desire those things. How like his angel to give up everything that mattered to her to save another. How much he hated the idea that a man like Donnatt had been able to threaten those hopes. A man should protect, not hurt.

'Not all men are asses, Thea.' He wanted to reassure her, to break down the walls she'd built. 'Your brother, your father, your sister Anne's husband, myself, if I might be so bold to add myself to the list.' A woefully short list. He wished he could do better.

'I can't marry them,' Thea snapped without thinking. 'Brothers and fathers don't count.' Neither did patients. All those men were obliged to like her. 'They have to put up with me. They haven't a choice.' They had to choose her. Proof that his earlier conclusions weren't wrong. She'd once wanted to marry.

Edward studied her, seeing the young woman who'd wanted to have it all: marriage, a family, a medical career. She wouldn't want his pity any more than he'd wanted hers as he recovered. 'I've never considered myself having to "put up" with you.'

Thea raised a doubting brow. 'Not even when I was forcing food down your throat? I seem to recall several nights when you wished me to perdition.'

Edward contemplated his glass. 'Well, maybe then.' He looked up with a smile. 'But I am still here.' He elected not to point out that he had nowhere else to go. It would have ruined the moment. The truth would insult them both and it would have quenched the ripple of undeniable electricity that jumped between them as their eyes held.

Do not indulge that chemistry, his conscience cautioned. *It can lead nowhere at present and result in nothing but hurt. It is late and you are both vulnerable.*

He swallowed hard and cast about for another distraction. Thea found one first. She grabbed up one of the books from the table beside his chair before he could stop her. 'What are you reading these days?' She studied the spine and raised a brow in an approving arch. 'Dante?' She reached for another. 'Voltaire? Hell versus earthly suffering at the hands of fellow man. Not exactly light reading. Both have a rather dark opinion of humanity.'

'I prefer "introspective".' Edward chuckled before offering more seriously, 'Dante suggests our afterlife will be commensurate with the level of our sins in this life.' With betrayal being the worst of sins in Dante's opinion, reserved for the most inner circle of Hell. He uncharitably imagined Clive Donnatt in that circle.

'Such contemplative reading. You've been soul-searching. But I doubt you've betrayed anyone.'

'How can you be sure, though?' Edward's expression echoed his doubt. What was in his past? Would that past shame him? Was that why he couldn't remember anything specific? Was his mind hiding cold truths from him, protecting him?

Thea reached forward and touched his knee out of her natural habit, the presence of her touch warming him. It was too rare these days. Did she realise how different that gesture felt now? She'd spent months touching him as he recovered but the more he healed, the less they touched. To touch him or to touch her now required an excuse, a reason of conversation. Frankly, Society didn't afford many reasons for an unmarried woman to touch a gentleman in the natural course of conversation.

'Because tonight you defended me against a man you didn't know and deliberately drew his fire.' Thea smiled softly as he tried to disabuse her of the uniqueness of his action.

'Any gentleman would have done the same.'

'No, they wouldn't have. They haven't to date.' She gave him a meaningful look. 'It's empirically true.'

'I don't count Donnatt and his stooges as real gentlemen.' He covered her hand where it lay on his knee and teased her with a wry smile. 'Perhaps that's the problem, Thea. You haven't met a real gentleman yet.'

'I've met you,' she whispered, but the words cost her, pulled them too near to what simmered between them. She pulled back her hand lest he read anything more into her warm touch than the support of a comrade.

She picked up the books from her lap, seeking refuge no doubt from the dangerous edge of the conversation. She opened Voltaire at a random page, perhaps to engage him in a philosophical debate that had nothing to do with hands on knees and dinner table champions, but he watched her eyes startle at the words on the page. She lifted her gaze slowly and Edward froze, knowing how fast that nimble mind leapt to conclusions.

'This is the original French.' She rapidly opened the Dante, letting recrimination show in her eyes. 'Most men can barely soul search in one language, let alone three. When were you going to tell me?' she accused and Dante's ninth circle of Hell yawned before him.

Chapter Eight

'Thea, I can explain,' he began, but she cut him off, rising and slamming the books down on the table beside his chair.

'The last thing I want right now are justifications wrapped up as "explanations". When were you going to tell me? How long have you known you could read French *and* Italian?' Anger replaced the dangerous softness that had welled up in her over the course of the evening, encouraged by his handsomeness of visage and manner. Dear Lord, she'd practically turned him into a knight in shining armour. She was supposed to be smarter than that.

He struggled awkwardly to his feet to meet her toe to toe. 'I was going to tell you when it *meant* something.' His voice was a growl. His hand gripped her wrist, begging her not to go until he'd had his say. He was angry too. Her anger had insulted him and the realisation was humbling, deflating even.

'It means nothing, Thea. It's no more than discovering I play the piano and understand music.' His hazel eyes blazed with emerald hues as he argued. 'I play the piano, I understand French and Italian—the last is not so surprising, given my apparent musical background. These are things I can do. They are not who I am. They aren't my name, my people, my place, where I come from, what I've done. They are not the things that matter.'

'You should have told me at once.' Her position was sounding weaker the second time around.

'I did. I told you I was working the equation backwards that day in the garden.'

'That's not specifics. You didn't tell me you'd discovered anything.'

'Because I didn't feel I had, and I would have told you eventually, when the time was right, when it mattered.'

'It mattered the moment it happened,' Thea snapped. Didn't he see? When good things happened, one celebrated them, shared them immediately in the Peverett family, where everyone was in everyone's business all the time.

'Why? Because you're my nurse?' He was challenging her, daring her to defy him, to give a name to the feelings that had punctuated the interactions between them ever since he'd been able to get out of bed, to say she wanted to be more than his nurse, or that she already considered herself to be more than that.

'Don't do that, Edward. Don't conflate nursing with friendship.' She wanted to back away, wanted to escape from his influencing touch that made her believe so much more was possible. 'We'll both be sorry.'

His eyes glittered dangerously, as if he wanted to dispute that, to argue with her, and the form of that argument might not be words but a kiss. Then his hand fell away from her wrist and he stepped back. 'I'm already sorry. I didn't mean to hurt your feelings.' He blew out a breath. 'I just needed some privacy, Thea. Something that was just mine for a little while.'

His voice was quiet like a meadow after a storm passed through. The anger was gone. 'I've not had anything that belonged just to me ever since this began. No memories except the ones you gave me, no history but what I've been told, and I'm smart enough to know that whatever I've been told is heavily based on speculation. My body hasn't been my own; it's belonged to illness and caretakers. Even now...' He stopped, refusing to go on, perhaps realising he was about to cross a line. He didn't need to cross it to make his point; she could fill in the unspoken sentences. Even now, she and her father required updates, asked constant questions about how he felt. How many times had she fussed over him tonight? She'd *not* thought about how it might have made him feel, how *unwanted* the attentions. What else was unwanted? The old doubts surged.

'Don't be downcast, Thea. It was all necessary, but that doesn't mean it doesn't chafe a man nonetheless.' He gave her a crooked smile and took her hand. 'Will you forgive me?'

She nodded. He always made it look so easy to be here, to fit in at Haberstock Hall. On the outside, he looked healthy and, dare she use the word—normal? Mental wounds were hidden, so easily dismissed for their invisibility. She'd forgotten how difficult it must be for him, a man who literally had nothing to call his own. Without that sense of ownership, he could not truly be at home in his own skin, nor would he be until his memories returned. He would not be whole without them, no matter what changes they would bring.

'Do you forgive me as well?'

He lifted her hand to his lips as he'd done on the terrace steps, but this time the playful teasing that had prompted the earlier gesture was gone. 'I'd forgive my angel anything.'

'Good night, Edward. I'll see you in the morning.' Thea smiled softly.

His eyes danced with mischief as he relinquished her hand. 'Maybe.'

In another time, another place, the night might have ended with a different kind of kiss, one on the mouth instead of on a hand. Goodness knew, even under the circumstances he'd been tempted to kiss Thea's mouth into submission along with her wayward thoughts— thoughts that did her no service. To show her that to a real man who was not intimidated by her dreams, her intellect, her forthright nature, she was absolutely as desirable as the Miss Rawdons of the world, perhaps even more so. At least she was to him.

Neither of them was ready for that kiss, although for very different reasons. She would think he was kissing her out of pity for her or out of his own desperation or the smallness of his world—a world where she was the only woman in it. And he would not take advantage of her or of their relationship while he dwelt beneath her family's roof, not after the generosity they'd shown him. It was not what a gentleman did. A gentleman did not kiss a well-bred woman until he had something to back his intentions with: a future, a cause, a pathway. He was working on that. Until then, the kiss had to wait. He would satisfy himself with her company. It would have to be enough. He'd have to settle for just dreaming of the rest.

The dream was vivid and frightening. Fog was everywhere, cutting companies and men off from one another, destroying all efforts to coordinate the battle. *Stay alive. Gather the men.* The messages of desperation and duty pounded through his head as he ran through the fog, calling orders, calling to men, his new-issue French Minie rifle at the ready to fire should the enemy materialise in front of him. A sound on his left sent him whirling, pulling up just in time to recognise the uniform, his heart thundering from the near mistake of shooting one's own, a very likely possibility under these conditions. Were they even in the right place? How could one tell in this fog?

The man yelled to him, 'The General is down!' and then chaos broke loose, the fog coming alive with the dark forms and gut-chilling cries of the Russians who seemingly swarmed from nowhere. Damn it, they were counterattacking! The flanking British troops would be trapped! Someone had to act.

'To me! To me!' he yelled, waving his rifle, trying to rally the men, trying to mount a defence among the chaos. Men ran everywhere, fell everywhere. It was the stuff of nightmares, fighting a never-ending stream of men materialising from the fog, their blood-curdling yells making them appear more like monsters than men. A man came at him, bayonet fixed for stabbing and slicing. He raised his rifle and fired without hesitation. He was not going to die here in the fog. The trigger clicked. No report. No spark lighting up the dark. Damn it! The fog had got to the powder. He met the bayonet with his rifle, wielding it like a quarterstaff, turning the blade aside in one move and bringing the rifle down on the man's skull with another.

A roar sounded behind him; he pivoted and faced another monster, and another, and another, wielding his rifle-cum-club until his arms ached and his throat was raw. Around him, men screamed, cut down in the melee. A light cut through the fog, a man wielding a torch like a weapon, setting everything on fire in his path, adding smoke to the fog. He brought his rifle up to fend off the torch, the heat threatening to scorch his fingers. He dropped the weapon, the musician in him instantly protecting his tools. It didn't matter, the flames caught his coat and he fell back, screaming in pain from the flame as the fire of a Minie ball sliced into his leg, bringing him down, burning and screaming even as his mind tried to marshal the last of his senses, firing rapid instructions to a body that couldn't respond.

Drop. Roll. Put out the flames. Drag yourself to cover.

He could do none of it. All he could do was meet the inevitable with screams.

The screams woke Thea. Instinct propelled her out of bed, had her grabbing her bag and racing barefoot down the hall, her mind assimilating bits of information as she ran. A man was in pain. *Edward* was in pain. *Extreme* pain. She threw open the door to his room. He lay thrashing on the bed, the bedclothes tangled about his legs, his nightshirt riding up, exposing his wounded leg, but it was his screams that tore at her. Whatever his nightmare was, it had reduced this brave man to blancmange.

She flew to his bedside, dropping her bag. She shook him. 'Edward, wake up, it's a nightmare. Wake up,' she instructed in stern tones, willing him to obey. Hazel eyes flashed open as he drew a sharp, startled breath. He tried to sit up, his body primed for the fight, his gaze hunting for that fight frantically in the dark corners of the room. 'Edward, you're safe, you're at Haberstock Hall. I am here,' Thea soothed, pressing him back to the pillows. 'You're safe,' she repeated, watching his eyes fasten on her, watching the fear recede.

She poured him a glass of water and helped him sip, his own hands trembling from the aftermath. Whatever he had dreamed of, it had wreaked havoc on his body. She could smell the nightmare's sweat on him, could feel him trying to control the rapid breaths. He was struggling to speak. 'Steady, you'll be better in a moment, Edward, relax,' she instructed, setting the glass aside. This was an old scene, the two of them at his bedside as he tried to construct words to express his world. She wrung out a cool cloth; his hand gripped her wrist as she laid it on his brow, his touch, his gaze full of urgency and insistence as his throat worked desperately to make words.

'Thea, *listen* to me.' The words were hoarse and forced. His eyes pleaded with her. 'I dreamed about the war.'

Thea stilled and sat on the edge of the bed, the import

of his words halting her ministrations. This had been no amorphous fever dream. This was a memory. 'Tell me, Edward. Tell me everything, if you can,' she whispered.

'I was fighting in the fog. I couldn't see anything until the enemy was on top of us, an unexpected counterattack. The General had been shot; there was no leadership, only chaos. I don't even know if we were in the right place.' The nightmare poured out of him, damp powder, torch and all. Thea listened, itching to write it all down and not daring to break the spell long enough to reach for a notepad in her bag. She would write it down later, sift through it for clues. 'And then I was screaming.' His grip clenched around her hand, the terror of the nightmare not entirely vanquished.

She had questions, she wanted to probe but this wasn't the time. She would wait for morning light and the calm it brought. She said only, 'It's all right now. You're healed, you're safe and well.' They would pick through the nightmare tomorrow. 'Shall I mix you a draught to help you sleep?' She hated seeing him like this. Why had they fought this evening? The quarrel seemed the height of pettiness now. She wanted only to help him.

'No.' His voice was stronger. 'No more poppy syrup, no more opium.'

'Staying up all night to keep the dreams away is no antidote,' she reasoned, seeing his stubborn intention immediately. 'You still need your rest. Sleep is a great healer.' She fixed him with a determined stare to ensure he didn't see through her strategy. 'I'm not leaving until I'm assured you're asleep.' He wouldn't dare ask her to stay, nor would he tolerate being treated as a child, so she volunteered it sternly, matter-of-factly, as if her remaining with him was more of a punishment than a pleasure. Perhaps after their quarrel this evening it was. Perhaps that quarrel had prompted the nightmare. Guilt poked at her. She should have been more careful with her words.

His response was gruff. 'Stay, then, if it pleases you.'

Thea smiled to herself as she settled into the chair beside his bed and took his hand. It pleased them both.

Chapter Nine

Thea was gone the second time he woke, her presence replaced by the morning light flooding his bedchamber, washing away the last of the night's darkness. She'd stayed the rest of the night, though. He'd woken right before dawn and she'd still been in the chair, asleep, her head lolling, her hand still holding his.

She didn't look as fierce in sleep as she did in life. The lamp she'd left burning cast her features in a soft light and the billows of her white cotton nightgown added to the glimpse of a younger, more innocent Thea, the girl who'd stood up against a bully for the sake of a robin's nest, her own vulnerability notwithstanding— one girl against a pack of boys. That was to the good. He didn't want her to lose her humanity; it was what made her passion so refreshing, so heartwarming. What was fierceness without caring?

Tonight, she had come to him, soothed him, despite their disagreement, despite feeling betrayed earlier, although in the aftermath he'd experienced no small amount of embarrassment over her seeing him helpless in the grip of his nightmare, his weakness on overt display for her. But she'd not made him feel that embarrassment in the moment. She'd not pressed him for details or for an immediate dissection of what the nightmare might mean, even though they both knew its import. She'd even left before he'd awakened for the day, so that he could rise in the dignity of the morning and face her questions with his self-respect intact. His angel had come to him and now it was time to go to her.

He found her in the little sitting room off the breakfast parlour, a room done in pink chintz and roses, a lady's room with French windows that opened onto the terrace and embraced the morning sun. She was at the writing desk, her head with its carefully coiled braid at her neck, bent to her task.

He cleared his throat in the doorway, drawing her attention and her smile. She stood and he noticed she was not dressed for work today in one of her serviceable dark gowns and aprons. Instead, she wore a white spring muslin decorated with blue flowers and a deep ruffle. The effect was decidedly feminine and lovely. 'I've come to thank you for last night,' he began. He would not let his embarrassment obscure what he owed her—gratitude, appreciation, even an apology.

'You look much better.' She gestured to the little cluster of chairs near the empty fireplace. 'Do you want to talk it over? I think we should.' Pretty dress aside, she was still his straightforward angel, although he thought today there might be a touch of vulnerability lurking behind the briskness of her tone. After last night, there was no ignoring that something more lay between them.

Thea took a chair, leaving him the settee. 'I think

there might be valuable pieces of information embedded in that dream.' He thought so too. Information that could unlock his memories, set him down a path of more intimate self-discovery than learning he spoke three languages and played the piano. He was torn about that journey. It was a journey towards wholeness, towards completeness. He owed Thea that; he owed himself that. But the achieving of it put this life at Haberstock Hall at risk. Once he knew who he was, he'd have to go back to that life. That life might require leaving Thea behind. It was an enormous risk— to regain a life he didn't know at the price of the life he had now.

She'd brought a notepad with her to the chair and he laughed as he sat. 'I see your question was merely rhetorical. You've already given the nightmare a bit of thought.' As had he as he'd dressed. His nightmare hadn't been a fabrication, not entirely at least, and there was already proof of that. He was reminded daily in his limp, in the soreness of his leg, in the scarred skin that marred his torso. The events in his nightmare were real. The question was, which of those events were real and which were fabrications of his mind, put there in hindsight, perhaps an attempt by his mind to make sense of it all?

Thea flipped open the notebook. 'I wrote down everything you told me last night. If you could remember where you were in the dream it might help us determine which division you were with, or what company you were in.'

He shook his head. It was only the first question and he was failing her. 'It was foggy in the dream. I kept thinking we were lost. I couldn't see my men or the Russians, not until they were upon us. I kept thinking we weren't in the right place. I'm not sure if that's real or if it's my imagination struggling with displacement.' He sighed. 'I'm sorry, Thea.'

But Thea didn't seem disappointed. She cocked her head, studying him and thinking. 'Did anyone ever tell you about the Battle of Inkerman? Perhaps a surgeon or anyone in the field hospital?'

'No, I was hardly in a conversational condition,' he reminded her.

'You're sure?' She leaned forward when he nodded, her excitement evident. 'Edward, the press has been calling it the "Soldiers' Battle" because of the fog and how disconnected the troops became. There was no way for officers to coordinate their troop movements.'

'That doesn't help us determine which company I was with,' Edward argued.

'No, but it *does* establish that the details in your dream are based on reality,' Thea encouraged in earnest now. Her enthusiasm was affirming and contagious. She believed in him. Lord, he didn't want to disappoint her. 'There *was* fog that day, there *was* confusion. You are not making that up.' She studied her notes. 'You said the General had been killed. We can track that. We can get a list of officers killed. There couldn't have been more than one or two Generals shot. It would help us determine at least what division you were with.'

He offered a smile only because he didn't want to disappoint her. 'I love your optimism, Thea, and your tenacity.' They made her beautiful in a sense that transcended her expressive whisky eyes and the striking angles of her face. Every day that optimism drew him in, made him hope not only that he'd walk again, ride again, but that he could have something larger—a life, a family, not one that he might be attached to out there somewhere in a world he didn't remember, but one of his own, one that he made with a woman he loved. Was that a new hope or a recovered hope? Something he'd always wanted or something he wanted now because of Thea? Because she'd given him a second chance to live.

'Are you not excited?' Thea's brow puckered, her eyes resting on him, trying to read his reaction. 'This is progress, Edward, and the reference to the General's death isn't all. You mentioned a Russian attempt to out-manoeuvre the flank. We can track you through that strategy as well. If you were part of the flank that would narrow down what portion of the division you were with. Don't you see, Edward? In a few weeks we will know, you will have your answers.'

He gave a dry chuckle. 'Are you that eager to be rid of me?' Once he knew who he was, he'd know his place in the world, his family. Even if his memories remained elusive, he would be their burden then. Thea wouldn't need to assume sole responsibility for him, which should come as a relief to him. He didn't like the idea of being a burden to anyone. Was that why she pressed so hard on his behalf? Was he holding her back? Where would she be right now if she wasn't here with him?

'I'm sure there are a thousand things you'd rather do than play nursemaid to me.' It was a confession and a test. She had her soldiers project and her work for the

Sanitary Movement. Was he the only one who both hoped and feared what his memories might reveal?

Thea had the decency at least to look appalled at the suggestion. 'You are not a burden, Edward, and you are welcome to remain at Haberstock as long as you like.' Not as long as he *needed* but as long as he *liked*.

He gave her a wry grin. 'That's a dangerous invitation, Thea. I might stay for ever.' It didn't come out as the jest he intended.

'Then stay for ever.' She wasn't jesting either, although they both should have been. This was impossible territory and they knew it. It was why they hadn't discussed it. There was nothing to discuss and there couldn't be until he knew who he was…or wasn't.

He tore his gaze away and fingered the head of his hawthorn stick. 'I have thought about it, Thea.' The unspoken 'what-ifs' hung between them. What if the family he remembered included more than parents, siblings and an assortment of relatives? What if that family included a wife, children? What if they were mourning him? Or living with the slimmest of hopes that he was still alive somewhere? If he remembered them, he could not walk away from them, not even for Thea or because of Thea. She would not tolerate dishonour in anyone she loved. 'What would you be doing right now if you weren't stuck here with me?'

'What I *am* doing right now with you here,' Thea insisted. 'Making rounds with my father, helping in the surgery when needed, which is not often enough. Writing letters, lobbying MPs on the sanitary conditions of the Crimean military hospitals. See, you are not disrupting anything,' she assured him with a laugh that faded too soon. She closed her notebook and rose, pacing before the fireplace before she gave him a considering look. 'May I be honest with you, Edward?'

'You may be anything you like with me.'

His usually assured Thea had something on her mind. He was just vain enough—or was that desperate enough?—to hope it was him.

'The truth is, I am in no hurry to see you go. As long as you're here, there's someone who knows where I've been, what I've done, what I've seen, someone I don't have to try and explain it to. People say they understand, and I know they mean well, but they weren't there. They didn't see the boatloads of wounded coming in, the conditions we faced, the piles of bodies, all the men I couldn't save.'

There was real, painful regret in her eyes, a plea for something—absolution, perhaps? She didn't need it, though. She'd done her best, more than her best. Surely, she understood that. But all he could give her were platitudes, so he said nothing; he just let her continue.

'You aren't the only one with nightmares, Edward. Sometimes at night, when I close my eyes, I think I can hear Menzies yelling, 'Living to the right, dead to the left'. Sometimes I wonder if I'll hear him in my head for the rest of my life.'

Thea made her confessions with strength, but the strong needed comfort and consolation too. Who consoled her? Who comforted her? Certainly, her family would try, but by her admission they would fall short. He knew in that moment what she needed: she needed him, *his* strength, *his* understanding. For the first time since November, someone needed him. That the person in need was his angel made the need all the more poignant.

He pushed to his feet and went to her, wrapping his arms about her, drawing her close against his chest, feeling her body give way and melt into his; he felt her hands at his back, digging into the fabric of his coat, the weight of her head against his shoulder. She did not collapse against him—his angel would never collapse, never cling—but he was gratified that she did lean into him, did take the comfort he had on offer.

'I'm here, Thea,' he murmured.

Hold onto me and never let go, for both our sakes.

It felt good to hold her, to be of use, to be of support. This was what it meant to care for another. The surge of emotion following the realisation nearly undid him. How wondrous it was to have the energy and strength to spare for another, to not have his own trials be the centre of his world, the sole focus of his energies.

Thea raised her gaze to his and he knew the surge of emotion went deeper than that. 'When I'm with you, Edward, I know who I am. I am accepted, flaws and all. You've never judged me. With you, I'm whole. If you leave…'

He pressed a finger to her lips. 'That makes two of us.' He might not know who he was, past tense, but he knew who he wanted to be. *Whole.* That was exactly the word for it. Standing there, his arms wrapped about Thea, knowing that she'd bared her soul to him with her confessions, he felt *whole.* Whole enough that he didn't want to release her even when his leg began to hurt—it seemed a small price to pay for what he felt right now— forgiven and whole. Whole enough that he would have stood there with her in his arms all day and he might have, if her mother hadn't walked in and demanded an explanation for the unexplainable.

Chapter Ten

'You were in his arms. Don't tell me it was nothing.' If it had been any other mother, the words would have been the prelude to a scathing scold, but Thea knew her mother well enough to know that she wasn't mad, she was worried. Thea supposed she had every right to be. The Peverett girls had not fared well in love.

Thea took a seat, schooling herself to present a calm front and deliberately trained her eyes to look away from the door through which Edward had recently taken his discreet leave. But inside she was anything but calm. The peace of those moments in Edward's arms had evaporated in the wake of her mother's suppositions.

'It was a moment of mutual support and that was all.' Did she sound calm enough, or did her mother see through the incomplete truth? It *had* been a moment of support, but it had also been so much more, two wandering souls finding one another. It was not like any connection she'd ever felt with another, and her insides were in tumult over what to make of it.

Her mother sat in the chair opposite—Edward's chair—the furrow of worry between her brows easing only slightly. She smiled and leaned forward, taking Thea's hand. 'My dear girl, it's natural for soldiers to fall in love with their nurses, to shape their gratitude into what they think is love. It is natural enough, too, for nurses to fall for their patients.'

Thea felt her cheeks heat. This was going to be worse than the procreation talk she'd had at twelve. Her only hope was to head her mother off. 'Love has nothing to do with it. Perhaps there is a friendly affection between us, but nothing more.' Why did it ache to belittle that moment? To try to downplay it as 'nothing'. To diminish the moment was to belittle herself and Edward, to belittle what she felt for him.

Her mother tilted her head, considering her oldest daughter with perceptive green eyes. She looked like an older version of Anne and Thea felt a wave of longing for her sister sweep over her. How she wished Anne were here now to be her confidante. Anne wouldn't understand going to war, but she would understand this confusion of feelings that had welled up in her. Alas, Anne was in London, busy with a new husband, a new babe and a new medical practice—Anne was living the dream, a dream Thea had once thought she could have.

'There is a very thin line between love and friendly affection, a line that is easily and unsuspectingly crossed.' Her mother gave her a knowing look, suggesting that her daughter's good heart had simply been taken unawares. 'Edward was eager to champion you last night and I've seen the way he looks at you.' Her mother paused. 'It's much the same way you look at him.'

'I watch him for symptoms of a fever returning, for

signs of fatigue. It is my *job* to watch him,' Thea protested, only to have her mother wave her reasons away with a dismissive gesture and a soft laugh.

'I may be a happily married woman and the mother of five grown children, but I still have eyes, Thea. I see what a handsome fellow our skeletal soldier has turned out to be. I see his fine manners. You needn't be ashamed of your attraction. I imagine many women would be attracted to such a man. Just be aware of it. Don't lie to yourself. Admit to it, understand it. Of course, you're drawn to him. The two of you have spent months in each other's pockets, you have a history together, one that no one around here shares.'

Normally, Thea welcomed her mother's rational mind but today all that logic only served to irritate her. She didn't like the idea of she and Edward being the result of a predictable set of factors that could produce such a result regardless of who the individuals were. She'd not felt like a factor when she'd been in his arms.

'It's only a moment in time, Thea. Have a care,' her mother cautioned. 'There will come a time when the moment ends and he will leave.'

'I can take care of myself,' Thea snapped, more sharply than intended. Her mother was only trying to help, trying to protect. But she was not Thomasia, who'd been blinded by the handsome façade of a man who'd been less than gallant and had left her with a child. 'I am twenty-seven years old, I've run a hospital ward, stood up to arrogant officers, I've been to war,' she reminded her mother.

'Yes, you have. That's why I worry, my dear. You've not been yourself since you've been home.' Her mother smiled softly. 'Do you realise this is the first time we've sat down together, just the two of us, and talked?' She shook her head, stalling Thea's protest. 'I know we've pounded herbs and weeded the garden. We've spent time together, but we've not talked about anything of substance. You've shared nothing, you've kept it bottled up inside.'

'There's been much to do,' Thea excused but her mother was having none of it.

'I haven't been to a battlefield, Thea, but I have seen a fair bit of life in my forty-eight years, and I *can* listen. You needn't feel alone here, among family.' In other words, she needn't rely on Edward; he needn't be her only outlet.

'Thank you, Mother.' Thea returned her mother's smile. Her mother meant well. 'It's just that Edward and I understand each other.'

'Do *you* understand him? You are a woman who has much to offer, both emotionally and in a practical sense, Thea. There are men who would take advantage of that. For a man who has nothing, not even a name, Haberstock Hall must look like heaven or at the very least the answer to a prayer.'

'Do not take Donnatt's side. Donnatt is a cad and he was out of line last night.' Thea bristled at her mother's suggestion. 'Do you think so little of Edward that he would compromise me in my own home? He's been nothing but honourable; you've said so yourself. He's shown every sign of being a gentleman in all ways.'

Her mother sat back and fixed her with a stare that made Thea feel as if she'd just walked herself into a trap. 'Don't you see how impossible it is, Thea, for there to be anything more than a moment between you? You must be on guard against the scoundrel *and* the gentleman. A gentleman has family, connections, responsibilities he will be required to return to. A scoundrel will want to stay but the gentleman cannot.'

She knew that, of course, but she didn't like hearing her mother put it so plainly. Was there truly no middle ground? Even her own mind mocked the idea. What would that middle ground be? Edward as a gentleman who never got his memories back? Who lived the rest of his life in limbo? All so that she could keep him here—but at whose expense? Certainly, it was at *his* expense. She was not so selfish as to wish a half-life upon him for the sake of her own happiness. It was all the more reason to write to Ferris and have him enquire about fallen generals at Inkerman, to take the next step in getting Edward's memories back. It would also be the next step down the path of losing him. Those memories would recall him to a life that might not have room for her in it.

'He has remembered some things.' She offered the news as a peace offering to her mother. 'Things about the battle at Inkerman that will help us determine who he is. I am sending a letter today to Ferris so he can gather the information. We should know in a few weeks.' Her time with him was limited. She'd need to get used to the idea and plan accordingly. She was being overly dramatic. That was not like her. She was practical and honest to a fault. Her heart came to the rescue.

You don't know what his memories will bring. You might not lose him. He might choose you.

And he might not have the choice. Even if he did have

a choice, men didn't choose her. She should not expect Edward to be different.

Her mother answered with a nod. 'That's good to hear. I am happy for him; that is progress.' She leaned forward once more, her cool hand at Thea's cheek. 'I'm proud of you too, dearest. It's for the best if you both know who he is before things and feelings go too far. You don't know who's waiting for him out there.'

No, she didn't know but, as for the former, it might already be too late for that.

Edward was coming to covet these late afternoon hours in the walled garden with Thea, especially since it was the only place he might sneak some time alone with her after the debacle in the sitting room. He walked towards the little door on the stable side of the garden, a twinge of guilt warring with a prick of excitement. No one, as in Catherine or Alfred Peverett, would see him enter from this direction—that was the guilt; he didn't like to think he was skulking around behind the backs of his generous hosts, and yet the idea of a 'clandestine' meeting with Thea did serve to quicken his blood in a manner that reminded him how very much alive he was.

He'd apologised, of course, to Catherine Peverett for the incident, and in proof of his sincerity he'd also made himself scarce at the Hall, spending his days at the vicarage making good on his promise to arrange music lessons for the school children. He enjoyed the work with the children and having a structured purpose to his days. It also added to his sense of purpose and to his expanding schedule.

In the mornings, he drove the pony trap to the village and taught lessons. In the afternoons, he took the offer of using the vicar's parlour to plan the lessons for the next day before driving home to the Hall, where he hoped to catch Thea in the walled garden before the family sat down to supper and the pursuits of a quiet evening: her father reading or engaging in a game of chess with him while the women did needlepoint or someone provided music on the cello or piano as a backdrop to their activities. He could imagine how these evenings would have once been in Thea's childhood, with all five of the Peverett siblings in attendance. It was no wonder she'd talked so fondly of her home.

He pushed the wooden door of the garden open and stood silently for a moment, taking her in: Thea in the green and white dress she'd worn the first day he'd come downstairs and sat at the piano. That day seemed a lifetime ago. He could hardly walk then, and now he was driving a pony trap to the village and looking forward to the day when he could walk the short distance on his own or even ride. He hadn't had a fever in eight weeks and the frustrated helplessness of living engulfed by illness faded a little more each day. All thanks to Thea. He owed not just his recovery to her but his health. If left to the whims of the Scutari hospital, his health might not have been regained so completely.

He was keenly aware of all he owed to his angel but gratitude was *not* at the heart of the current feelings roused by the sight of Thea in the garden. These were far deeper and more complex feelings. This woman called to his heart and his heart answered with ever more elaborate fantasies of the life he might build with her: of coming home to her, of sharing a meal with her, of making love to her and doing it all over again the next day and the next.

There were holes in the fantasy, of course. Where would they live? How would he provide for such a life, not just practically but ethically, as a man with no memories? He pushed them away, content to pretend she was his for the moment.

She was absorbed in the task of training the lilac over the arch of a trellis, her arms raised, the fabric of her gown pulled tight across her breasts in a blatant reminder that Thea Peverett *had* breasts. They were not the first feature a man noticed about Thea, only because there was so much more to her than how she looked. An appreciation of her physical charms came later, after one had fully appreciated the keen wit and intelligence on display.

Most men would never get that far. Donnatt, the idiot he was, was proof of that. She was unique and she'd been made to pay for that uniqueness by people who didn't want to accept that a woman might be more capable than they. She wasn't for everyone, but she *was* for him. His body knew it, his heart knew it. She'd washed her hair earlier and now it hung in damp tendrils down her back, loose and curling. His hand twitched, his fingers wanting to tug at the curls and watch them spring back or wind themselves through the twisting spirals.

Edward walked towards her, announcing himself with the rhythm of his uneven gait. 'Let me help you with the lilac. I can reach that better.' He set aside his cane long enough to tie the last errant bough to the arch. A book lay on the glider and Edward smiled to himself, knowing what she'd been about. She'd been hiding out, taking a moment away from her self-assigned responsibilities. 'You've spent the afternoon here,' he commented with a nod.

'I needed to dry my hair and I wanted to take advantage of the sun.' She paused, looking a little guilty. 'I also wanted some time to myself,' she confessed. 'The Hall was busy today. We had the ladies over to finish preparations for the May fair. They make such a fuss. I don't know why. It's the same every year: the same vendors come, there are the same games, the same races, even the same winners.'

She laughed but he heard the exasperation in her tone and sought to meet it with consolation. He slid onto the glider beside her. 'Normality is a gift, Thea. How wondrous it is that we can sit here and talk of such things, that life can be this simple.'

'I know.' Thea sighed. 'I'm ungrateful. I have the world and yet I want more. I thought this year we could have a booth to raise awareness of household cleanliness. We could do demonstrations about how to clean with hot water and soap or how to disinfect a cut or how to brush teeth.' He saw her shoulders slump even before she delivered the verdict on how those ideas had gone down. 'But the ladies thought no one would want to hear about those things at a fair. They said we shouldn't abuse a captive audience.'

'It's still a good idea. Perhaps there will be another venue later?' Edward encouraged. How hard it must be for her, to have had a glimpse of the life she wanted running the hospital ward, and then to be returned to this life of limits. In some ways, she had no more idea what she might be, here in the countryside of Hertfordshire, than he did. She might be a local midwife but that would hardly challenge her skills and she could see beyond that. She *knew* she could be more.

Thea suddenly brightened. 'I almost forgot. I had a letter today from a woman whom I'd written to on behalf of her son in Scutari.' One of her soldier projects. 'She lives nearby in Hoddesdon and has invited me to call on her on Wednesday.' She paused and slid him a considering glance, asking the question with her eyes.

'Yes, I'll come,' he offered before she had to ask him. 'I don't have a uniform to wear, but perhaps she would appreciate the gravitas of having a soldier present.'

She reached for his hand and squeezed her gratitude. 'Thank you. I wasn't sure if you would feel up to it.'

He flexed his leg as if to demonstrate he was indeed up to the day trip, but he knew she hadn't meant physically. In customary Thea fashion, she was worried about the emotional toll.

'Who knows? It might trigger something,' he offered. He wasn't sure he wanted the trip to trigger something or not.

'I *am* sorry there's been no word from Ferris yet. The waiting must be difficult.' Not as difficult, though, as it was to know that every day brought a chance for his memories to come back. He went to bed each night feeling a mix of relief and failure: relief that he hadn't remembered—it meant another day with Thea without his past intruding—and failure over the same: that he *hadn't* remembered, hadn't made any progress towards complete healing.

'It's of no note. I did not expect to hear from Ferris until the end of the month. It's not the waiting that bothers me, Thea. It's the not knowing, and then it's the knowing. I can't decide which one bothers me most,' he confessed honestly. 'The waiting itself has been good, a gift really. It's allowed me a chance to think about what I want, to have control over at least a few decisions.' He twined his fingers through hers, the warmth of her skin sending a ripple of awareness up his arm.

It was time to stop tiptoeing around the obvious attraction between them, and the obvious obstacles to it. 'I don't mind not knowing my own name as much as I mind not knowing what goes with it, *who* goes with it.' He looked down at their linked hands. He wanted to do so much more than hold her hand, wanted to be so much more than a patient, than a guest, than a new friend. Catherine Peverett was right to worry over that embrace in the sitting room. It had not been entirely chaste, at least not in his mind. It signalled a desire to pursue the deepening of this relationship. 'Do you ever think about that, Thea? What happens to us if…' He couldn't bring himself to say it.

'If there is a prior claim?' She held his gaze, both of them fully aware they were stepping over the line into the forbidden territory of things left undiscussed. To admit to worrying over a prior claim also meant admitting the existence of a relationship between them, of wanting that relationship.

Edward took the final step. 'I don't want there to be a prior claim, Thea.' It was an awful truth. 'What sort of man does it make me to wish away a wife and children? Yet I cannot play the coward and hide from either my past or my feelings regarding you.' He wanted her and what they could have together. What sort of man didn't fight for his own happiness? For his right to love? To make his life his own? It was a terrible position to be in. The only position worse would be to know un-equivocally that he *was* married, that a wife and children were indeed counting on him to do the right thing and return to them.

Thea's gaze was steady despite the emotion rolling through them, between them. He saw in her eyes that his admission had brought joy briefly and sadness deeply. 'We would honour the prior claim, Edward.'

He nodded. It was what he'd come to expect from Thea. She would not want a man who was so dishonourable as to leave his family for another woman, even if that woman was her, even if it was her happiness at stake. Such a man would never make her happy. In truth, such a man would never be happy in himself either. There was only misery in that direction. And yet he knew how much the decision cost her, to know that she would not be chosen. Even though the reasons had nothing to do with being acceptable to him, the outcome would be the same as it had always been and it would reinforce Donnatt's cruel lessons, although nothing could be further from the truth.

'*Do* you think there's a prior claim, Edward?' Thea asked quietly. He could see in her eyes that she was hedging her bets, wondering how much of herself she could risk and how much she needed to protect herself against the possibility. It was one thing to invest in a man with no name who might have the luxury of a blank slate on which to start again, or even to invest in a man who might have responsibilities to a family: sisters, a mother, aunts, cousins. There might be room for her in that life. It was another to invest oneself in a man who could never be hers, who already belonged to another. There would be no room for her there.

'You'd think I would know.' Edward shook his head at the impossible question. 'One would think a man couldn't forget something like his family or someone he loved, that I should *feel* them somehow. But I don't.'

'It bothers you; I know. I am sorry, Edward. I didn't mean to cause you pain.' Thea was all sincere concern for another, for him, when he was the one slowly breaking her heart, risking her heart.

'No, don't be sorry. It's an important question. We owe ourselves an honest answer to it. I *am* old enough to be married, perhaps to have been so for a few years, long enough to have had a child or two, assuming I didn't marry at a very young age.' If he had, he could have been wed for a decade now. He was banking on the idea that he was a gentleman and gentlemen didn't usually marry until their late twenties or early thirties. If so, he might even now still be unattached. 'What do *you* think, Thea? Am I married?' He watched her intently and waited. It mattered what she thought. If she thought he might be free, there might be a chance. If she thought there was no chance of that, however…they would be finished before they even started.

Chapter Eleven

She lifted their twined hands, examining his long fingers. 'I don't know. I admit it seems unlikely, and my bias may be shading my opinion. But a gentleman of your age going to war *while* being married and a father doesn't fit. Although the Duke of Cambridge went to war. He was at Inkerman. Gentlemen, titled gentlemen even, go to war. It's their duty to England.' She was thinking out loud and he loved watching her sharp mind work. 'There are plenty of lords in the British army.'

'But a country gentleman, not a titled gentleman, with a family would be unlikely to volunteer or be required to serve. He wouldn't be conscripted.' Thea argued back against her own premise. 'The military is for younger sons who can afford commissions, looking to make a place for themselves. A married man would already be sure of that place. He wouldn't be able to offer for a bride otherwise,' she reasoned. Those were the very same reasons why he could offer her nothing now. His sense of place had been destroyed with his memories. The irony was not lost on him that the one thing he needed in order to come to her without empty hands was also the one thing that could take him from her.

He nodded. 'You make a good point, Thea.' One he desperately wanted to believe. How much simpler this would be if he knew he were free. Then it would just be up to them. 'If there was no prior claim? What then?'

Would you have me?

She shook her head as if he'd spoken the last out loud. 'Don't, Edward, that is a cruel question with no good answer and it's only hypothetical.' She made to rise from the glider; spring dusk had fallen and it would soon be supper, but he wasn't ready for her to go inside. He rose and halted her with a hand at her arm. She scolded him with a look. 'Don't ask these things, Edward.'

'Why not? What happens to us if I *don't* ask them?' he challenged. 'Do you deny the connection between us? Am I truly just a patient to you? *This* is how regret happens, Thea.' The conversation was escalating to parts unknown, but now that the lines had been crossed there was only going forward and that path seemed clearer to him than ever.

'You will have your memories, Edward.' Thea's eyes flashed, equal to the battle. 'Whether it's tomorrow, out of some sudden chance encounter like it was with the piano and the books, or if Ferris finds something that jogs them, or if they come back in a year or two. The point is, they will come back. Even if you don't have a wife waiting for you, you will have a life waiting for you—a life I was not part of. I am only part of the life you have now and that life is temporary.' Their hands had found their way back to each other and her grip on him turned her knuckles white. He was torturing her with these questions. He could tempt her with a single suggestion.

'What if Ferris finds nothing? What if I never remember?' But even he knew he was grasping at straws.

'Never? That's an unlikely scenario. I wish it could be otherwise, Edward.' She was in the right. He'd either remember on his own, his memories triggered by Ferris's information, which seemed likely based on his recall experiences so far, or he would be handed a life he had to embrace whether he remembered it or not. Someone, somewhere, knew who he was.

'We are agreed that real life starts when Ferris and Anne arrive at the end of the month,' Edward summarised for her. The Treshams were due with their new infant in tow for a visit. He had two weeks.

Thea nodded. 'Yes, I think it does.'

It would be over before it had really begun, this life he'd started to make at Haberstock Hall. Edward would cease to exist. Perhaps not all at once. Ferris wasn't likely to produce a name and a biography, but he would produce leads to follow and one of them would lead him to who he was and where he was from. Ferris's arrival would be the beginning of the end. Each day 'Edward' would diminish and a new man would emerge until Edward was obliterated entirely. He would miss Edward.

'There's only one thing to do then, Thea. We must enjoy the present to its fullest. If now is all we can have, we must make the most of it.' He managed a smile. 'Starting with our trip to Hoddesdon. Pack a lunch. We'll make a day of it.' A whole day in which to have

Thea to himself, or nearly so. It was a luxury, given the circumstances. Those circumstances had always been there, had always underlaid this relationship, but now that they'd been spoken out loud, they had become far more real.

Thea nodded solemnly. 'These days that await us won't come without the potential for guilt later if…' If he had a wife, despite their careful calculations which trended towards no.

'To not act exacts its own price too. The price of missed opportunity, of time wasted, of throwing away happiness,' Edward answered. He'd had this argument with himself as well. 'I can't control what awaits us in the future, only what happens now. If the choice is between guilt and happiness, I will choose happiness and stand the guilt.'

Thea gave another serious nod. 'Then I shall too.' She slipped her hand from his and headed towards the house, alone. He watched her go, memorising the natural sway of her hips, the soft swing of her hair. He would make mental pictures of her, of them, in these days that remained. There would be the picnic, the May fair, Sunday church in the Peverett pew, suppers and music afterwards and he would commit all of them to memory. Even when his other memories came back, he would not forget these.

He made his own way back to the house, the lights shining through the windows guiding him like beacons. This was the only home he knew. It should disconcert him. But tonight, he wasn't bothered by it. Tonight, he had no desire to know another home. He'd come all this way, through war and sickness that would have slayed a lesser man, only to discover he didn't want the world to find him. He looked up at the house and paused, taking it in as if seeing it for the first time. Life became more precious when it was limited, everything rare and beautiful. He felt that way now, like a man who'd been given two weeks to live.

Two weeks to live. That was what all the words, all the arguments had boiled down to. The impact of Edward's carefully couched message thrummed through Thea throughout dinner, possibilities pulsing in her veins long after everyone had said goodnight. What might she do with those two weeks?

Thea brushed out her hair before bed, the rhythmic task bringing much needed calm to her racing mind. Two weeks not only to live but to love, if she dared. Edward had firmly put that decision in her hands while making his own intentions clear. Edward wanted her, wanted to *be* with her. *Her.* Shrew-tongued Thea Peverett whom the neighbourhood had firmly declared unmarriageable because she wanted it all. Even now, hours after the realisation, the thrill of it ran through her.

Edward wanted her. Thea set her brush aside and stared at the woman in the mirror. She was not unattractive, but she was no grand beauty, not like her sisters, Anne or Thomasia. But tonight, the sharp eyes and the even sharper angles of her face held a hint of wantonness. With her dark hair drawn forward over one shoulder, she looked almost pretty and with the lamplight shining through the thin white material of her summer nightgown she almost looked alluring, a seductive siren.

Was this what Edward saw when he looked at her? Would he be disappointed if she took his offer? She ran slow hands over her body, up past the slight curve of her hips, the narrow waist, up to the mere handfuls of her breasts, cupping them through the fabric of her nightgown. Would Edward prefer larger? It seemed most men did. Hers was not a build that men liked. In her teen years her build had been termed neat and trim. There'd always been the hope that she would bloom late. But her twenties were nearly over now, and no lushness had arrived to round her out. She was still neat and trim, but it would not last. She'd seen such women in their forties and fifties. On them, 'neat and trim' had become angular and spare as they aged. These women looked more like dried-up sticks. She did not want to be them in looks or experience, although she'd begun to despair of it being otherwise. Her work didn't leave room for romance and her past foray into such hopes had only reaffirmed how unsuitable she was for love in looks, temperament and dreams.

She could still hear Clive's words as if he were in the room with her, as if his humiliation of her had been yesterday, not a decade ago.

'Did you really think someone like him would fall for someone like you? So tall, so mannish, and with a viper's tongue.'

Edward didn't think so. He enjoyed sparring with her. He was never put off by her opinions or boldness. He might be her only chance, incomplete as it was, to know physical and emotional happiness with a man. It wouldn't last but it promised to be wonderful while it did. Perhaps it was the temporary nature of their association that made such wonder possible. She need not worry where it led, or how it would end, because it *would* end. Because of that, she could set aside her fear that this was somehow another prank, an abuse of her trust. She was not naïve this time.

Thea planted her hands, palms down, on the vanity. No. She was many things, but she was *not* desperate for a man. She faced the image in the mirror. *If* she did this thing it would be because she was a free woman. She would do this because she chose to do it, consequences and all. These would not be the usual consequences—the loss of virginity, the potential of a child, although she knew how to reasonably protect against that—these were more far-reaching consequences that extended into the murky areas of ethics and morality.

How did morals apply in the case of a man who did not recall if he had a wife? Did that wife really exist? Was she non-existent until he was told of her or recalled her? Thea had no desire to be an adulteress, no desire to steal another woman's husband. Her only desire was for Edward.

She shook her head and left the woman in the mirror. Who would have thought she, Thea Peverett, who'd never had a serious suitor, would have to navigate such personal complexities? Married men and secret passions were for the demimonde and fast widows. She was neither. She was not a decadent woman, just the woman who might be falling in love with Edward of the no last name, the woman who must weigh her passions against the guilt, should it become necessary.

Chapter Twelve

'What's the name of the woman we are visiting today?' Edward stretched his leg out in the pony trap and picked up the reins. The sun was out and the day showed every potential of being perfect for a late spring outing as they set off for Hoddesdon. Breakfast was behind them, the day before them. A whole day with Thea. It seemed like an eternity at ten o'clock in the morning. He wondered if it would seem that way at five o'clock tonight, when the day had sped past. 'Do you have everything?' He made a final note of Thea's bag and basket tucked beneath their feet and the picnic hamper strapped in the back of the trap like a Pandora's box, a temptation daring them to open it. Was that only his own heated imagination, filled as it was with the possibilities of picnicking alone in a meadow with Thea?

He clucked to the horse and they were off, her skirts pressed against his thigh on the narrow bench. He didn't mind. Did she? Had she thought about his offer yesterday, that they spend the next two weeks living to the fullest and setting aside any guilt that might ensue later? What had she decided? Had she realised how indecent his proposition was beneath the careful words and decided to refuse him outright? Or had she, too, spent the night wrestling her moral demons into an outcome that would permit them a certain freedom born of being in limbo? He shifted his leg slightly and Thea was all immediate solicitousness.

'Are you sure your leg can handle a journey of this length? This is not a short jaunt to the village.'

He slid her a smile to soften his words. 'My leg is fine. At this rate, I expect I'll be able to ride by June,' he assured her. He was eager to be back in the saddle. He wondered if that was because he'd always ridden and had an affinity for horses or if it was simply because it was another step towards recovery and the freedom that came with good health. He'd not been on horseback at Inkerman as far as he knew.

The horse was well behaved and the road easy. He needed only one hand for the reins. He reached for Thea's. 'Promise me something, Thea. Today you won't be my nurse.' It would be hard for her. Enquiring after people's health was her usual conversational opening. He wasn't sure he'd ever heard her start a conversation without such an enquiry. How many mornings had she come to his bedside in Scutari with the words, 'How are you today, Edward? Did you sleep well?' He didn't want nurse Thea today. He wanted Thea the woman and he would have her if he could just get her to come out. She gave him a dubious look. 'If I need something, I'll ask,' he promised. 'Now you—you promise me you won't be my nurse today.'

Their gazes held for a long moment. 'All right,' she said at last. 'I promise.'

He gave her a grin. 'Good. Now, tell me about this woman we're visiting.'

'Mrs Middlethorpe,' Thea began. 'Her son died of fever at Scutari. He had wounds but it was the fever that did him in. I have the letter he dictated, and I have his small belongings, the things that came with him.' She sighed. 'That box seems so insignificant now. A man's life fits in a box beneath my feet.'

'Not his whole life,' Edward offered. 'Memories don't fit in a box very well anyway. They're too big. The box is just things.' It was a good thing he hadn't died. He didn't even have a box. If he did, it was lost, left behind at a military camp or on board a ship somewhere. There would have been nothing to send to the family.

'He was polite always, I remember that,' Thea continued. 'He said thank you for even the smallest of comforts: food, a drink of water, for someone to fluff his pillows so he could sit up. I remember, too, that he was young. Very young. Too young to die.'

'Tell Mrs Middlethorpe about his manners. That will mean more to her than battlefield heroics.' He squeezed Thea's hand. She was worried about the visit, about being equal to Mrs Middlethorpe's grief. 'You will have the right words, Thea. You always do.'

'I wish I could have done this for all of them.' Thea offered him a grateful smile. 'I would have liked to have visited their families. A letter isn't nearly as personal.' It would be, though, if she wrote it, Edward thought. Everything was personal to Thea. It was part of her passion that she was neutral about nothing. Whatever she chose to invest in, she did it whole-heartedly. She held nothing back. He'd had a taste of that passion—she'd invested in him.

Mrs Middlethorpe lived outside Hoddesdon on a small dairy farm, neatly kept and prospering for its size. She was outside, just coming from the barn when they arrived, and she bustled forward to greet them. She invited them inside the cottage and Edward joined the women for a few minutes of small talk, long enough to express his condolences. When the conversation turned more serious, he excused himself to look around the grounds while Thea did what she did best—comfort and healing. The visit didn't take long, perhaps three-quarters of an hour, but Edward could see it meant the world to Mrs Middlethorpe, who walked Thea to the pony trap, their arms linked as if they were the best of friends.

'I trust it went well?' Edward asked once they were on their way. Thea was quiet.

'Yes, I am glad I went.' There was simmering frustration beneath her words. Edward waited, knowing more would come. 'The army told her nothing, Edward, just a formal note informing her of her son's death. It was all very official, and of course when she wrote to enquire for more information there was none forthcoming. She hasn't the time and resources to pursue it further.' Not like him, who'd had the good fortune of being taken in by a nurse whose sister was married to a duke's son. He was acutely aware of just how good his fortune was.

'She had you and now she knows all there is to know,' Edward consoled. Knowing Thea, the woman probably knew more than she wanted. Perhaps Thea had also recruited a new champion for the Sanitary Movement today as well.

'Don't look at me like that,' Thea scolded. 'I did not recruit her for the cause.'

'Did you discuss conditions at the hospital with her?'

'Only because she asked,' Thea said solemnly. 'I told her the truth. She didn't know if she could believe the papers.' She sighed. 'Sometimes at night I can still see his face. He should not have died. If conditions had been better, if I had been there sooner, I think he would have lived. I should have been able to save him, Edward. It was just a fever.'

'Not any fever, though.' He thought of his own fevers, his own bout with brucellosis. To a man already weakened by poor rations, the rigours of battle and the sea journey from Sevastopol to Scutari, the Crimean illness, as it was called, would be fatal. It nearly had been for him and he'd had the benefit of Thea's care from the start, the hospital already improving from Florence Nightingale's innovations when he'd arrived.

'It angers me, Edward, to see the army treat human life so callously and not be made accountable for it. I don't think for a moment this war and the way it's been conducted behind the scenes is an anomaly.' There was that passion again, roaring to the fore.

'Have you thought about going to London? The Season's underway and Parliament's in session. Everyone you need to see in one spot.' He knew she was already advocating for the Sanitary Movement and for Florence Nightingale's cause by letter, but Thea Peverett in the flesh would always be more compelling than a letter, no matter how well written it was. She would be a force of nature in person.

She shook her head. 'I'm not the ballroom type. I doubt I could fill my dance card, let alone get anyone to listen to me while we waltzed.'

He scrunched his brow. That made no sense. 'Your sister's mother-in-law is a duchess. I imagine people would listen to you.' Maybe those connections hadn't been there previously, but they were now.

'No,' she said firmly. 'I think London is better off without the Peverett girls for a while.' There was something more behind that but he was smart enough not to pursue it. She was protecting someone. The way she referred to the Peverett girls, he didn't think she was protecting herself but perhaps one of her sisters. Surely not Anne, the sister with the ducal connections. One of the other two, perhaps? But it wasn't his business. It wasn't part of the two-week arrangement. She was hardly going to divulge family secrets to a man who'd be gone in two weeks.

He nodded towards a stand of trees in the distance. 'Shall we pull over there for our picnic? I think I sighted a stream as well on the way out.' It was time to test the two-week proposition. It was a given they'd spend the time enjoying one another's company, but it wasn't clear just what form that enjoyment might take. Would she want as much as he did? Would she allow herself to claim that enjoyment? He would understand if she didn't, but it wouldn't make the wanting of her, the regret of losing her any less.

They stopped at the stand of trees and he helped her down, picnic hamper on one arm. It was time to open

Pandora's box. They set up their little camp on the grass, a short distance from the stream, laughing as the breeze almost took away their blanket. It was something of an effort for him to get down on the ground. He wasn't certain he'd be able to get back up. For a moment he thought Thea would say something.

'Don't,' he warned her as he stretched out and found a comfortable position to lounge in. 'You promised.'

'So I did. I'll regret that if you hurt yourself.' She grimaced and busied herself instead with setting out the lunch: the slices of ham, the wheel of cheese, the bottle of white wine. He liked watching her work, liked watching her busy hands.

'Middlethorpe was the last soldier, wasn't he?' Edward asked as she fixed him a plate of ham and bread. 'What will you do with yourself now if you won't turn politician and you have no more letters to send? Will you go back to the Crimea?'

She shook her head. 'I suspect the war could be over by the time I got there, and Florence needs me here. I suppose I'll keep lobbying MPs from a distance. I have great hopes our Mr Rawdon will be of use.'

'That doesn't sound like you, Thea.' There was a decided lack of enthusiasm behind those plans. Since when did Thea Peverett allow someone else, especially a man, to be her mouthpiece when she was fully capable of making her own arguments?

'My father needs me here.' Thea sliced him another piece of bread. That also didn't sound like her.

'And when William comes home? Will there be room for three Doctors Peverett in Hertfordshire?' he asked lightly, but it was a serious question. Her brother and her father had diplomas—they were 'real' doctors. Would Thea be happy here playing second fiddle to them, limiting her skills to delivering the occasional baby? Something shifted inside him, something that went deeper than the attraction he felt towards her. He didn't want to leave her here when these two weeks were over. What would happen to her here in this place that didn't fully appreciate her?

Thea played with the fringe on the edge of the blanket. 'I can always go back to the hospital on Harley Street. We implemented Florence's strategies at the hospital long before we set sail for Scutari. I can always take up my old post there.' That was a very different London than the one he envisioned her in. It would not be a London existence of ballrooms and state dinners. It would be an existence of serving others, a humble existence that was hardly worthy of her.

Edward gave her a grin. 'I think you should run all the hospitals in London.' He leaned forward, unable to resist the little crumb that hovered at the corner of her mouth. He brushed at it with his thumb, letting his thumb linger long after the crumb was gone. 'You are a marvel, Thea Peverett,' he said in low tones. 'I wish you saw yourself as I do. You are deserving of so much more.' He'd lay the world at this woman's feet if it were his to give, and if she'd want it. He had a feeling she'd far prefer to go get the world herself rather than have it offered to her.

She gave a small breathy laugh, her whisky eyes dropping from his, a little blush staining her cheeks, this woman who was never flustered. 'You're flirting with me, Edward.'

He tipped her chin up, forcing her eyes back to his. He wanted her to see him when he answered. 'Yes, I am, and, with your permission, I don't mean to stop there.'

Don't stop. Don't ever stop.

The words pounded through her mind, coursed through her veins in the moment before their mouths met. The kiss, when it came, was equal parts claiming and offering, the press of his mouth welcomed by the openness of her own. He tasted of white wine and wishes, the kiss a manifestation of long, quietly nurtured want.

His mouth moved against hers, his hand cupped her jaw, aligning her mouth more firmly with his, the kiss deepening, gaining urgency, and her body quickened to it in answer. This was what it meant to be alive, to thrill to another's touch. She was not alone in that thrill. Edward whispered her name between kisses, his voice a hoarse rasp at her throat, a testimony to the power of the kiss, the power of the connection between them.

'Sweet heavens, Thea, how I want you. How I *have wanted* you.' His eyes glittered, green and sharp, two shards of emerald desire. She could see herself in them, a woman whose hair was falling down; she looked ravished and wanton, all from a kiss. She hardly knew herself, this woman who was so undone by passion, by this man. Thea leaned into him; all she wanted was for him to kiss her again and again. Or perhaps she might kiss him.

This time it was she who took his mouth, she who led the kiss, who wrested a guttural moan from him that came from deep inside. 'Thea, you'll be the death of me.'

She smiled, feeling playful and free. It was easy to be with him, to be honest with him. 'I think I've already died and gone to Heaven.' Had she ever felt this way? She didn't want to leave. She wanted to stay on this picnic blanket for ever, perhaps with fewer clothes on. Clothes were fast becoming a restriction. Perhaps Edward felt the limitation too. The next bout of kisses contained a new urgency, as his mouth sought the tender spot of her ear, her jaw, her throat, with an intensity that spoke of a new frustration, a new desire, and her body echoed it with an ache of its own. Kisses had not satisfied their appetite for one another. They'd merely whetted those hungers for another course, another taste—a decadent, intimate taste. But she knew Edward would not push her for it. Any escalation would have to come from her. She would not be shy. There was no time for it.

Thea reached for him, sliding her hand over the hard length of him, tracing him through the fabric of his trousers. This was the length of a man in his prime, vigorous with health, hard and hale and wanting. She felt his breath catch as her hand gripped him.

'Thea...' He exhaled her name, managing to coax and caution at once.

But she was beyond caution. She leaned into him, her mouth at his ear, her hand at his phallus, and whispered the ancient temptation. 'We can have more.'

Chapter Thirteen

More. Just the thought of what that one word offered
would have him spending in his trousers before it could
become a reality. Thea was intoxicating like this, her
hair falling down, her lips puffy with his kisses, her
hand stroking him, inviting him. And, oh, how he
wanted to be invited, how he wanted to take that invitation, risk and consequences be damned. They'd spent
days, weeks, letting those consequences stand in their
way. But not today. Today would be just for them, for
Thea and Edward; the future held no sway here. There
was only now.

'Take me in your hand, Thea.' It was a plea more than
an instruction. It was driving him mad to have her so
close and yet so far. He wanted her bare hand on his bare
flesh and soon he had it, his trousers open, her hand on
his hot length for as long as he could stand it. Her gaze
held his as she worked him, the faint curve of a knowing smile on her lips. 'You like this, don't you, minx?'
he growled. 'Being in charge, watching me suffer.'

Her smile broadened. 'I don't think suffer is the word
I'd use. You seem to be enjoying yourself quite well.'

He pushed himself up on his elbows. This had gone on long enough. Any longer and he wouldn't be able to reciprocate. He gave her a wicked grin, the only warning she'd get. 'It's your turn now.' He caught her about the waist and bore her back to the blanket, coming over her in a careful move, cautious of his leg, but he'd be damned if the first time they made love he'd make her do all the work, riding him astride. *He* wanted to take her, wanted her to know the pleasure of being taken by a man who loved her, cherished her. She was not a game to him nor was the desire between them.

He pushed her skirts up, his hand finding the warm, damp core of her as her eyes went wide. She gasped at his touch, a sound of awe and delight.

So, this is what it should be like. This is what love feels like, her gaze said as he watched her mind process the sensations.

He pressed a kiss to her mouth. 'Don't think, Thea. Don't seek to understand it, just feel,' he murmured. 'Give over to it.' Lord knew he was giving over to it, losing himself in it. His fingers parted her folds, finding the hidden nub of her, his thumb gliding over it in a rhythm that drew increasingly ragged breaths from her, her back arching as the sweet tension of his caress mounted in her, and then it was gone, obliterated in a shattering moment as the pleasure took her, sweeping away the rising ache. Her whole body shook with its passing. The sight of her in her pleasure was intimate and overwhelming, ratcheting his own desire. It gave him pleasure to see her *in* pleasure, to know he'd provided it for her, that he alone had given it to her.

He kissed her hard on the mouth and whispered his wicked promise. 'We're just getting started.'

She answered, moving against him, her hips lifting to meet his, her eyes flashing with whisky-hued mischief as she smiled up at him, urging him on. Her thighs opened for him, took him within their cradle in proof that she wanted this, wanted *him*. It was all the assurance he needed. He moved into her, slow, steady, sure, aware of her need for deliberate, measured progress even if she wasn't. He was her first, and she was Edward's first. He liked the thought of that. Whatever and whoever lay out there in the larger world waiting for him, this beautiful intimate act was just between them.

He moved within her, inching forward until he was fully seated and the rhythm began, the eternal surge and ebb of lovemaking, slowly at first, the tempo increasing as the need for one another grew. He felt her long legs wrap about his waist, holding him close, holding him deep within her as if she never wanted him to leave. He would need to withdraw though, at the last critical moment, to keep her safe.

That moment was fast approaching; it was there in the signals of her body as it tensed beneath him, gathering itself for climax, her back arched, her head thrown back, the muscles of her neck exposed as they worked to articulate the sounds of her pleasure. His own body gathered, warning him of his own impending release, his breathing ragged, and somewhere in the midst of his own pleasure there was the distant nagging pain in his thigh. He pushed it back, willing the muscles of his arms to hold his weight, willing his leg, his body, to hold out a few moments more to ensure her pleasure.

He thrust once, twice more, and was rewarded by her cries, an exultation shouted to the skies as he spilled into the verge at the blanket's hem before he collapsed, gathering Thea to him.

His breathing came hard, as did the emotions swamping him in the aftermath. What he felt now, the sensations of wholeness, completeness, of rightness and the overwhelming sense of being utterly alive coursing through him, were as strong as the primal urges driving the lovemaking, perhaps even stronger. He was meant to be with this woman. His body knew it, his heart knew it; they cared nothing about the logic of his mind that said it was impossible. He pushed the reminder away. No, not today. Today, nothing was impossible.

The sleep of an exhausted lover crept over him, claiming him with a final thought. Whatever he'd endured to get to this moment, to this woman, had been worth it. A man would do anything he had to in order to get home. He was there now, with her. Whatever his life had been or could be, this was the life he wanted. He'd be damned if he'd give it up without a fight.

The best weapons to fight a fantasy were time and distance. Thea was counting on the morning bringing much-needed equilibrium, but the soreness between her legs proved to be a delicious distraction from reclaiming reality. Edward had pulled reality entirely out from under her like a rug.

Thea sat at the writing desk in her room on another sunny spring morning, unwilling to risk encountering her mother or even Edward until she had her thoughts straight. If her mother guessed what she'd been up to she would be disappointed in her after their last discussion, and a single look from Edward would set her thoughts spinning with impossibilities. Dinner last night had been torture enough. She'd spent the meal wondering if her face gave away what had transpired on the trip to Hoddesdon, wondering if anyone could *see* the change in her. She'd changed her dress and fixed her hair, careful to eliminate any trace of what they'd done. But she could not eliminate the sense of being lit up from the inside out, of feeling life tingling through every inch of her.

She still felt that way, which had her up and pacing every few minutes. She could hardly sit still, could hardly marshal her thoughts into any order. The page in front of her remained blank. She'd not expected lovemaking to affect her like this. She'd committed to it, gone into it with her own understanding. It was supposed to be a culmination of the feelings that had grown between her and Edward. Because of their circumstances, it was to be a *farewell*, the beginning of the end. It was *not* to be the beginning of anything new. But making love had not sealed her feelings as much as set them free.

Did Edward feel the same way—that this was no longer an ending? If so, did that change anything? That was the real question, assuming that they both wanted to change the rules. What was possible? Perhaps nothing. Feelings aside, the circumstances hadn't changed. But how was she supposed to walk away from this? How was she to let him go? And yet what choice did she have? Ferris and Anne would bring the information he needed to find his old life and reclaim it. Using that information was what they had agreed upon.

It was the right path. But there was no room for her on that path and she would not be so selfish as to suggest he not follow it. In truth, there was no room for her on the other path—a path that had him remaining nameless and placeless, at least for the time being. One could not marry a nameless man and, ironically, having a name might prevent that just as effectively. *Marry.* That was a strong word to use simply because they'd made love. In their situation, marriage did not necessarily follow as a logical conclusion for many reasons.

That prompted a thought. A list was in order. Thea wrote in crisp letters across the top of the paper: *Reasons why I can't marry Edward.* She let her mind work through the practicalities of the subject. Reason One: banns could not be called. How could they be if a man had no surname? For that matter, he had no 'real' name. In fact, Edward was a fiction, a made-up name. But such considerations were a hypothetical exercise only. There'd been no discussion of marriage between them. That made a good Reason Two. Edward had not proposed. It was hard to marry a man who hadn't asked. Reason Three: they'd promised themselves this affaire would end. Ending had been the key premise on which they'd entered into it, the one way they could countenance the decision. It was *not* going to lead to marriage. Reason Four: did she even want to marry? Her pen paused. That was a question, not a reason.

She'd spent years talking herself out of it, and she had succeeded. Marrying would mean leaving the hospital. She would not go back to her Harley Street work.

Marriage would likely mean staying here in Haberstock, where she had yet to find a place. If she married, this would be her life. Would she spend it following her father on his rounds? Would that be enough? That and Edward's affections?

Ah, there was reality; it had shown up at last. Thea sat back in her chair with a sigh, surveying her list. Reality had done its job. The choice had become clear. It would have to be medicine or a man. But not any man. Edward. Would she give up the hospital for him? Would she settle for life in Haberstock as the wife of Edward? Would Edward be different? Would he ask such a thing of her? The reasons on her list depended on it. If not, her list was moot.

There should be no choice. One path was straightforward and embodied her long-held dream of providing health care to others, while the other was ladened with risk. What logical woman would throw it all over for a man whose future was uncertain and his past unknown? Even without Anne and Ferris's prompting, his memories could return at any time and what those memories might reveal could shatter the life they'd built in Haberstock.

Refusing Edward and choosing to end the affaire when the time came was the practical decision. The matter was settled, right there in front of her on the page, but that didn't translate to her heart. Despite the facts, her heart wanted to do something else entirely. Never before had she wanted to disregard logic. It had always been her refuge in a world that seldom made sense. But now she'd let her logical guard down, allowed him to slip past her defences, and she couldn't help but feel that she'd broken promises to herself. She'd promised to protect herself and here she was, opening herself up to have her heart broken.

Heavens, she needed counsel! She was missing her sister. If Anne were here, they would talk it through. She drew another sheet of paper from the drawer and began to write, the next best thing.

Dear Anne,
I must tell you something in strictest of confi-
dence. I may have fallen for Edward...

That was when she knew, seeing those words in ink, that she was in trouble. A healer was never supposed to fall for a patient. It was the gravest of infractions, but for Edward she would do it again.

The trouble with problems was that he felt compelled to solve them. Edward turned the pony trap off to the side of the road, steering it down a path that led to the stone cottage just visible from the main road between Haberstock Hall and the village. He'd spied it the first day he'd driven to the village to give music lessons and it had stayed in his mind every day since, looming ever larger, especially given what had transpired on the way home from Hoddesdon and the feelings it had left him with.

Those feelings had been the first problem to solve. He didn't want to leave Thea, which had prompted the obvious solution: what if he didn't leave? It was a possibility. Perhaps Ferris's information would reveal his family connections were such that he was free to pursue his own life. If so, he could stay. Nothing needed to change. It was a hope he fell asleep to every night, especially after making love to Thea. But staying wasn't a cure-all. It was simply a decision that created a host of other problems. To stay and court Thea, he had to be a man of means. He needed a name and he needed a home, the latter for several reasons. He needed a home for decency's sake. He couldn't court her and continue to live under her parents' roof. It would lead to talk and ultimately it would be her reputation, not his, that would be injured by it, no matter how the future worked out. More than satisfying the superficial needs of society, he wanted the cottage to act as tangible proof to Thea of his respect for her and the honesty of his intentions. He would stay if it were at all possible.

He was keenly aware of the special nightmare this situation posed for Thea. *No one chooses me.* He would choose her. Only a prior marriage would prevent him from making that choice. To rent a cottage, even month to month, was proof of that choice. A house symbolised his intention to stay. A house was no small commitment, especially when he was less than two weeks away from facing his past. He couldn't think of a better way to show his intentions than this.

Edward set the brake and struggled down from the seat, careful to use his cane. If he fell here, there'd be no one around to help him back up. The cottage looked abandoned. He called out to be sure before peering into the windows. The place was in good shape, although in need of cleaning. He shaded his eyes and looked out across the fields. He could hay if nothing else to generate some income. It would be a start, although he'd need to hire help. He wouldn't be scything any hay this year, not with his leg.

He made his way over to the small adjacent barn, counting stalls. Five. Whoever had lived here had probably kept a cow and a horse or two. It would do. He would talk to Dr Peverett this evening after supper to determine who held the deed on the property. He couldn't buy it, but perhaps he could lease it, or establish a tenancy in exchange for hay and crops.

That would be one problem solved, but it caused another. How could a man with no name sign a deed? To get the cottage, he'd need a name, a real name, to sign for it. Officially taking it on might have to wait until Ferris's news, assuming that brought him a name. If it didn't, he had a plan for that too. He'd speak to the vicar about it tomorrow, once he knew more about the cottage.

Edward took a final look at the cottage. What would Thea think of it? It wasn't as grand as Haberstock Hall, but perhaps she would see its potential as he did. This was a place where they could begin. He did acknowledge he might be putting the cart before the horse. Would she even be interested in beginning? It wasn't what they'd promised each other. He was changing the rules drastically.

He levered himself back up onto the bench of the cart, steering the patient horse towards Haberstock Hall and turning his mind to the third of his problems. Would Thea want the same things he wanted? And would she want them as badly? He understood he had everything to gain but she had everything to lose.

How did one go about persuading a headstrong

woman used to her own independence to trust a man who barely knew himself? Not with words, he knew that much. Thea was a doer—she would not be impressed with poems and flattery. She would be impressed with actions. He would start there, with the cottage. He would show her that he could make a life for them, then he would let her decide. Society had decided too much on her behalf so far. It was time she knew she was desirable, a woman who was worth waiting for.

Chapter Fourteen

Edward waited for Dr Peverett to say something. He'd shared his interest in the cottage as they sipped their port in the quiet of the dining room after supper, the ladies already gone to the music room. He tried to read the doctor's face and couldn't. Dr Peverett was a master of the carefully cultivated neutral expression. He did not take that neutrality for apathy. Alfred Peverett was devoted to his children.

'There are some who might find your enquiries about leasing a cottage illogical, given that you could be leaving us in two weeks,' Peverett replied, raising a grey brow in question.

'It's a fair question, sir.' Edward wasn't surprised by the query. Peverett was an intelligent, thoughtful man and he'd sat across the chessboard from him often enough to know Peverett was not precipitate or impulsive. He drew a breath and met the older man's gaze with the strength of his own. Dr Peverett would not appreciate hesitancy. 'Leaving is not a foregone conclusion, of which there are three. First, my memories, should they return, might show that I have no reason to leave, that I am free to stay, or they might mean that I need to leave to settle immediate affairs and to apprise a family of my well-being, but that I would be free to return. Only the third option would preclude me from being able to remain in Haberstock.' The third option tacitly acknowledged the potential existence of a wife.

Peverett's brow knitted. 'Remaining in Haberstock is your dearest desire? A small village in the middle of nowhere?'

The man was going to make him say it. 'I stay for you daughter, sir. I want to court her, but I cannot do that while remaining beneath your roof, nor will my conscience allow me to court her empty-handed. I want her and her family to know that I can provide for her.'

Peverett took time refilling their glasses. 'This cannot wait another two weeks, once Dr Tresham visits?'

When you might have a name and memories, when we might be more aware of the consequences surrounding a courtship.

'I am a man who has stared death in the face, sir. I do not want to wait, especially since, as I have laid out above, two chances out of three suggest there is no need to do so.'

'You are gambling with my daughter's reputation,' Peverett said bluntly. 'I would not like your intentions made public, only to have it revealed that you have a wife and children somewhere.'

Edward fingered his tumbler. Peverett had a point. 'I think that's all the more reason I should take the cottage. If that were to be the case, to be out from under your roof would preserve her reputation. I think, either way, taking the cottage is the honourable route now I am healthy and able to live independently.' He was thinking, too, of Donnatt's cruel words that he was sponging off the Peveretts' generosity. He would not want it to be said that he'd married Thea for her settlements, whatever they were. Such rumours would only feed Donnatt's claim that she was not a woman men wanted for herself. He would not do that to her.

Peverett seemed to give that serious contemplation. 'As it happens, that cottage and a few others are attached to the estate. I have jurisdiction over them, which would certainly mitigate the need to sign a name to a lease document in the near future. I can give you the key tonight and we can settle lease details later.' Later implicitly being once he had a name to call his own legally, and later being when Ferris Tresham's information was revealed and decisions could be made about his future without guessing, without jeopardising Thea's reputation.

Peverett gave a fatherly sigh. 'I like you, Edward, but I *love* my daughter. She is priceless to me, a unique, beautiful person, full of strength in some ways and vulnerable in others. Oftentimes I think it would have been better if she'd been born a man. Haberstock has not been a place where her talents can thrive. What does she think about these plans?'

Edward shook his head. 'She does not know. She fears I will leave, sir. I want this cottage to show her otherwise, that I will stay if it is humanly possible. Then, I want the decision to be hers.' If she wanted to stay in Haberstock, he would stay. If she wanted to go to London, he would go there. If she wanted to study medicine at a German university like her namesake, he would go there too.

Peverett nodded at his words. 'Then you understand her. You are perhaps the first man to do so.'

Edward opted to be bold as they rose to join the women. 'I more than understand her, sir. I love her. Her happiness is of the utmost priority to me.'

Peverett gave him a stern look. 'Do not make promises that are beyond your control to keep, son. There is to be no public mention of courtship until after Tresham's visit. I am doing this for the sake of my daughter's reputation.'

'So am I, sir.' Edward went upstairs a few hours later to spend his last night in his room at Haberstock Hall, the key to the cottage heavy in his pocket, waiting for the right time to share the news with Thea—perhaps tomorrow. It would be market day and they'd have time together. He had the key to the future in his pocket, quite literally, and tomorrow couldn't come fast enough.

Was there any better day than market day in Haberstock, with blue spring skies overhead, money in a man's pocket and the woman he loved on his arm? Edward was hard-pressed to think of a more pleasant day to be had as he strolled—yes, *strolled*—around the open-air market on the Haberstock village green with Thea by his side. The vicar had, with thoughtful foresight, paid his wages today and, for the first time since Inkerman, he had money of his own. Today, in fact, he felt in possession of an embarrassment of riches, not all of them monetary. He strolled with a limp and a cane, but he did stroll, something he would never take for granted again the rest of his days.

'You're smiling.' Thea shot him a sideways glance as she stopped at a vendor's stall to look at soaps.

'Is that such a surprise? I am happy.' He *was* beaming. There was no reason not to be. Thea bent over a bar of soap to sniff it, her eyes closed, the elegant length of her neck exposed by the gesture, her dark hair curling about her face, framing her exquisite profile, and he let the fantasy take him: he and Thea walking through the market always. A man could make a good life here and he'd just about figured out how he could do it. Those details had dominated a large part of his thoughts since their trip to Hoddesdon and an afternoon spent on a picnic blanket embracing the inevitable: he was meant to be with her. The key to the cottage was an obvious weight in his pocket.

He had to tread carefully, though. They'd not talked of the afternoon nor repeated it in the interim but the sensations it had imprinted on him still remained. He did not want to leave her here. He wanted to stay. Lord willing, such an option would be possible.

They moved on to a stall selling ribbons. Thea studied some green lengths of grosgrain he could already imagine trimming the straw hat she wore with her green lawn dress on Sundays. Perhaps he would buy them for her, but before he could reach for his coins a woman touched him on the arm. 'Sir, what luck to meet you here. Might I seek your advice for a moment?' It was the mother of one of his best students at the vicarage, the son of the squire, a man of some means. He murmured to Thea and stepped aside with the boy's mother. She'd want to discuss extra lessons and the boy's chances of attending a conservatoire in the autumn.

He was just agreeing to the extra lessons when Thea joined them, her ribbon purchases complete. 'I am free in the afternoons, Mrs Hanson. I can come out to your home and teach him there on Tuesdays and Thursdays,' he offered, excited about the opportunity to help the boy grow his skill, and excited about what it meant, not just the extra wages, but the acceptance it signalled. He had value to the community.

They said goodbye to the squire's wife and Thea slipped her arm through his, wearing a knowing smile as if she'd read his mind. 'You're making an impression. Everyone knows you,' she said as Edward nodded to a few passing ladies, mothers of his students. There was pride in her voice. She was proud *of* him, and proud to be seen *with* him. He was proud too. Not only to be seen with her but because he was becoming a person in his own right. He was no longer entirely dependent on Thea and the Peveretts for an introduction. Every day he was standing more and more on his own two feet, literally and figuratively. It was a step towards being more independent, towards having a place here.

'Thirsty?' They stopped for refreshment, Thea taking the opportunity to introduce him to buttered beer. 'Hertfordshire is known for its dairy and for its brewing.' She handed him a small tankard. 'So, it's no surprise that the two have been combined.'

Edward gave the thick foam a dubious glance. 'It's good, but just take a sip,' Thea counselled. 'It's got a very sharp taste. This is chilled for warmer weather, but normally it's served warm.' She sipped her own in demonstration, perhaps hoping to convince him while her eyes laughed at his reticence.

He took a swallow and found it tolerable enough for a second and then a third. 'It's an acquired taste but I think I could become used to.' He grinned.

'You're staring.' Thea blushed under his perusal and the teasing entendre of his words.

He leaned close and breathed in the lavender scent of her, whispering at her ear as they began to walk. 'You're a beautiful woman, Thea. Of course, I'm staring.' She *was* beautiful. He wished she would acknowledge that, and he wished he had good reason to pummel that idiot Clive Donnatt for leading her to believe otherwise.

They neared the end of an aisle selling produce. One vendor had lemons from Italy, a luxurious find in a small village, and Thea's excitement was evident. 'I don't know how fresh they are, but let's get some and I'll make lemonade for old times' sake.' Thea selected six lemons and put them in her basket.

'It does seem like a very long time ago.' They hardly talked of the Crimea these days, beyond reading the politics in the papers. It was not the only thing that bound them together anymore. They had a new history between them now. Their conversations were dominated with topics like his music lessons and her rounds with her father, plans for the approaching May fair and a hundred other things that populated daily life.

Those conversations helped obscure other topics too, like the impending visit from Anne and Ferris Tresham, which would bring answers—answers he wanted less and needed more with each day. He no longer feared learning something unpalatable about himself, as he had earlier. He liked the answers he'd discovered for himself, about the French and the Italian, and the music. But he did fear discovering the details, details which had the power to take him from Haberstock for ever, from the life he'd built on his own, starting from scratch, with Thea here. He tried not to think about it, not on this marvellous, magical day.

'Oh, chocolates!' Thea exclaimed suddenly, dragging him to a spontaneous halt in front of a stall sporting cases of beautifully decorated chocolates drizzled in a variety of coloured icings. He'd not needed his cane much today, but he was glad for it now as he steadied himself against her enthusiasm. 'Do you have cremes?' Thea was asking the vendor. She was usually not given to such excitement. He liked the flush on her cheeks at the discovery of an unexpected treasure.

'We have your favourite today, Miss Peverett—' the confectioner, a white-aproned, rotund older man grinned back at her '—the raspberry cremes. Shall I make you a box?'

Thea seemed to prevaricate. 'Perhaps just a few pieces. A dozen seems extravagant. I don't need a whole box.' But the look on her face suggested otherwise.

Edward intervened. 'Yes, you do. We'll take a box for later and a half dozen for now.' He put the necessary coins on top of the case, a look passing between him and the confectioner while Thea protested ineffectually. His angel had a sweet tooth. The discovery was nearly as delicious as the chocolates themselves and he hugged the fact to himself like the greatest of treasures. How wonderful to learn something so uniquely personal about her. He filed it away, right next to her favourite colour—blue-violet. Favourite chocolates—raspberry cremes drizzled with pale pink icing. It was a short list, but it was growing.

They tucked the chocolates into her market basket alongside the lemons and her ribbons. 'Let me take the basket; it must be getting heavy,' Edward offered, although it meant he had no arm to offer her. 'Where to now, Thea?' They'd finished their perusal of the stalls, but he was loath to let the afternoon end. He was still looking for the right moment to tell her about the key.

'Can't you guess? You're the one who ordered chocolate for *now*,' Thea teased him with a smile. She smiled often when they were together, something she did far less in the presence of others. 'We are going to eat chocolate under that tree over there.' She gave him an exaggerated sober look. 'We can't let the chocolate melt, after all.'

The tree was a thick-trunked oak and it served its purpose admirably, giving them privacy to talk quietly without being overheard while making them visibly public. No one could accuse them of impropriety while they were in plain sight.

Edward leaned against the tree, grateful for its support. His leg was starting to ache from the exertions. Other than nearly falling over at the chocolate booth, he'd not needed his cane much today, a sure sign that Dr Peverett was right. He would eventually walk again, mostly without a limp. He was looking forward to that day, but it wasn't today.

He reached into the white bag of 'now' chocolates and held one up for Thea, and the semi-arousal he'd been experiencing all day turned to something more than a state of pleasurable alertness as she bit into it, revealing the pink filling. Eating chocolate had never been so sexy.

'Your turn.' Thea snatched the bag and selected a piece for him, holding it to his lips as he tasted it. He liked this playful Thea who was enjoying *herself* instead of worrying over others. She was a wicked tease when given the opportunity. His body was aptly remembering just how wicked, and just how much she'd enjoyed herself the last time they'd been alone.

He finished the chocolate and raised her hand to his lips, kissing her palm. 'Mmm. Your hand smells like chocolate.'

'Someone might see!' she scolded, but he could tell from the flash in her eyes that she didn't mind the attention. She liked his flirting, liked his touch today as much as she had on the picnic blanket. He would take encouragement from that.

'Let them see.' Edward laughed. 'Do you think there's a single soul in Haberstock who would be surprised?' He'd promised Dr Peverett no declarations, but this wasn't a declaration. It was akin to sitting together in the Peverett pew and walking through the market. She did pull her hand back at that, some of the mischief in her eyes quenched. 'What is it?'

'We should disabuse them of that. They should be surprised,' Thea said with a sternness that betrayed her seriousness. She meant it. Surely, she wasn't regretting what they'd done, what they'd committed to? Goodness knew he wasn't. 'When you leave, Edward, there will be those who will say it was a matter of course that another man has left me just when it looked like it was getting serious.' He could see the thought hurt her although she tried to shrug it off. 'I shouldn't care. A woman is more than the man she's attached to. I don't *need* a man.' But she did need redemption. Clive Donnatt would find a way to make her a laughingstock. Protectiveness rose. Edward did not relish the idea of leaving her open to ridicule, but neither was he compelled to hide his feelings.

'If we distance ourselves now,' Thea was saying, 'perhaps we can convince people they misunderstood, that there was nothing more than friendship between us.' He did not like that idea at all. It would waste what time they had until news came.

'Or,' Edward drawled, holding her gaze, letting her see that his next words were not to be taken lightly, that his heart was in his eyes, open and naked for her, wanting and waiting for her approval, 'we can try to be optimistic. You are determined to plan for a scenario where I must leave. What if you and I start to plan for a scenario where I stay?'

'But we can't,' Thea insisted. 'We've been through this before. You are changing the plan.' She was protecting herself. 'Why set ourselves up for disappointment?'

'Because I would rather have a little time dreaming of Heaven than to consign myself prematurely to Hell, Thea.' Did she see it that way? He thought of Dr Peverett's question last night, *What does she think of these plans?* 'Would you want me to stay?' He would not pretend there was any other reason for staying but her.

'You know I would, but...' she began, rallying the old protests, the old arguments. 'Surely, you've not forgotten all the barriers that have to be overcome?' And yet there was no heat to her objections. She leaned towards him, her body betraying her. It had not forgotten how it felt to be in his arms, or how much she wanted to be in his arms again.

Edward pressed a finger gently against her lips. 'No, say nothing, Thea. Come with me, listen to me before you leap to debate, but not here. We will not discuss such a thing in public.'

Chapter Fifteen

Come with me. A thrill of excitement rippled through Thea. She was intrigued and drawn by this commanding version of Edward, a man who took charge. The stubborn patient had been replaced with a man who wore authority well and expected to be obeyed, no matter how politely he asked. The combination was a heady one, an arousing one even. There was no question of denying him as he led her back through the market towards the pony trap. Her curiosity was far too piqued to mount a resistance now. She wasn't even sure she wanted to.

'Where are we going?' Thea could only remain silent so long, instructions or not, especially when it seemed as if they were merely going home. Perhaps he meant them to take refuge in the walled garden for their discussion.

Edward gave her a laughing scold. 'You are not terribly good at following directions, are you? We were to say nothing until we get there.'

'Wherever that is,' Thea shot back. She was more than a bit edgy. Patience had never been her strong suit. It was practically non-existent in the wake of his words, *What if... I stay?* He couldn't just drop those words into the conversation and then make her wait, make her hope.

'We're here.' Edward turned the trap down a short drive that led towards a stone cottage set off the main road.

'The Anderson place?' Thea gave him a quizzical look. 'No one has lived here for over two years. Mr Anderson passed away and his widow went to stay with her sister's family.'

Edward halted the trap and Thea clambered out on her own before he could be foolish enough to try and help her down. He shot her a scolding look that said she should have waited for him. He stopped at the door. 'It will be locked,' Thea said, only to be answered with a grin.

'Thankfully, I have the key.' He grinned back, entirely too smug for her taste. Something was afoot, something she'd not been told of. She felt distinctly and uncharacteristically out of control. He fitted the key to the lock and pushed the door open, ushering her inside with a sweep of his hand.

Inside was dim and empty. Mrs Anderson had sold most of the furniture or given it to her grown children when she'd left and the place smelled musty after having been closed up. But it was a good space. It was a sturdy cottage, as Thea recalled. There was a parlour to the left of the entry and a kitchen to the right that also served as a dining room.

'A good sweeping and some window-washing would have this place set to rights.' Edward stood in the doorway of the parlour, letting her walk about the room and look out of the grimy window. 'I can imagine a fire in the fireplace, a braided rug on the floor, a few chairs, a settee perhaps, a bookcase against the wall. It would be a cosy room.'

Thea laughed. 'Shall we have a dog on the floor too, just to make the image complete?' The picture he painted was tempting. It was too easy to imagine so much more than furniture in the room, but people too. Specifically, him and her. She could see him in a comfortable chair, reading one of his favourite Italian texts, while she sat with some sewing or the latest medical tract, perhaps reading out loud when she came across a particularly interesting bit.

'Shall we see the rest of it?' Edward offered her his arm and they made their way to the back of the cottage, where a room served as an office for record-keeping and another served as a work room that might be put to any number of uses, from laundry to distilling herbs.

'Or a surgery,' Edward put in as she surveyed the room, plucking the very thought from her own mind. It would make an excellent surgery. With cleaning, it would have good light. His fantasies were catching, apparently.

'Who would come here to see me, though, when my father is just a half mile up the road?' She was quick to squelch the fantasy. If she wasn't careful, Edward would have her believing all kinds of impossibilities—he could stay, she could practise medicine, they could live happily ever after. Fairy tales, all of them.

'Expectant mothers?' Edward offered. 'I would think they'd prefer to have a woman looking after them.'

She gave him a half-smile. 'I'm to be a midwife, then?' She'd been trained to be so much more. But Edward had the right of it. Staying here, her choices would be limited when it came to practising medicine. Staying here assumed she wouldn't go back to the London hospital, no more running of a ward even if it was just for ill gentlewomen and governesses.

Edward slipped a hand around hers. 'It's a *start*, Thea. You can begin as a midwife, but you could eventually expand. Women who had a good birth with you would be compelled to turn to you for other needs, and their children's needs as well as they grew. You can specialise in women's health, like the women of Salerno you were telling me about. If it was possible in the fourteenth century, surely it's possible in the nineteenth. Women caring for women.' Damn him for making it sound so *possible*, so realistic when she knew better.

'Shall we go upstairs, Thea?' More temptation.

'With your leg? There are only bedchambers up there.' Thea hesitated. 'It's not necessary.'

He grinned. 'We'll take it slow. I can manage the stairs.' She wasn't sure she could, though. She didn't want to think about Edward and bedrooms all at once. It was sure to send all of her other thoughts scattering.

There were three bedrooms, two of them empty, but her mind was already leaping ahead to what the dormered windows would look like with curtains and what a coloured bedspread on an iron bedstead might do to brighten the room. The last room was larger and it held the only piece of furniture to be found in the house: a carved oak four-poster bed, complete with mattress and covered in a dark quilt that had been left behind, too big to be of use on an ordinary bed.

'The bed is too big to get down the stairs,' Edward surmised. 'It's an elegant piece of furniture, though. Mr Anderson must have assembled it in this room. If it couldn't go down the stairs, it certainly isn't likely to have gone up.' He pressed a hand down on the bed, testing it. 'This room must get magnificent sunsets with the two windows facing west.' He chuckled. 'I think Mr Anderson must have been a romantic with this big bed and the west-facing room. Not only would he have had lovely sunsets, he'd have been able to lie abed a bit longer in the mornings before sunrise found him.'

Thea laughed. 'I think the romantic might be you, Edward. I would not have guessed it. You're an irascible patient.' She should not flirt with him; she should not encourage him to spin his fantasies—it would only lead to disappointment. But before disappointment it might lead to something else.

'I might be, when it comes to you, Thea.' He had an arm about her waist, pulling her to him to steal a playful kiss. It didn't stay playful for long. Between a day at the market eating sweets and spinning homely fantasies, desire pulled at them. 'You taste like chocolate,' he murmured, deepening the kiss until she wanted nothing more than to fall with him onto the bed, to make love until the sun set.

'You taste like butter beer.' She ran her tongue across his bottom lip and watched his eyes go dark. Her hands went to his neckcloth.

'What are you doing, Thea?' His question came out as a hoarse rasp.

'I'm undressing you,' she whispered, kissing his throat. 'It would be a shame to let this light, this bed, this privacy, go to waste.'

'Thea, are you sure? Are you sure you want to see me? You needn't, you know. I'll understand.' His hands came up to cover hers, to stop hers from revealing him.

She held his gaze, touched by this brief glimpse of his vulnerability, his humanity. Her voice was soft when she spoke. 'Yes, Edward, I want to see you, burns, scars and all.' With slow hands she pushed back his jacket from his broad shoulders, her fingers working the buttons of his waistcoat, then his shirt until he stood before her, bare-chested, the muscled, sculpted perfection of his left side in stark contrast to the puckered, scarred tissue on the right, but it didn't matter to her. Of course, she'd seen the scars when she'd nursed him—a patient held few secrets from a nurse—but this was different. They were lovers now and she understood that he wanted to please as a man pleased a woman. She ran the palms of her hands up over his torso, revelling in every ridge and plane, and back down again. 'Edward, you're beautiful,' she breathed, her hands finding the fastenings of his trousers. She paused, thinking. Only Thea would stop in the middle of undressing a man to think. 'Perhaps you should sit; we should do your boots first.'

She marched him backwards to the bed and divested him of his boots while he laughed. 'You like this, don't you? Bossing me around.'

She tugged down his trousers until she had all of him to feast on in his naked glory, and what a feast it was, a feast of lean hips and long legs, of curling hair nestling between his thighs, and a proud phallus rising ruddy and red from its dark roost. She stepped back to gaze at him. 'I was wrong; you are not beautiful, Edward, you are magnificent.' He was all man, all healthy, hard man, a warrior in truth.

He levered up on his elbows, eyes glittering, sharp emeralds, ready to exact his revenge, his voice a sexy growl. 'Your turn, Thea. Take off your clothes.'

He was not going to make it easy on her and take her clothes off himself. He was going to make it deliberate on her part. A thrill of arousal and anxiety ran through Thea. This was new territory, both exciting and frightening. What if he was disappointed in what lay beneath her gown?

'Thea, you will be beautiful,' he whispered. 'Shall I tell you how to start? Take down your hair. I love it loose; it's the colour of carob and coffee.'

She pulled the pins and watched Edward's eyes darken in appreciation as it fell. 'Take off your dress,' came the next command, his eyes following her hands to the buttons of her bodice. 'Front-buttoning gowns are very alluring, Thea—' he offered an intimate, low-voiced commentary '—I don't know why more women don't wear them. They're efficient *and* tempting.' Her gown slid to the floor, leaving her decidedly exposed in the failing rays of sunlight and her chemise. It took all of her courage not to cover herself, to stand there and let him look his fill, to raise her gaze and see his reaction.

'Come here, Thea.' He reached out a hand for her and she came, standing between the vee of his thighs. 'You are a goddess.' His hands reached for the hem of her chemise and tugged it up over her head until she was fully revealed to him. His eyes were full of reverence. She looked down at herself, wondering what he saw, watching his hands skim up from her waist to cup her breasts.

'They're not very large,' Thea began.

He silenced her with a kiss. 'They're perfect—*you* are perfect.' His thumbs ran over her nipples and she felt them strain in delight at his touch like the rest of her body strained, yearned. She wanted his hands everywhere. He fell back on the bed, a little puff of dust rising as he took her with him, his hands at her waist, her legs settling on either side of him. 'Ride me, Thea.'

What a delicious proposition that was. She bent forward, kissing him on the mouth as she raised her bottom up and over his phallus, feeling his hands guide her, settle her so that his phallus brushed her sex, her moisture mingling with his.

'Dear Lord, Thea, you're so wet.' The words thrilled her, the groan that followed thrilled her, fuelling her own arousal, her own confidence. *She* aroused this man. She sat back and took him into her sheath, revelling in the moan she wrung from him, the shudder of his breath as she began to move, the rise of his hips as his body rose to meet her. She experimented, giving a little swivel of her hips, and was rewarded with a guttural cry of pure delight.

This was sheer heaven to simultaneously give pleasure while seeking her own, a pleasure that was quickly escalating out of her control, her own breathing as ragged as Edward's. His hands dug into her hips as his body tightened and gathered. His neck arched. She moved up and down his length once more, the final sheathing pushing her into her pleasure. She collapsed against his chest while Edward shuddered deep within her, filling her with warmth. This was so much better, to complete the act with him. She lay against his chest, his heart thumping beneath her ear, his phallus resting within her, his arms about her, his lips at her ear. 'I did not plan for that to happen.'

'It will be all right,' she whispered. In these moments it felt as if everything would indeed be all right. This was contentment, to lie here with Edward. How could she want for more? Everything she needed was right here. His breathing settled. Carefully, she rolled to his good side, tucking in against the length of him. She felt his arm come about her, holding her close as sleep claimed them.

Chapter Sixteen

He'd not planned for it to be this way. Not just what had happened at the end, the total loss of control on his part, but the whole seduction. Thea's bottom shifted against his groin in a rousing reminder of how spectacularly his plan had gone awry. Not unpleasantly awry, but awry all the same. He'd meant to show her the house and make his case. He'd only managed to show off the house. His case remained unstated, at least in the fashion he'd intended. Which wasn't to say that what had occurred hadn't been persuasive. Perhaps his arguments would only pale in comparison to what had happened in this room. Still, in all fairness to Thea, he wanted to make them anyway, to show her how intently he'd thought on this, to show her that his solutions were not just reactions in response to an immediate want. These were solutions if the future was willing.

She woke in his arms just as the sun was sinking in the sky, bathing the late spring sky in pinks and purples where its light flooded the room, turning the shadows of the room to shades of blue-violet. 'Mmm. I think you

might be right. This room does get the best sunsets.'
Thea stretched and rolled over to face him, her hand
soft at his jaw. 'How are you, Edward?'

'Good…' He kissed her forehead and couldn't hold
back a grin. Had he ever felt this fulfilled in his life?
'How are you?'

'Wonderful.' She arched and he let his gaze roam
over her long, slim limbs. What a sleek beauty she was.
His body was wanting her again but this time he felt
compelled to resist. It was getting late and they *must*
have time to talk, especially now.

'This afternoon turned out better than planned,' he
began, liking this intimacy of talking quietly and lying
skin to skin, nothing between them but all the time in
the world.

'But it was not what you'd planned?' Thea's finger-
nail drew a circle on his chest, sending a ripple of desire through him. At this rate, he'd be forgetting himself
once more.

'No, not what I'd planned. Do you like the house?
I am thinking of taking a lease on it.' He watched her
expression change, ease turning to wariness. He reminded her of the purpose that had prompted the visit.
'If I stay, I'll need a place to live.' He debated his pro-
noun. What if he said 'we'? Would it assume too much
too soon? He was keenly aware that Thea's obstacles
might be best dealt with gradually.

She tilted her head and studied him. 'That's not
something you can choose, Edward. Just like you can't
choose to give the squire's son more music lessons. You
can't really promise the squire's son you'll be there to
teach him until he's ready for a conservatoire. He will

be devastated if he loses you.' The squire's son was a convenient diversion. He didn't think for a moment this concern was really about one boy's music lessons.

He heard what she was truly asking: *How long will you be able to be here? What happens when your memories come back? When Ferris brings information about who you are? We could be destroyed.*

He laced his fingers with hers. Eating chocolates under the oak tree seemed ages ago instead of hours. 'I don't have to acknowledge any of it. Who's to say I'm not Edward?' He gave her a moment to digest all that was implied in those simple words.

'Why would you do that?' she pressed. 'Why would you give up who you are and just be Edward?' Awe glittered for a moment in the depths of her gaze, suggesting that she suspected the real reason and wasn't sure what to make of it. Any step he took affected them both. Whether she was ready to fully accept it or not, they were already intertwined, like their hands, the choices of one affecting the other.

He was not afraid to say the words, only of her reaction to them. 'For you, Thea. I would stay because I hope for *you*, for *us*. If Edward is the only way to get that, then Edward I will be.' He hoped it wouldn't come to that. That would be a drastic, dangerous measure to take and it would involve a lifetime of denial.

'Edward with no name?' she challenged softly, proof that perhaps she'd toyed with this scenario too.

'No, I'd be Edward Luckman, a man who can be baptised into the Anglican church, and thus into reality. The vicar is amenable to it. A man must be born anew and all that.' Not just to enter the kingdom of Heaven but to enter Society. He watched her take it in, registering the privileges that came with a name. 'The banns could be called, should we decide or should we need them.' It would not hurt to remind her they'd not been careful today; it might become an issue of the latter, something that was out of their control.

'At the expense of our future happiness and possibly someone else's?' she queried with a softly voiced cynicism that said she too found such means drastic. 'A happy life cannot be built on subterfuge. We could not live with ourselves for long if we were cheating another.' This was a more tangible form of the guilt they had discussed before.

'It won't come to that.' It was time to fell one of Thea's most important obstacles. He held her gaze, willing her to see the truth in his eyes. 'I don't think there's another's happiness at stake. I think there is only ours.' He bent his forehead to hers, the closeness of their bodies cocooning them in a private world of their own as he laid his case. 'I would have remembered if there'd been anyone when I kissed you. I remembered Italian and French when I opened those books. I remembered playing the piano when I was confronted with music. It seems logical that I would have remembered someone I was committed to when I kissed you, but there was nothing, only you. I work with children every day and they trigger no memories for me. Thea, I don't believe I'm married, I don't believe I have children. What I *do* believe is that I am yours.' And he hoped he was right. So much hinged on it.

She wanted to believe that. His logic was careful and her heart revelled in it; it swelled in the hope that there was a middle ground after all. His argument fitted with their earlier discussion that he was unlikely to have chosen military service if he'd been attached to a family who was dependent on him.

What if they were wrong? What if he simply couldn't continue to uphold the choices he'd made today?

'This is not something we can be only partially right about, Edward. Even if there's no wife, no children, you belong somewhere else. There *are* people, there *is* a place that would claim you.' A mother, a father, a brother, sisters, perhaps. 'Could you deny them the knowledge that you're alive?'

'For you? For the family we could make? Yes.'

The words shook her. She'd heard tales of men who'd walked away from everything for love, but this was beyond that.

'You would never wonder about them? Never wonder who you might really be?' He wouldn't just be turning his back on a family but he'd be turning his back on himself, giving up the quest to know his name. He'd be Edward Luckman for ever. Only he might come to believe he wasn't so lucky as the years passed.

'I already have the answer to that, Thea. I am Edward, the man who loves you. *That* is who I really am.'

'What if there is no choice, Edward? It's not as plain as telling Ferris to leave his findings at home. What if your memories return one day of their own volition?' They'd not addressed that possibility out loud between them. That would be a special kind of torture for them both to live with, to know that one day, tomorrow or ten years from now, he might wake up, his past fully restored to him. It could happen at any time; any little thing might trigger it, in the middle of church on a Sunday or at a family dinner. He would be forced to face those memories.

Her comment stung him. 'I've already said I'd disavow them. I don't have to acknowledge them whenever or however my memories return. Although who is to say that I cannot take you into that life with me, should we choose? Why should my memories returning preclude including you in my old life?' He was growing frustrated with her; she could hear it in his voice. There was a sharp edge underlying his gentle persuasion. He wanted to be rewarded for his efforts and perhaps he deserved to be. All she had done was raise objections.

It was hard to argue with his responses. They were evidence of how long he'd wrestled with the subject and how much thought he'd given it. She'd grappled with the situation and come up empty-handed, but he'd come up with solutions. On one level, it was an intoxicating relief to not shoulder this burden on her own. On another level, though, it was novel and dangerous, especially wrapped as it was in the pictures he'd painted downstairs of comfortable chairs and braided rugs set before a hearth, of a surgery bursting with possibility. Those were beautiful images but they were sirens, lures, that didn't come without cost. They would require her to dash her own dreams against the rocks.

'It's not just you giving up everything, Edward.' While they were on the subject of walking away from the past she might as well throw her own into the mix.

'I know,' he said solemnly. 'That's why I wanted to show you the house, to show you the surgery.'

'You wanted to show me the possibilities, you mean,'

Thea corrected. 'I'd have to give up the hospital.' It was a valid point, but it seemed hardly enough to tip the scales against his promise to disavow his past.

'It would be a new life for both of us,' he soothed. 'It excites me, Thea, to build that new life with you.' It excited her too, which was an enormous problem. Excitement obliterated logic and reality. His hand was moving in gentle circles at her hip in prelude of another bout perhaps of reason-shattering argument with his body. No, not now, when she needed to think. Intuitively, she knew if she didn't leave the bed before that happened, reality would be lost and she with it. Before her willpower deserted her entirely, she scooted away and swung her legs over the bed.

'Thea—' the sound of her name embodied a frustrated groan '—what are you doing? Come back to bed.'

She picked up her chemise and gown from the floor. 'I am preserving my sense of reason.' She slid her chemise over her head. 'You do not fight fair, Edward.'

He levered up on his elbows, gloriously nude as he watched her dress. 'I don't fight fair? You, my dear, should have been a barrister instead of a doctor.'

Their comments were spoken both in jest and scolding.

Thea's temper flashed as she fumbled with the buttons of her bodice. Dammit, her fingers would not work. 'This is not what we pledged to, Edward. We promised each other two weeks of living to the fullest, and now you're breaking the rules! You're renting a cottage and spinning images of a future that wasn't supposed to be.'

Edward gave a bark of laughter. 'You cannot say you've never broken the rules when they've proven not to serve your purpose, Thea Peverett. You, my dear, are the original rule-breaker.' He swung himself off the bed, reaching for his cane as he came to her, naked and laughing. His hands batted hers aside, his voice soft. 'Let me do it, Thea. Your hands are shaking.' He kissed her when he finished, drawing her against him, his body deliciously warm with health and calm. 'I did not mean to upset you, truly. Do you know why I want this cottage so badly? I want you to see what you mean to me. I want to give you hope, Thea. I want you to know that I will choose you.'

She nodded against his shoulder and wrapped her arms about him. Had anyone ever cared for her the way this man did? Would anyone ever again? She felt beautiful, whole, normal when she was with him. He saw her differently from how she saw herself. She was stubborn and headstrong; it was hard to like her.

'I don't know why, Edward. I am difficult and in my determination, I run roughshod over people.' She'd continually argued against him at every turn today and still, here he was, comforting her when she ought to be apologising to him.

She looked up at him. 'I want to believe in everything you said but I don't want to see you hurt, Edward. It's one thing to make promises based on theory. It's another to stick to those promises in reality. Today, you *think* you can disavow your past, a past you don't even know. You may not feel that way, or be *allowed* to feel that way, once you know it, no matter what you say today. In truth, I don't want to be hurt either.'

She felt his arms tighten about her as if he feared she would slip away. 'Where does that leave us, Thea?'

What a gift those words were. He'd recognised he'd come to the limits of his argument, that the rest was up to her. He'd done his part and now he was putting *them* into her hands. He was entrusting her with his heart and she would be worthy of it.

'I need to think, and you do too. For now, take the lease on the house. My mother and I will come to clean and make it into a proper place, Edward.' His eyes gleamed a soft green that said he understood the enormity of that assent. 'But we will wait for Ferris's information before we decide anything further, for both of our sakes. It is only another week.' She held him close, unaware of how much she sounded like her father. 'I know you are in a hurry, but we have time. There is always time to do things right, Edward.'

'Yes.' He held her gaze with all the solemnity of a bridegroom taking his vows. 'And will you do something for me? No matter what Ferris finds, you will see the victory, not the battle? You're not a woman who accepts the impossible. Don't start now.'

Chapter Seventeen

Omnia cum tempore. All things with time. The Latin phrase had popped into his head from the void that was his mind, but the words fit the week, becoming his motto as Edward waited for Ferris Tresham's arrival with all the enthusiasm of a condemned man waiting for the judge. Did Tresham realise all that hung in the balance with the news he'd bring? His future with Thea, his future in Haberstock, the man he would become—all of it waited in a limbo tinged with anticipation and dread. He both wanted Tresham to arrive and be done with the waiting, and he wanted the man to never arrive at all.

The week erred on the side of speed, flying by in a flurry of efficient activity that gave him hope even as it reminded him that judgement was growing closer. That efficiency was marked daily by the progress on his cottage. Thea had been true to her word. She and her mother had not wasted a moment in coming down to clean and to set his cottage to rights. *His cottage.*

In a week of emotional upheaval as he worried over the future, those two words were a lifeline, his one step forward, his one step closer to a life with Thea. The cottage metamorphosed before his eyes, changing every day. Catherine and Thea arrived each morning as he left for the vicarage and they worked until he returned.

Edward chirped to the horse to pick up the pace. The cottage would be coming into view soon and he was eager to see what had been done today while he'd been off teaching music lessons. Each day, Thea remained behind after her mother returned to the Hall, to tour him through the evidence of their progress. The first day, the women had devoted themselves to cleaning the front parlour and the kitchen. Thea had met him that evening to show off the gleaming windows and swept floors. A pegged board had been installed in the small foyer for coats and cloaks and he'd made instant use of it, being sure to brush the dust off his boots before venturing further.

In the kitchen, the old stove had been cleaned, the worktable scrubbed, and a small dresser had been added. That dresser was thoughtfully stocked with everything needed for a home: dishes and cups on the shelves, pots and pans below, behind the dresser doors, and various utensils in the drawers. The pantry was stocked too, and soup simmered on the stove in anticipation of a simple dinner for two.

Edward refused to see this outpouring of largesse as anything—first and foremost—but a gift. He'd been with the Peveretts long enough to know they were a generous family. But he could also not ignore the subtle message behind this kitchen. Soup and a full pantry meant there was no longer a reason to take his evening meal up at the Hall.

Dr Peverett was holding him to his word that he would call at the Hall only as a suitor. There would be no more opportunity for lingering night walks with Thea or visits to the walled garden. The Peveretts were taking no chances with Thea's present or her future. If things *did* work out, Alfred Peverett's daughter would have a real home to go to as a bride but, until such things were established, Edward was to be given no more freedoms than any other eager suitor, except that he might steal Thea for supper before walking her home to the Hall ahead of nightfall.

The parlour had stopped Edward in his tracks. It had been empty and dusty when he'd left that morning. Now, it was his simple fantasy come to life. The floor had been swept and adorned with a braided rug. Two over-stuffed chairs were set by the hearth and a bookcase set against the wall. Already, one shelf was full of titles. Edward ran his hand over the spines. 'You brought my favourites.' Voltaire, Dante and others populated the shelves, no doubt taken straight from the Haberstock Hall shelves.

The furniture was old, probably pieces scavenged from the attics. The bookcase bore a few scars, enough to make it interesting. The chairs and the rug were worn. None of it mattered to Edward. What did matter was the story these pieces told: Thea had listened to him and, despite her own reservations about their circumstances, she'd dreamed with him and brought this room to life.

'I'm trying to see the victory, Edward,' she'd said softly.

That first day set a pattern for the week. The second day, Edward had come home to find his office set up with a desk and chair and small bookcase. The third day, he was welcomed home to the master's suite. Curtains hung at the two west-facing windows and a wardrobe and a bureau had been added with his personal items arranged within. A jar of blue violet pansies sat on the nightstand beside the bed, proof that this was Thea's doing. The fourth day had been devoted to the other bedrooms, each one now containing a small chest of drawers and a quilt-covered iron bedstead.

Efforts had moved out of doors on the fifth and sixth days, establishing a garden full of neat-rowed vegetables and herbs made from starts from Catherine's own garden at the Hall. The front of the cottage had benefitted as well. The weeds had been pulled and flowerbeds defined. That would be Thea's work, he'd surmised, recognising the new starts from flowers in the walled garden.

And on the seventh day, they'd rested. He turned into his drive, searching for signs of today's efforts and for signs of Thea. What was there left to do? He saw it immediately. A bright blue door and shutters met him. They'd whitewashed the stone and painted the door. Just in time—in time for the May fair tonight in the village square and in time for Ferris and Anne's arrival tomorrow. His cottage was ready to meet his future. Tonight, though, he was fully intent on appreciating the present.

He took time to brush down the carriage horse and see to the horse's dinner. It would be back in harness soon enough. Then he made himself ready. He was expected at the Hall to escort Thea to the fair and he wanted to look his best. He washed and shaved and fussed over his clothes until he laughed at himself for such foolishness. He was acting like a nervous bridegroom. Perhaps that wasn't too far from the mark. Perhaps this time tomorrow he would know if that was a role he could aspire to.

He arrived promptly at the Hall and found Thea waiting for him, dressed in her green gown, a white fichu tucked about the neckline and her new green ribbons trailing from her hat. He drank in the sight of her. Taking her hand, he raised it to his lips. 'Thea, the cottage looks marvellous,' he began, but words suddenly seemed inadequate to the task and there was no time to say more. Her parents joined them in the foyer, her father shaking his hand and enquiring after the cottage while informing him, they would follow them down to the village in their own conveyance.

'Are we never to be alone?' Edward groaned as he helped Thea up to the seat of the pony trap. At least their conversation would be private as they travelled but he was sorely missing their quiet suppers in the cottage.

Thea smiled as he settled beside her and took up the reins. She slipped her arm through his. 'We might manage something later,' and he smiled back, warmed by the promise in her voice.

'I've had some news from London,' she began, leaning her head on his shoulder. He loved the feel of her weight against him, the rightness of her beside him. There was a touch of excitement to her voice that made him smile. 'My article, the one about the Crimea and the medical conditions there, has been published in *The Times*. Rawdon wrote to tell me, and he sent a copy.'

'Well done, Thea,' he complimented. His Thea was unstoppable. 'The first of many, I assume. Florence will be pleased to hear the news.'

'Not everyone will be pleased, though.' Thea laughed.

'I'm sure if anyone can bring them around, it's you.' Edward gave her a friendly nudge with his elbow. For a moment it seemed as if she wanted to say more but the village came into view and the fair claimed their attention. Further discussion would have to wait.

The village green was bustling with festive energy when they arrived. They left the trap at the vicarage and joined the throng of villagers, walking carefully to avoid a collision with any of the young merrymakers who darted through the stalls and squealed with delight at the holiday. 'Tell me again what we're celebrating,' he asked Thea. Not that it mattered. Haberstock could celebrate whatever it wanted as long as it gave him a reason to walk out with Thea.

'Springtime. It's our farewell to winter,' Thea explained. 'A lot of villages do the same thing around May Day. But in the sixteen-hundreds Haberstock thought it was too pagan, too close to Beltane. So, being the good Anglicans they were, and also appreciating the importance of a good party, they designed their own festivities and moved them later in the month. There's better weather at the end of May anyway.'

'This has been going on for two hundred years?' Edward liked the idea of that, the stability of enduring tradition. 'It's something to count on,' he remarked. 'So, this was all your doing this year? You and your com-

mittee?' He was actually surprised by the scope of it.
There were games at one end of the green, vendors for a
night market at the other, and in the centre of the green
a giant bonfire had been built to be lit later in the evening, along with trestle tables and a space for dancing.
They passed the tables and Edward caught the scent of
roasting meat.

'Later!' She laughed and tugged at him. 'Games first,
then food.'

There was a ring toss, dart-throwing, and a chance
to knock down wooden bottles with a ball. 'Are there
prizes?' Edward asked as they watched young men attempting to impress their young ladies with their ball-
throwing prowess.

'Pies—the ladies have been baking all week.' Thea
pointed to a protected area off to the side of the games,
containing tables loaded with the delectable prizes. 'The
money from the games goes to the church poor fund and
winners can claim a pie to eat for dessert after dinner.'

'Did you bake a pie?'

'Yes, it's the rhubarb one in the second row.' Thea
seemed content to downplay the pie, but Edward stared
in frank amazement at the elegant lattice work that
criss-crossed the crust.

'That pie is beautiful.' He gave her a grin. 'I think
we must have it.' He put down a coin. 'Three balls to
knock down three bottles, is that right? And the pie is
all mine?'

Thea blushed furiously. 'You don't have to do this.'

'Why not? The other fellows are doing the same for
their ladies.' Edward shrugged out of his jacket. 'Hold
my coat.' But Thea seemed suddenly and uncharacter-

istically shy. 'What is it?' he asked quietly, folding his coat over her arm. They were talking in whispers now, just the two of them.

'It's just that no one has ever wanted my pie before,' Thea confessed and it occurred to him that, for all her worldliness, Thea had never strolled a festival ground with a beau beside her, never been the recipient of impetuously bought gifts or fed chocolates from another's hand. She'd been a virgin when she'd come to him, but many gently bred women were. He'd not guessed just how untouched she truly was. The simple pleasures in life had passed her by because of the cruel prank of some louts.

'Not wanted your pie before?' Edward said in low tones. 'Thea, I do believe that's quite the naughty innuendo you've made.' She went positively scarlet. He moved his mouth to her ear. 'I'll tell you a secret. I like your pie and I am looking forward to having a slice or two later tonight.'

Amid her embarrassment she found her wit. 'Now who's making naughty nuances?' she scolded. That was better. He liked Thea's scolding better than her self-doubt. He liked that the self-doubt was in less evidence these days.

'There won't be any pie if you don't let me throw these balls.' He gave her a smile, rolled up his sleeves and stepped to the counter. He hefted the first ball, feeling its weight. Not as heavy as he'd like, a sure sign the bottles were probably weighted. The ladies committee wasn't giving away their pie for free. Then again, losing was for a good cause. That ladies committee was shrewder than he'd given it credit for, although he should have expected that with Thea on board.

He was just about to throw the first ball when a drawl stopped him in mid-throw. 'Isn't this lovely. Miss Peverett is walking out with her mysterious soldier.' There was a bout of laughter at the implication behind the unfriendly words.

Edward set his ball down and turned to face the newcomer. 'Good evening, Donnatt, gentlemen.' Donnatt and the young men with him looked as if they'd already been at the free ale quite heavily. 'Are you any good at these games? None of you seem to have a lady fair to champion.' Edward watched Donnatt stiffen at the implication while Thea bristled beside him, wanting to take Donnatt on herself. He could not allow that. His Angel didn't have to answer to a half-drunk cad.

'Are you suggesting a cripple with a bad leg would be better at this than I am?' Donnatt's gaze was steely. 'Boys, did you hear that?' There was a burst of laughter at his expense, but Edward ignored it.

'I am suggesting just that, Donnatt. A friendly little competition. First one to knock down three bottles.'

'Six bottles.' Donnatt countered, slapping coins on the counter and took up his spot in the lane beside Edward. 'Unless that's too rich for you?'

'It's never too rich when a lady's honour is at stake.' Edward found another coin and six balls were stacked up in front of each of them.

The signal to go was given and Edward threw his first ball, hitting two of the bottles while Donnatt's first throw went wide, missing entirely. The man was drunker than Edward had thought. He threw again, knocking down his third, and waited for the bottles to be quickly set back up. He moved to throw again, when someone purposely jostled him, causing him to lose his balance, his fourth ball missing the target. 'Tell your boys to keep their hands to themselves,' Edward growled to Donnatt, who'd managed to knock down his first three at last. They'd gathered a crowd and people were starting to cheer. Someone booed at the foul play. Donnatt and Edward were both down to their last two balls and Donnatt had caught up while Edward had recovered his balance. One more throw might decide it. He was not going to lose to this cad who sought to insult Thea at every turn, but he might if Donnatt got to six first. He just had to make sure Donnatt didn't have six bottles to throw at. Edward grabbed his fifth ball and threw it hard. Not waiting to see the results, he threw the sixth ball at Donnatt's bottles, knocking them down along with his own.

'What the hell do you think you're doing?' Donnatt exploded.

'Helping you out. Looked like you needed it.' Edward grinned. 'That's six bottles for me. I'll take the rhubarb pie, if you please. My lady and I are off to eat.'

They filled their plates with roasted meat and opted for mugs of cider over ale and found two seats at a long table. Thea set the pie between them and cut two pieces to add to their meal. 'You should not have done that to Donnatt,' she scolded as she served up the prize, 'but I am glad you did.'

'He's an odious man. You shouldn't have to put up with him.' He smiled as she forked a piece of pie and held it up. 'Don't worry over Donnatt, Thea. Tonight is for us.' The very last night that they might be able to claim, but he tried not to think of that.

She smiled, but the shadow in her whisky eyes echoed his silent thoughts. She was aware, too, that the sand might be running out of their hourglass. 'Eat your pie, Edward; the bonfire will start soon.'

Chapter Eighteen

The bonfire made him uneasy. He couldn't share the general enthusiasm for it. The flames licked high into the night as the village burnt an effigy of Old Man Winter while people cheered and danced. For once, Edward was glad his leg kept him from joining in. He didn't want to be that close to the flames or the noise.

'Edward, are you all right? I know it's still rather pagan.' Thea was studying him carefully. He tried to school his features, tried to find a calm centre.

'It's not that.' He couldn't shake the growing anxiety that had settled on him, although he felt ridiculous. There was no reason to respond this way. Fires in the hearth had not affected him. But this fire, a fire out in the open on a dark night, had his mind racing with fear, his heart pumping with trepidation until he had to get away. He lurched to his feet, his hand gripping his cane for dear life. 'I have to leave. I need a moment.' His panicked brain sent him lurching into the dark, seeking a destination beyond the fire, until he saw the oak tree at the fringe of the green where they'd eaten chocolates.

He stumbled in its direction, nearly tripping over a tree root in his haste. Thea was there to right him, but he shook her off, crossly. 'I'm fine, leave me be. Go back to the party.' He didn't want her to see him like this, on the brink of breaking down, on the brink of an unnamed terror, just on the brink... The unknown loomed.

'I am not leaving you. You are clearly not fine,' Thea insisted, but he was leaving her. The fear was riding him hard now, forcing his eyes shut in one last attempt to push it away, but there was no hiding from this. It was in his mind and it was going to have its way.

He was at Inkerman again, his coat on fire, his leg bleeding, his body writhing on the ground, smothering the flames, but not before the damage was done.

He was unable to move, but someone was coming, someone was calling out.

'Leopold Swann! Wychavon, where are you? Matthew Corkley! Andrew Biles!'

Someone was looking for the fallen. He tried to make his throat work, tried to call out, I'm here, I'm here.

But the words wouldn't come.

No one would come.

No one would hear.

Don't leave me. I am here.

'I am here. I won't leave you.' It was Thea's voice in the darkness, Thea's arms that held him, Thea's stern command that called him out of his fear. 'Open your eyes and look at me.' How many times had he heard her make that same command in Scutari? To open his eyes, to see the world, to belong in it? He had no choice. He knew from experience she wouldn't take no for an answer.

He forced his eyes open and was rewarded with her cognac gaze, her own eyes steady, willing him to find strength. He clung to her. He was breathing hard. 'I was at Inkerman, on the ground; soldiers came looking for the living. They were calling out names. I tried to answer but they couldn't hear me.' He couldn't stop the sobs now, couldn't hold back the abject horror of those moments of knowing he was going to be left behind to die, that no one would find him, no one would hear him, just as no one had heard him or seen him the day he'd been unloaded at Scutari.

'I am here, Edward,' Thea whispered fiercely against his ear, her arms tight around him. 'You've been found. I found you.' Yes, she'd found him, she'd found his single tear, she'd pulled him out of the pile of the dead. 'I will never let you go.'

That was a promise she might not be able to keep but, at the moment, Thea didn't care. She only cared that Edward was hurting and there was only her to stand between him and that hurt. Tonight, his fears had broken free, interwoven with a memory. The best way to exorcise fears was to confront them with logic.

'Edward, you were not lost. Someone at Inkerman *did* find you and they took you to the field hospital. I found you at Scutari. You were found both times,' she reminded him, rubbing small circles on his back to soothe him, 'when you needed it the most, you were not left…you were not lost. I was there and I am here and you are with me.' She repeated it over and over until she felt his breathing become even and his pulse steady. She was loath to release him, but he would want his space and time to process his thoughts. After a while, reassured that he was all right, she sat back and simply waited.

'They were calling names, Thea,' he said at last. 'Leopold Swann, Wychavon, Matthew Corkley, Andrew Biles—there were other names too.' He shook his head, trying to clear it, clarify it.

'Do you think one of those names was yours?' she asked quietly, even as something akin to excitement and anxiety surged within her. A name, perhaps, after all this time. This latest recollection was so much more well-defined than his previous ones. She could not let such a specific detail slip away unexamined, not when so much hinged on it.

'I don't know. I suppose it's possible. Leopold Swann…' He tried the name out thoughtfully, but not the others. They both waited, perhaps thinking enlightenment would strike. Nothing came. Edward shook his head. 'In the moment, in the memory, all I could focus on was being left behind.' Even now, knowing that he was safe, she could see him shudder against the realness of the recollection. 'The names were secondary, something in the background. I suppose we'll know soon enough—tomorrow. Perhaps Tresham will bring word of those names and we might understand them better.'

He reached for her hand and squeezed it. 'I wonder if those men were ever found? I wonder if they were as lucky as I am?' He paused and sighed. He passed a hand over his face, still obviously uneasy and doing his best to overcome it. 'I am sorry. We were having a wonderful night. I thought about tonight all day.'

She had too. It would be the last time they'd be to-

gether before Ferris came, before everything changed
in some way. What would tomorrow bring? She leaned
close to him, breathing in the soft herbal scent of his
soap, a light *fougère* that smelled of healthy male and
springtime. 'I want to make love tonight,' she whispered at his ear, her teeth nipping at the tender flesh
of his lobe in invitation. 'Right here, beneath the oak.
No one will see.'

He answered with a low, warm chuckle. 'Yes to the
first, no to the latter. I want you in my bed tonight, if
only for a couple of hours. Will you come to bed with
me, Thea?'

She let her heart sing with all the joy it had bottled
throughout the week. 'Yes, take me home, Edward.
Home to the cottage.' She would give herself permission to indulge the fantasy one last time. She would let
herself imagine they were going home in truth, that
somehow they were able to be man and wife, without
the worry of what the past held and what the future required.

That was the daydream she'd nurtured all week, as
she'd put the cottage together for him, for them, in the
hope of a few stolen moments. They had a few hours.
Her parents would be caught up in the festivities, and
busy treating injuries from those who'd been careless
with the bonfire and the games. She knew from past
experience that turned ankles and minor burns would
abound. Her mother and father would be busy.

They travelled in silence back down the road towards
the cottage and Haberstock Hall, the festive sounds fad-
ing in the distance as they left the party behind them,
the rest of the rhubarb pie tucked beneath the seat. The

silence suited her. She leaned her head against Edward's shoulder, watching the stars overhead, listening to the night birds. It was a peaceful evening, or perhaps *she* was at peace and that made all the difference. Despite his earlier episode, Edward seemed peaceful too. So much of her life had been about a fight—fighting for the lives of others, fighting to make a place for herself, fighting to understand herself and what that place might be. What happened if the peace she'd been looking for wasn't to be found in a place after all but a person? What happened if she lost that person?

The realisation made Ferris and Anne's visit more imperative than ever, and more terrifying. Even so, Thea could hardly wait for her sister to arrive. Whatever news Ferris had, she didn't want to face it alone any more than she wanted Edward to. And there was still the other piece of news from Rawdon to share with Edward. Change seemed inevitable; it waited for her on all fronts, whether she wanted it or not.

Perhaps lulled into a false sense of security by that peace, they were caught unawares, too wrapped up in their own thoughts to sense the danger until it was upon them. It was the horse that gave the first warning, neighing into the night, ears laid back as they approached the turn to the cottage, but it was not warning enough. A rider blocked their way, moonlight catching the glint of a pistol resting across his arm, a scarf obscuring the lower half of his face.

'Stand down, hands in the air!' The man waved his pistol, motioning for them to climb down. Not on her life. Indignation coursed through Thea. She was not going to have her evening ruined by a ridiculous prank.

'A highwayman in Haberstock? Really? It's hardly a lucrative pastime, compared to the risk. Folks around here don't carry enough coin to make it worthwhile.' Thea crossed her arms and refused to budge, although Edward had tensed beside her. 'Did Clive Donnatt put you up to this?' She was worried about Edward; his gaze was riveted on the masked man, his posture posed for action. Would being faced with imminent danger trigger other memories?

'Get down!' the man barked, 'or I will shoot you where you sit, soldier-boy.' He jerked the pistol at Edward and swayed in the saddle. Good Lord, the man was drunk, Thea realised. 'I'd hate to miss and hit the girl by accident.' Which he might do, regardless of Edward's compliance, thanks to the influence of whatever he'd been drinking.

'Don't do it, Edward. It's a bad joke,' Thea insisted. Donnatt would know how awkward it was for Edward to get up and down from the trap. Next, he'd have him down in the dirt grovelling and aggravating his leg. 'He won't fire. Gunshots are loud and would call attention,' she challenged boldly. How like Donnatt to not think the prank through. She wondered which of his cronies was behind the mask. 'He's drunk, Edward.'

'All the more reason to comply, my dear,' Edward said in low tones, his assessment the same as hers. The real danger was the influence of drink on the man's judgement and his aim. Judgement impaired by drink made any prank dangerous, a prank with a gun even more so.

'Climb down!' the man growled, his anger rising at Edward's resistance to comply, and at Thea's antagonism. 'Your tongue is just as shrewish as I've been told, for all that you're pretty enough.'

Edward shifted beside her in response to the changing tenor of the altercation. 'Thea,' he murmured, 'I think I must get down.' To protect her, to draw this man's fire away from her, the way he'd drawn Donnatt's verbal fire at the supper party, and at the fair tonight. Only this fire was so much more deadly. Fear came to Thea for the first time since the horse had neighed.

Edward clambered down, taking care to stand as far from the trap as possible. He kept up a string of conversation, another protective measure, she realised, to keep Clive's drunken friend on the horse distracted so that she might pick up the reins and be prepared to fly. As if she would leave him! She would no more desert him if the highwayman were real instead of this drunk prankster. Prank or not, though, the situation had its own seriousness. Loaded guns waved in supposed jest were just as dangerous as guns waved in earnest murder. Something must be done to relieve this prankster of his weapon, and if not the gun at least his power to threaten them.

Edward put his hands up and took an awkward step towards the mounted man. 'I haven't anything of value, just a few coins. The lady has nothing,' he said, playing along, while Thea reached beneath the seat with slow, unobtrusive movements and grabbed the only weapon available to her.

'It's not your riches I'm after, it's your pride. You humiliated my friend tonight. Might be kind of hard to do that again if your other leg was hurt too.' The man raised his pistol. Donnatt had gone too far this time, sending a man to do such an injury. But she could already hear Donnatt excusing it in the bright light of morning as nothing more than too much drink and a prank gone bad, and at least no one was dead. A man like Donnatt would have little inkling of what a 'mere flesh wound' could do.

Edward did not flinch. Thea heard the pistol cock. It was all the provocation she needed. No one was going to shoot Edward down in the road, not when he'd come so far.

Thea threw the pie, sending it flying like a disc. It hit the horse squarely in the side. The spooked animal reared up with a startled squeal, its rider dropping the gun and grabbing the reins for dear life as the horse tore off into the night, the prankster effectively routed. But not the terror.

Edward rounded on her, 'Good God, Thea. You could have got yourself shot.' His face was white in the moonlight. 'What if you'd missed? What if he'd shot at you as a knee-jerk response to that pie?'

'What was I supposed to do? Let him shoot at you?' The thrill of the fight surged through her along with the fear, and the anger. 'It was a horrid prank.' Only a drunk man with a gun was never a prank. Donnatt had gone too far this time and she had too. Some of the fight left her. She sank back down on the seat of the trap, realisation settling in. 'I could have killed him. He could have fallen from his horse.'

Edward was beside the trap, his hands reaching for her, drawing her down into his arms. 'Shh. Everything turned out fine. We got lucky. No one was hurt. I'm fine, you're fine, Donnatt's crony is fine. His horse has probably stopped running by now and nothing more is hurt than his pride.'

'I'm a healer.' Only the warmth of his body kept her from shaking as her mind calculated how near it had been. Drunk men were easily unseated from rearing horses. 'I'm supposed to seek to do no harm.' But tonight, she'd done violence. 'He might have fallen, broken his neck.'

'But he didn't, Thea,' Edward soothed, taking care of her as she'd cared for him, soothing him under the chocolate-eating tree. He kept an arm around her, his other hand at the horse's bridle as he led the horse and trap towards the little barn.

She was glad for the work of putting the horse away for the night. Brushing him down gave her something to do while Edward put the tack away, and the work steadied her nerves.

'Are you better, Thea?' He came up behind her and wrapped his arms about her. 'You are my fierce warrior, although I'd prefer you let me be yours.' He placed a kiss along the column of her neck, the press of his lips sending a thrill of desire through her. This was what they'd come here for.

She turned in his arms and wrapped her arms about his neck, her body pressed close against his. 'I will always fight for you, Edward.'

'I will always fight for *you*, Thea. Tell me you believe me,' he whispered before his mouth crashed down on hers, possessive and hot.

How could she not believe that kiss? It consumed her with its heat, its intensity, and she answered it with an intensity of her own, her hands tangling in his hair, their bodies acting in the knowledge that men did not die only in war or after a long lingering awareness of their mortality lying in a hospital bed with time to come to grips with it. Men died on dark roads, suddenly and unexpectedly, laughing one moment and dead the next. It could have happened that way tonight, all because a drunk man was out for petty revenge. How ridiculous that would have been. How senseless.

His hands were at her skirts, her hands ripping at his neckcloth. There was no time to waste. Too much had been wasted already worrying over futures that weren't guaranteed. They would not make the bedroom at this rate. John Anderson's big carved bed across the small garden and up the stairs in the cottage seemed miles away, too far for their passion. It would not wait; it demanded to be fed.

Edward was of the same mind, dancing her back to the barn wall, but the healer in her rebelled at the idea. His leg would pay for their passion. 'The stall, the one with the fresh hay,' she murmured, pushing at his chest to redirect him. He was in no mood to argue.

The hay was soft at her back, the scent of spring tickled her nose as he followed her down into the impromptu bower; the strength of his shoulders took the weight of him as he thrust into her, sure and swift. She arched into him, her body revelling in the hard use and determined to drink everything from it before it was lost. This thundering pace could not be maintained for long, nor would she want it to be even if it were possible. Her body wanted completion with his; wild, storming, majestic completion and she had it in three shuddering thrusts that left her gasping her pleasure to the rafters.

This was what it meant to be alive, this was what she'd been made for. In the moment, nothing more mattered, not even that one last bit of news from London she had yet to share with Edward.

'What is it, Thea?' Edward's voice was drowsy beside her as his fingers idly picked straw from her hair. The sweet peace of post-coital alliance swaddled them still, but they dared not lie here much longer, for fear of falling asleep and forgoing any chance of seeing her safely home before her parents returned. There would be the devil to pay but at the moment she wouldn't mind the toll. Lying in Edward's arms was heaven. 'You are thinking, my dear.'

This wasn't the time to bring it up, but Anne and Ferris arrived tomorrow. There might not be any more time, let alone a better time.

'It's nothing; it's just that Rawdon, in his note, asked me to come to London to speak to some groups he thinks would be amenable to the Sanitary Movement and to our work in the Crimea.'

Edward shifted in the straw, levering up on one arm. 'That is wonderful news. Miss Nightingale will be thrilled; it's what she sent you home for, to build allies and support.'

'Perhaps I can engage them from Haberstock,' she began, skirting the implications of Rawdon's invitation.

Edward sat up. 'But why? You should go to London.'

She sat up slowly, the last of the peace falling away from her. *I will always fight for you, Thea.* How short-lived those words were. He wasn't fighting now. He was gently pushing her away and making it seem as if it was her idea. 'I can't possibly leave Haberstock at the moment.'

'Because of me?' His brow knitted. 'I'll be perfectly fine, Thea,' he went on, smiling. 'If you're worried about whatever news Ferris Tresham might bring, I assure you it does not impede you going up to London for a few days, or even a few weeks. Go for the rest of the Season if need be.' He brought her hand to his lips. 'I will be here when you return, if it is within my power.' He kissed her knuckles with a smile. 'Perhaps I shall go to London with you, if you desire it.'

She met his humour with confused silence. To be here. To go to London with her. Those were not the words of a man preparing to set her aside and they confused her.

He drew back in confusion of his own. 'What is it, Thea?' She felt his gaze linger on her for a long moment. 'You thought I was encouraging you to go to London so that I might slip away?' He gave a bark of a laugh and waved his arm to indicate the barn. 'I am going nowhere, my dear, just as I promised. What did you think this cottage was about? What man takes a home a week before he needs to depart? Certainly not someone who means to leave.' He grabbed both of her hands in his. 'A man who takes a home is a man who means to stay, Thea. Don't you see? This cottage is for *you*; it is proof that I will not leave you of my own volition.' He paused, their eyes holding, emotion shimmering between them. His voice softened. 'I choose you, Thea. Nothing that happens tomorrow, or whenever my memories return, can change that, even if they might change what I can do about it. I love you.'

I choose you. I love you.

Once, she'd longed to hear those words. Once, she'd given up hope of *ever* hearing them. Now they came when she'd least expected to hear them and perhaps when she was least prepared to give into them, no matter how her heart clamoured to the contrary. She pressed a finger to his fine lips.

'Edward, we shouldn't talk of such things tonight, not when so much is still unsettled. Words can only hurt us, disappoint us until…until we know more.'

Loving Edward in theory was easy. Loving Edward in reality would be more difficult. But that was for another day, a day that might not come. There was only tonight and the small amount of time that remained to them.

Chapter Nineteen

Anne and Ferris arrived shortly before luncheon to much excitement. Thea and her parents stood on the steps, eagerly awaiting them to disgorge from the carriage, baby and all. But Thea could only wait so long before meeting Anne halfway and grabbing her sister up in a hug, leaving Ferris to show off the baby to his grandparents. No matter what the afternoon held, this visit was first and foremost a reunion.

'I thought you'd never get here!' Thea exclaimed, laughing and crying as she and Anne embraced. She'd not seen Anne since the wedding last May. After years of having Anne with her every day, it seemed as if a lifetime of events had happened since: Anne's honeymoon, followed by Anne's pregnancy, her own departure for the Crimea and the birth of Anne's son early this spring. She'd missed so much of it!

'I've missed you too.' Anne smiled through her own happy tears, taking Thea by the hand. 'Come meet your nephew.' Anne laughed and tossed her coppery curls, hazel eyes dancing. Her sister was radiant with apparent happiness and Thea felt her own heart swell at Anne's good fortune even as it ached with its own wants. Anne took the baby from her father's arms and deftly passed him to Thea. 'This is Benjamin Albert Tresham. The Benjamin is for the Scottish surgeon Benjamin Bell, of course.'

'Of course.' Thea looked down into the little face peering up at her from the blankets and her heart melted. Was there anything as sweet as a baby? Especially this one. 'He has your hair, Anne.' She smiled at her sister and brother-in-law. 'And your eyes, Ferris.' She did not miss how close they stood to one another or the subtle linking of hands, nearly hidden in the folds of Anne's skirts. One could not mistake the look of love.

Anne moved to stand beside her and the baby. 'Would you like me to take him?'

'No, I could hold him all day.' Thea was entranced with everything about her nephew. She'd delivered babies before, held them as they took their first breaths, but this was different. Little Benjamin was hers in a way, a new member of her family. 'I am sorry I wasn't there for the birth,' Thea said in quiet tones. 'Did it go well?' As wondrous as this precious child was, she hadn't liked the idea of her sister labouring without her, never mind that her sister's husband was a capable physician.

Anne gave a low laugh, her gaze flitting to her husband, who was deep in conversation with her father. 'I think it was more difficult for Ferris than it was for me.'

The two sisters moved apart from the others, taking a short walk for privacy and giving Thea, always the healer, a chance to pepper her sister with questions. Was Benjamin sleeping through the night? Was he nursing well? Was his weight all it should be? They might have been apart for a year of enormous changes for them both, but that year fell away as they strolled in the walled garden showing baby Benjamin the flowers until he fell asleep against Thea's shoulder.

They settled in the glider to rock the sleeping infant. Anne leaned her head back and looked up to the bright blue sky. 'This is heaven, isn't it, Thea? To sit and rock the baby, to have good weather and to be back home with those I love.' She sighed. 'Has it been lonely, though? Being here without all of us?'

'Yes, absolutely,' Thea confessed. 'This house is too big, too empty without everyone underfoot. But I've been busy with the Movement, with projects on behalf of my soldiers and, of course, with Edward. Still, I wish Thomasia was here. I have hopes Rebecca will convince her to come home at the end of the summer.'

Anne squeezed her hand in sympathy. 'Yes, the new cousins should be raised together and have all their aunts and their uncles to dote on them. We'll both hope she comes home.' Anne was quiet for a moment before adding, 'You weren't entirely alone though, as you say. You had Edward, after all. Is he around? I was surprised he wasn't out to greet us since the visit is in part on his behalf.' It wasn't a very subtle probe, but subtlety had never been a Peverett trait.

Thea felt herself smile at the mention of Edward's name and a slight blush crept up her cheeks. 'He didn't want to intrude on the family. He thought it would be best to give us time together first. He didn't want his situation to upstage your visit.' She adjusted the baby and tried not to think of last night in the barn stall. Edward had not achieved his wish of having her in a bed. They hadn't made it that far.

'Then he's a thoughtful man and a perceptive one.' Anne hesitated before pushing forward. 'Thea, I was so thrilled to get your letter and to hear that you and Edward have perhaps formed an attachment. I can see from your face that you have. Love always shows. I am so happy with Ferris in ways I never thought possible for me. I want you to be happy too. It *is* possible, Thea, I want you to know that.'

Thea nodded. She was happy for Anne too, but she wasn't her sister; her circumstances were different. 'I know you mean well, Anne, but it's complicated. It's not just a matter of us choosing to be together.' They'd already made that choice and it wasn't enough. Today's news could see that upended.

She met her sister's gaze. 'We may not be able to make the choice to stay together; it may have already been made, years ago.' She dropped her voice. 'That's my fear, Anne. That he's married, that he'll have to go back to…to that life. It's what we decided. It's what would be right. I've spent the last few weeks worrying every day that it will be the day he remembers, and now that day has arrived. Whether he remembers or not, information is now available that will change everything.'

If he were married, there'd be shame and guilt over what they'd done. She didn't want their memories tainted with that. She shook her head. 'Anne, there are so many ways to lose him. I don't see how this works out for me.' She swallowed. 'Edward says he'll walk away from it all for me, that we don't have to acknowledge any of it—' she looked at her hands '—it's a gallant gesture but it's no way to live, to spend a lifetime hiding in Haberstock, hoping no one discovers his secret.'

Anne patted her hand. 'Let's just wait and see what happens. Shall we go into lunch? Mother won't like it if we're late. Besides, maybe Edward is here by now. I confess to being inordinately curious to meet the man who has stolen my sister's heart.'

Edward was waiting for them in the drawing room, already in easy conversation with her father and with Ferris. The sight of him did wondrous, strange things to her stomach and put a soft, gentle ache in her heart. It was not just the sight of him, although he was turned out well in his good blue coat and fawn trousers, the sun picking out the highlights in his dark blond hair. It was the way he stood with the other men, as if he were already part of the family, as if he belonged here with her—with *them*. As if he were a Peverett.

He caught sight of them and excused himself from the group across the room, leaning casually on his cane as he approached them. One hardly noticed the cane or the limp when he smiled like that, as if she were the sole object of his attentions. 'Ladies, good afternoon.' He made them a small bow—a gesture that had been months in the making. 'Lady Tresham, I am pleased to meet one of Thea's sisters at last.'

'You must call me Anne,' her sister insisted with a smile, clearly taken with him at first glance.

'And who is this?' Edward peeped into the blanket while Thea made the introduction. 'Another physician, no doubt,' he congratulated Anne. He turned to Thea. 'May I?' He took the baby from her, settling him easily into the crook of his arm as Benjamin woke. 'Hello, little fellow.' Edward gave him a finger to play with and Thea's heart clenched, filling with emotion as it had so many times already today. To see Edward with the baby was torture and pleasure. Torture because of what it might indicate. A man so natural with a child might have children of his own already in another life. Pleasure because of the possibility of what might be. It was too easy to call forth images of Edward with their child, playing on the braided rug in the blue shuttered cottage or rocking the child to sleep. It was a future that might be snatched from her at any moment. The old fears rose again. Perhaps they'd been wrong and their careful reasoning had only been an excuse to justify what they'd wanted—to be together for however long they could.

Thea was worrying again. Edward smiled at her over the baby's head, wanting to soothe her. She was thinking of the battle to come, of all that was at stake, of all that they could lose. He wanted her to think about all they could win. Thea's mother entered and announced lunch was served. Edward handed the baby to Anne and moved to escort Thea in. 'Chin up, my dear. Whatever happens, we'll see it through together.' He dropped his hand to the small of her back, where it fitted as if it had been made for that space alone. 'Did you sleep at all last night?'

'A little,' she admitted. 'Did you?'

'Some.' He'd spent most of it haunted by the name Leopold Swann, feeling that he ought to know it, that recognition hovered just beyond his grasp. He held her back as the others filed past into the dining from. 'Thea, there is nothing to worry about. Love does not change.

Love finds a way.' He said it for them both. He believed the words, but he also knew that love's journey could be made much more difficult depending on what Ferris Tresham had found. It had taken all his willpower to stand there with Tresham and Thea's father and talk nonchalantly about the weather and Tresham's mobile health clinics, knowing that Tresham likely knew more about himself than he did. He was not sure how he'd get through lunch. Just the sight of the well-set table, loaded with fresh bread and ham and spring vegetables, was enough to turn his stomach. How would he manage a bite?

He held Thea's chair and took his own seat beside her. Tresham and Anne were across from them, the baby on Anne's lap. Tresham caught his eye and raised a dark, questioning eyebrow, taking pity on him. If he wished it, Tresham would bring the business up at the table. He gave a nearly imperceptible shake of his head. What was one more hour? He'd rather wait and do it in private. He had questions for Tresham: why had this happened? What had caused him to lose the memories? Could it happen again? He didn't want to dominate the lunch conversation with his queries.

He was worried, too, about what it would feel like to remember. Would the memories come gradually— some today, some later? Or would they swamp him all at once? The latter seemed more likely. He'd felt his memories pushing against him since last night's attack. But nothing came, just amorphous images full of tension, a reminder that perhaps nothing would come, that his memories might be beyond reclaiming.

The family bowed their heads for the blessing. He

felt Thea reach for his hand beneath the table and they held on tight to one another, lending each other their strength. He let the family carry the conversation, most of which was about London news and the baby. 'Snow has isolated the germ he claims causes the cholera outbreaks,' Tresham was saying excitedly. 'Vibrio cholerae. It's an absolute watershed moment for controlling sanitation. The pump handle has been removed from the well that started the outbreak last autumn.' He addressed Thea. 'I think the Sanitary Movement will need to acknowledge germ theory now.'

'You are preaching to the converted here, Ferris,' Thea replied. 'Like you, I don't see the Movement and germ theory as mutually exclusive. Think how powerful the two would be if they would unite their efforts. It would revolutionise public health care.'

Edward joined the conversation, 'Thea's been invited to speak to some groups in London about the Sanitary Movement.'

'Have you, Thea? That's wonderful. You must stay with us,' Anne enthused. 'Why didn't you say anything?'

'I haven't decided if I will go or not.' Thea's slippered foot kicked him beneath the table. 'I think we need to see how things work out here first.' She slid him a stern look, not appreciating the attention he'd called to her.

Tresham folded his napkin and the baby took the opportunity to fuss. Anne handed off the baby to a maid. 'He needs to be changed. There's witch hazel for his bottom in my valise for you to use,' she murmured in quiet tones, but Edward's ears pricked, drawn to the words. *Witch hazel. Wychavon.* They sounded alike.

Last night's memories pushed hard at him. Who was Wychavon? Was it him? Why did he feel he ought to know the name, just as he should have known Leopold Swann? *Was* that him?

'Are you well, man?' Tresham was leaning forward in concern. 'You've gone pale.'

Edward drew a deep breath, prepared to give the polite lie that he was fine, and then thought better of it. 'Your wife's mention of witch hazel reminded me of something I remembered last night.'

Tresham's gaze became alert. 'You had a memory? Of what?'

'Nothing new, just more details about Inkerman, a few names, and one has stayed with me, although I don't know why it's important to me.' It felt awkward to try and explain things at the lunch table. He was doubly glad now he'd put off hearing Tresham's information.

Tresham nodded, a knowing look passing between them. Tresham rose. 'That seems the perfect prompt for the two of us to adjourn to the music room, perhaps? Unless you'd like to have Thea come?'

'No, the two of you should go alone.' Thea spoke up before he could invite her. She gave his hand a final squeeze and he knew how hard it was for her to give him the space to face his past on his own, should that be what occurred, as well as the gift of trust that he would tell her all once it was sorted. His heart surged with love for this woman, who was strong enough to let him go. He rose, a bit shaky from the realisation and from the tumult of his mind.

Chapter Twenty

The music room was filled with sunlight and warmth. It did much to steady him and Edward was glad Ferris had chosen this room. He had happy memories of this room, as he did of most places at Haberstock Hall. He took a chair, grateful to sit, and Tresham wasted no time in bringing up the subject. 'If it's all right, I'd like to share what I found when I followed up on your account of Inkerman.'

'Actually, I have questions first,' Edward answered. 'As you know, I received no detectable head injury, which begs the questions why did I lose my memories in the first place, and could it happen again?'

Tresham nodded. 'Those are good questions and I don't know that my answers are equal to them. What you are experiencing is as old as the human race; it's not a new phenomenon but our study and understanding of it is in many ways. Perhaps it will bring you peace to know you're not alone. Warriors for millennia have experienced what I believe you are experiencing.'

Tresham was a kind man. Whatever the outcome of today was, he owed this man who sat across from him in Thea's chair. 'Thank you for that,' Edward offered sincerely. 'Does this memory malaise have a name?'

'Many names.' Tresham smiled. 'Or cardiorespiratory neurosis, *Vent de boulet*— We have Napoleon's wars to thank for that.'

'The bullet wind,' Edward translated absently, easily.

'Yes, soldiers reported falling to the ground after a cannon ball passed or when they feared a cannon ball would pass by, and doctors took note.' Tresham's tone was conversational. 'Thea mentioned you like to read. Are you familiar with Goethe?' Edward nodded although he only read Goethe in English translation. Tresham continued. 'He fought in the Battle of Valmy and for years afterwards he reported about the eerie, frightening pre-emptory sounds of incoming cannonballs. More interesting, though—' Tresham leaned forward, thoroughly engrossed in the topic now '—he talked about the feelings that would come upon him, the way his vision changed and the way his body responded.' Tresham reached for his valise. 'But you are wondering why I am telling you this, no doubt. Because I've been researching this for some years. I volunteer my services at the Chelsea military hospital down the street from my home. I saw soldiers suffering with all types of neuroses: nightmares, sleeplessness, recurring shock set off by an overturned dray in the street, and I wanted to know why that was and why it seems to vary from man to man.'

Tresham drew a book from the valise. 'Look at this.' He opened the book to where a thin silk strip marked the page and passed it to Edward. 'It's part of the *Hip-*

pocratic Corpus, the collection of medical works attributed to Hippocrates.'

Edward scanned the page and looked up while Tresham grinned. 'Hippocrates was noting war traumas in the fourth century BC. Lucretius mentions them in his poem *De Rerum Natura*. There's more too, but we can discuss literature another time. The point is that writers, physicians and historians have been chronicling this for millennia and the symptoms vary. I have read several reports of nightmares repeating real events, like the nightmares you've mentioned. I've come across accounts of people who have lost their physical vision, which is attributed to a desire to 'block out' their experiences. I think that is what happened with you. The trauma of Inkerman, of being left on the field, of being wounded: one or all of those circumstances has contributed to the blocking of your memories. The nightmares are a means by which those memories are trying to leak out.'

Tresham gestured to the valise at his feet. 'May I?' He reached inside and extracted a set of folders while Edward drew a deep breath to steady himself against whatever lay inside it.

'You're nervous,' Tresham said matter-of-factly, setting aside the first folder.

'The man I am, Edward, loves Thea Peverett,' he said baldly. 'Whatever is in these folders, it means Edward will cease to exist because he never was. I don't know that the person who will replace Edward will have the luxury of acting on that love and yet that man cannot be ignored. I cannot pretend he doesn't exist.' Although he'd offered to do just that for Thea's sake. She had immediately understood how impractical that was; hopefully she also recognised the depth of his commitment to her in that offer. 'But I also fear that whatever you've found isn't enough. I've had remembrances already: the piano-playing, the languages, and they triggered nothing further. Why would this be different? As you can see, I am a conundrum of hope and hopelessness.'

Tresham smiled kindly. 'After six months, it's no surprise. As for those other skills, the music and the languages, I'm not sure they really classify as remembrances. Our body contains physical memory and our minds contain what I think of as implicit or unconscious memories, among them procedural memories about how to perform certain skills. Both of your supposed 'remembrances' would fall into that category. Just think of all the things you did 'remember' how to do, that you probably didn't even have to recall: using the bathroom, getting dressed, how to eat at a table, your manners. Once you were in a situation that demanded them, those skills were easily recalled.'

Tresham leaned forward, hands on his knees. 'I also have a theory that they were not affected because they were not attached to the trauma. Your name, your sense of place, being lost and all that might be lost with you: a family, a home—those are definitely attached to the trauma, especially if you have strong feelings about them.'

Tresham reached once more for the file. There was no more putting it off. 'Whatever is in these files, we'll face it together, shall we?' He opened the file, laying out a newspaper clipping. 'You mentioned being part of a flank in your dream. There was indeed a flanking movement during the battle, although it wasn't well coordinated, nor was it in the place it was anticipated. The Fourth Division lost their direction in the fog and overshot their destination. They ended up in a ravine, struggling with unexpected Russians. This is an account of that.'

Edward picked up the clipping. He scanned the story, which was uncannily similar to his own recollection and yet he was sure he'd not read about it before, had not borrowed his recollection from another source. He remembered Thea's queries weeks ago after his nightmare. No one had discussed the battle with him in the field hospital; he'd barely been conscious and the nurses in Scutari at the time were too far removed to have that kind of detail.

Tresham nodded his approval. 'This only reconfirms that your dream had a level of accuracy to it, that we can trust your dreamed recollections.' Tresham took back the news clipping and, growing more serious, said, 'Thanks to the recollection Thea sent, and being able to confirm its accuracy, I was able to track down the roster of troops involved.' Ferris held his gaze, perhaps warning him, preparing him. Edward felt his body tense. 'The Fourth Division was headed by General Cathcart, who was killed in the ravine.'

The General is down!

Those were the words from his dream. Cathcart. Yes. 'His horse was shot out from under him,' Edward supplied without thinking, without hesitation. 'He was my general, I was his aide de camp.' Memories pressed in his mind with renewed urgency. He closed his eyes briefly, pushing them back out of reflex. He didn't want to go into the darkness.

'Let them come, if they will,' Tresham counselled gently. He felt the other man's hand rest encouragingly on his knee in support. He would be strong for Thea and let them come. The future lay through these memories. He could not claim her until he claimed them.

'I have a list of the dead or missing from the Fourth Division.' Tresham was pushing the discussion to the next level. 'You recalled a name last night?'

Edward opened his eyes and met Tresham's steady gaze. 'A few.' He named them for Tresham. 'The soldiers were calling for them after the battle.'

'You will find this list interesting then. What else do you remember?'

'Nothing at present.' He took the list from Ferris, reading down the names, seeing the names of those who'd numbered in his flashback last night at the bonfire. 'Wychavon isn't on the list,' he murmured as his eyes lit on the one name that had haunted him. *Leopold Swann.* Sadness gripped him. He passed the list to Tresham. 'Apparently, they never found him, poor sod,' he whispered. The old fear of loneliness, of being left behind gripped him on the man's behalf. Had the poor man lain on the battlefield until even hope deserted him and he'd simply given up?

Tresham sat quietly. Watching, waiting. What did the man expect? What had he himself expected? That this information would be an instant trigger? That his world would be restored at the snap of fingers after months of wandering in a fog of forgetfulness? Yes, he did suppose he'd expected that.

'Why doesn't it mean anything?' he groused sharply at Tresham. If he remembered nothing now, then when? How? Would he spend the rest of his days chasing something he couldn't catch? What could he offer Thea without his memory? Could he ask her to jump into the abyss with him? The disappointment left him feeling oddly empty, oddly calm, the way a man felt in the space immediately before battle began, when the world seemed surreal, too quiet to believe that in a moment all hell would break loose. Yes, just like it.

Tresham spoke to his frustration. 'Don't worry; there are other things we can try. It takes time.' But how much time? It had been six months. He didn't hear what else Tresham said. The world had suddenly come into sharp, vivid clarity, his senses seeing and hearing everything at its most vibrant. Hell was starting to break loose. He rose, thinking to get away from it. His legs were unsteady. He bumped into the side table by his chair in his clumsiness, irrationally seeking to run, to flee the chaos.

It was too late. The turmoil had him, surrounded him, absorbed him. He gripped the table, looking for purchase against the chaos, but it was already breaking out of its cages, claiming him, and he *had* to walk through it. But he was not walking alone. Tresham had his arms around him, supporting him as he sank to the floor, a sobbing, shaking wreck as the memories took him, walking him through the aftermath of Inkerman one more time.

'Leopold! Leopold Swann! Lieutenant Swann!'
The voices came and relief swept him amid the pain.

They would find him soon and there would be help. He called out, horrified to find he had no voice, able to make only the merest of croaks. He tried again, summoning all the volume he could.

'Here, I am here!'

'Damn. I can't see a thing in this murk,' someone swore. 'I thought I saw him go down here. Poor man never had a chance, two to one. One man threw a torch at him. I saw him go up in flames before he dropped. Still, we should take him back even if he is dead.'

I'm not dead. I'm right here.

He tried again to lift an arm, to make a sound, but he had no strength. No, the voices were moving off; they were leaving. He was going to die here. He would never see Arthur or Wychavon with its hills rolling down to the sea. He'd never play the piano again and he could do nothing to stop it from happening.

He'd lain there long into the evening, hope deserting him as his strength waned and night was all that came. They did not come back for him. They did not call for him again. Leopold Swann was lost.

Only he wasn't. Clarity and reason battled with chaos, Thea's logic from last night, inserting itself into the madness. He was not lost. He *had* been found. Someone had come and taken him to the field hospital, someone who had no idea who he was, which wasn't surprising given the disorganization of the battle and the fog. No one was where they were supposed to be, certainly not the Fourth Division, which had been way off course. His jacket had been burned away, the only thing that would have offered some indication of his rank. It was no wonder he'd been lost. He forced his body under control, tried to suppress his trembling as he opened his eyes. He was aware he was still gripping Tresham's hand.

'They didn't find Swann, did they? Because I *am* Leopold Swann. Lieutenant Leopold Swann of the Fourth Division.' He was supposed to be running messages out of the thick of the fighting but he'd become lost in the fog. Perhaps that had saved him. Otherwise, he would have been with the General.

'Breathe slowly. Let it all settle,' Tresham instructed in low, calming tones. He did as he was told. It was a lot to take in. He had a name: Leopold Swann. He had a rank: Lieutenant. He'd been in the wrong place at the wrong time and he'd been shot down. He'd lain on a field and nearly died there for having been overlooked. The pieces fell into place and for a moment there was the beautiful clarity of understanding, that he'd been seeking for months but never finding, and then the consequences of that knowledge rolled over him. He wasn't just a fallen soldier rescued from the field.

'I have a place,' he began. 'Wychavon. It's my home. Arthur is there; my family is there. My sisters are there.' He smiled, remembering them. He had a family, a large family, three sisters and a brother, all younger. But then he furrowed his brow. He'd heard the men calling for Wychavon. 'Wychavon is a place, not a man's name.' He tried to sort through it. That part didn't make sense.

'It's both,' Tresham said quietly. 'And you are the Earl, the missing Earl of Wychavon. I have the news clippings if you're interested. Society was fascinated with the story for a while.' He reached for one of the five files he'd brought. 'I did what research I could on each of the men, just in case. This is Swann's folder.'

Edward waved away the offer. He didn't need the clippings to tell him what he already knew—*finally* knew. He held his head in his hands as if by doing so he could keep the memories in some semblance of order, to process them one by one instead of letting them bombard him all at once. What an unbelievable series of years it had been. His father had passed away. Suddenly he'd been the Earl at twenty-five, and hardly ready for the responsibility, his Grand Tour, his chance to play the piano in Europe's great capitals cut short. People expected him to marry, to take up the Earldom seamlessly.

He'd done his best, burying his own disappointments for the sake of the family. His sisters were coming out, Arthur was at Eton, his mother in mourning, the Marquess of Stryde pushing his daughter in Leopold's direction, and then the war had risen. It had been the perfect escape; by all accounts, it was to be a short war far from home and there were lords like himself going by the dozens. He'd have adventure from a safe distance as an aide de camp. He'd serve his country and his own desire for travel all at once. The military would make a man of him in ways London never would. He'd come home ready to settle down with Elizabeth. A pit formed in the bottom of his stomach.

He hazarded a glance at Tresham. 'The Marquess of Stryde's daughter, Elizabeth; is she still waiting for me?' Nothing had been decided, he was sure of it, but there had been an implicit understanding between the two families. Surely, after two years, she would not be waiting on him.

Tresham shook his head. 'I don't know. For Society news you'd have to ask the ladies. Stryde's in Town, of course, to sit his seat. He was causing a rumpus over the war effort when we left. He sees nothing wrong with letting the military operate without accountability to the public, although his man, Aberdeen, is out of power now. You'll be on opposite sides of that debate, of course.' Perhaps that would make him less welcome as a prospective son-in-law. 'The Dowager Countess of Wychavon is in Town with her daughters, according to what Society news I have heard.'

His mother. Sweet emotion filled him at the thought of his family, followed by a rush of questions: how was she bearing up, having thought she'd lost her husband and then her oldest son in the span of a few years? Had his supposed death hampered his sisters in making good matches by throwing them into mourning, cheating them of their Seasons? He hoped not. He had to go to them at once, had to show them he was alive and found. He would take Thea to London... His head was a whirl of thoughts, of next steps, until it wanted to explode. He needed quiet. He needed to sort through it all and put it into order.

'Are you all right? Can I get you a drink?' Tresham asked. How long had they sat here on the floor? Hours? Minutes? Tresham had been patience itself.

Edward—no, he was Leopold now, an earl, a man with a family—glanced over his shoulder to the French windows leading out into the garden. 'No, thank you. I need some time.' He managed to get to his feet. His leg ached. He looked about for his cane. Dammit, he'd left it at the table in the dining room, but there was no way he was going back for it. He wasn't ready to face anyone yet. But they deserved…something. How could he keep them in the dark?

'Might I burden you with one more favour?' he asked Tresham.

'Anything.' Tresham was sincere.

'Will you share some of the facts with them? My name and situation, perhaps? Nothing to worry them, but something to soothe them. I am not so self-centred as to think I am the only one reeling.'

'Gladly, and with all due discretion,' Tresham assured him, clapping a brotherly hand on his shoulder.

'Thank you, we'll talk more later,' he told Tresham with a confidence he didn't quite feel. It was too soon; there was too much to think about. He didn't have all the answers but he had the one he wanted the most. He could act on his love for Thea. He carried that one hope with him into the walled garden as he sorted through the rest. What would she think of all this? He yearned to be with her, to send for her and wrap her in his arms and take her strength, but that was selfish. He had to make sense of it all before he could expect Thea to do so. He needed all of this to slow down. He needed just a few hours.

Chapter Twenty-One

He sat in the glider, reacquainting himself with Leopold Swann, the lieutenant, the aide de camp to General Cathcart who'd translated messages, making use of his French. He'd enjoyed serving the General. He wondered if he was still in the military? Perhaps technically. That would have to change now that he was found.

A lot of things would change. Edward was no more. What happened to Edward's life? Did it die with him? The excitement of discovery faded in the prospect of that consequence. Yesterday he'd been Edward, a tutor with nothing more than his weekly wages in his pocket for a local country fair. Today he was the Earl of Wychavon, a man who commanded a fortune and multiple estates. There would be no more blue-shuttered cottage, no more teaching music lessons to village children, no more market days, no more of the simple pleasures Edward had come to enjoy, to covet. Those would be replaced by the House of Lords, a Mayfair mansion and the estates. He was Wychavon now, or *again*, at the expense of Edward.

He pushed at the glider with his foot. People were

counting on him. He could not delay his departure, and yet he would linger here as long as he could, perhaps giving Edward the send-off the man deserved. Tomorrow, he would force his emotions to settle and he would decide on his next steps. He would write the necessary letters. But not tonight.

Such tasks would require going back to the house and that was the last place he wanted to be, despite the fact that it was too dark now to legitimately stay out any longer. He'd already been out here for hours but he couldn't go back in. His thoughts were still too new, too raw and too unfocused to be the subject of conversation. They would want to discuss the news, they'd want to know how he was feeling, and what he thought it all meant for him. He didn't want to be fussed over. He wanted to sit with it all for a while longer. It wouldn't truly be real until he went back inside and said the words out loud.

Leopold leaned back in the glider and stared up at the early stars, stifling a yawn. His body was overriding his mind at last. He wanted to sleep, to rest. He'd close his eyes for a moment and then he'd go in, at least to see Thea. How was she bearing up after today's revelations? She had Anne and her mother for support, and surely she knew he'd come back to her once his mind settled. But when he opened his eyes again it was to a bobbing light and a figure clad in luminous white emerging from the darkness. He smiled for the first time in hours. His angel was coming just when he needed her.

Edward had not returned. Thea paced her room. She'd forced herself to go through the ritual of getting ready for bed. She'd combed out her hair and put on her nightgown, just as she'd forced herself through the rest of her day since the moment Edward had left the dining room with Ferris.

Every healing instinct in her had cried out to follow him, to protect him. It had taken all her willpower to let him go alone. She'd known she had to resist the impulse, just as she'd had to resist the impulse to seek him out when Ferris had returned alone. He'd quietly informed her that Edward was in no condition for company. So she'd gone through the day, playing with her little nephew and smiling bravely for the family. Edward had not come back for dinner. Ferris had gone to the cottage to check on him, only to discover that Edward was not there.

That was when the worry had set in. It was fully dark now. Had he fallen somewhere? He'd left his cane and that had concerned her. Was he even now lying in the dark unable to get up, reliving the horror of Inkerman? She could not imagine how that would feel to him if that was the case. She was concerned how that might affect his already agitated mind.

He was not the only one reeling. Ferris had been charged to reveal some of the news. Her unknown soldier was an earl. He had not only a name but a title to go with it. It was far beyond what she'd predicted and it left her in the lurch. She had no idea what that meant for them. Would he even want a country doctor's daughter now that he was an earl? But no, she would not think on such petty things. It was selfish of her to be wondering about the status of their relationship when he had so much more to grapple with. She counselled herself to patience. What mattered was finding him, making sure he was safe.

Where would he go? Where would she go? She'd want a place to be alone, a place to think and sort out her thoughts... Then she knew where he'd gone—the very place that she'd given him weeks ago when the world was simpler. How many times had she taken refuge there when the world had disappointed her? Thea gathered up a lamp and a quilt in one hand, his cane in the other and raced barefoot across the wet grass to the walled garden.

She found him in the glider, waking and healthy. Relief suffused her. He was safe and unhurt.

'You have been sleeping while I've been worrying,' she scolded. 'You must be cold.' She shook out the blanket and settled it about him. 'You'll catch a chill out here, Edward...' She said the last without thinking, too late to correct herself. 'Leopold, I mean.' She felt self-conscious. She was used to fussing over Edward, not Leopold. Did Leopold even want her fussing? Despite Edward's protests of constancy last night, would Leopold want her tonight? Unexpected tears threatened. Edward was no more. He'd slipped away this afternoon without saying goodbye. She tried to blink back the tears. She was being ridiculous. Edward was just a name. The *man* was still here, right in front of her.

'Thea, what's wrong? Don't cry.' He was reaching for her, drawing her to him, tucking her in beside him on the glider and it was all too much.

'Edward's gone,' she choked on a sob. 'And I miss him.' She was angry too—angry at him for somehow stealing Edward from her, stealing her happiness.

'I know. I miss him too. I've been out here mourning him as much as I've been out here thinking about everything else. I don't think anyone but you would really understand that, Thea.' Edward—Leopold—Wychavon the Earl—ran his hand up and down her arm in a reassuring stroke. Yesterday he'd had only one name and today he had so many more. 'It's all right, Thea. I imagine I will have difficulty getting used to being Leopold too.'

She let the heat of his body warm her and some of the tension in her began to ease. His name might be different but he still *felt* the same. He still felt like Edward, the man she knew and loved.

'Have you begun to make sense of it all?' she asked quietly, laying her head against his shoulder.

'Hardly. There is so much to wrap my head around, so much to celebrate, Thea, and so much to grieve. It will take time to get it sorted out.' He sighed and lifted her hand to his lips. 'Do you mind if we don't speak of it tonight? All that matters at the moment is that I want to hold you, and for the first time I am truly free to do that.'

She opened her mouth to speak, to say they weren't really free, but he quieted her with a kiss. 'Not tonight, Thea,' he murmured against her lips and she relented, letting herself bask in the echo of Edward's ghost one more night before she had to face the Earl.

It took time to digest it all. There were so many moving parts and so many things that needed to be done all at once but he had a supportive crew at his disposal: Tresham and Anne, Thea and her parents. They spent the next few days working through the lists of tasks in the library. First, and most important, was a letter to his mother explaining what had occurred, that her son was alive and home in England and would call on her shortly in London.

London. That was the next issue and they—he and Thea—were dancing around the inevitable. He would have to go. There would be paperwork to file, his commission to resign, reports to make, the estate solicitors to see, and it simply couldn't be done efficiently from a distance. There was also the consideration of his seat in the House of Lords, which meant this wasn't a quick dash to Town on the train. It meant a more permanent trip to Town, one from which he wouldn't be coming back. After the Season, he would need to travel to his estates. He was loath to go. As long as he stayed in Haberstock, Edward still lingered, as did the life he'd built.

London would swallow up the last of that man. He didn't want to go alone. He wanted Thea to be by his side. His name, his status, his story might have changed in the last few days but his feelings hadn't and yet he sensed that Thea had become more reserved.

He rose from the library table where he'd sat for an hour writing the requisite letters and walked to the window overlooking the herb garden. Thea and Anne were outside with the baby, taking a morning off from helping him as the paperwork dwindled. There was little left to do now but pack up and go.

They made a pretty picture, both in dresses of white summer muslin, one dark head, one copper, bent over the baby in Thea's arms. She was forever holding the child, filling his mind with images of her holding *their* child, of what life might have been like in the stone cottage had they ever had the chance. Would Thea come with him? She had her invitation from Rawdon to conduct her own business in London. Surely that made the decision to join him in London an easy one, and yet he felt Thea drift further from him each day.

Tresham come to stand beside him. 'You're distracted. Did you hear a word I said?'

'No, I'm sorry,' Leopold apologised. His head was too full of Thea to focus on business. For all that he had grappled with in the days since his memories had returned, he and Thea had had little time to discuss the particulars of their situation.

'I asked, what are you and Thea going to do?' He clapped a hand on Leopold's shoulder and Leopold felt the comfort of his commiseration. If he were to marry Thea, this man would be his brother-in-law. Tresham was a good man. He'd enjoy having this man for a brother.

'We've not discussed it yet. I think we are both still mourning what has been lost. I had a life here that I liked, a life that I wanted, with her. Now, we have to reconfigure what that life looks like. What can we be together as the Earl and Countess of Wychavon?' When he had spun his scenarios for Thea, that had not figured in his plans. He'd been adamant that nothing precluded them from being together, whatever his past life had been. He'd not counted on being a peer and neither had she. He had no qualms about making her his Countess, but he sensed she did. 'She may want the man, but I'm not sure she wants the title.' He'd be more sure if he actually talked to her about it, but then he'd know and, in truth, the answer frightened him. He didn't want to lose her, not now, when they should have had the way swept clear before them.

Ferris chuckled. 'The Peverett women are stubborn to a fault. I had difficulty with Anne. They love their freedom. But you must talk to her about it, no matter how hard.'

And soon. He couldn't put off returning to London much longer. He had a duty to his family. One might argue he should have returned immediately, not even delaying the few days that he had. Wychavon was worth protecting, worth loving as a living, breathing legacy of his people and history. It had been an essential lesson patiently drilled into him by his father.

Thea spied him at the window and raised her hand to wave, her face wreathed in smiles as she held up the baby for them to see. Tresham immediately made a fool of himself, pulling silly faces through the windowpanes for his progeny.

Lord, how he wanted that. In that moment he envied Ferris Tresham, a man who'd found a way to have it all. He'd told Thea to focus on the victory, not the battle, but he was having a hard time taking his own advice. Everywhere he looked, he saw only what he was losing, what he was leaving, and he didn't know how to save it. He only knew he couldn't do it on his own.

'Let's go down and see the ladies,' Ferris suggested. 'I have a powerful urge to play with my son and you have a long-overdue conversation.'

Chapter Twenty-Two

Thea, we have to talk. Those were ominous words to open any discussion with, even when one knew that discussion was coming. Thea relinquished the baby and took Leopold's hand, letting him lead her deeper into the garden. He looked tired, his features drawn after what the last few days had demanded of him and what was demanded of him still. She'd not wanted to add to his burdens.

'We must talk about London, about us,' Leopold began when they were out of earshot of her sister's happy family. Of course they must. This was a discussion that should have happened sooner but hadn't. There'd always been an excuse to put it off, another letter to write, another list to make. Time had slipped away from them and now any decisions, any farewells that had to be made would be hurried. Perhaps it would be better that way. This was a necessary conversation, but its content was not unexpected.

Thea stopped beside a lavender bush and busied herself cutting sprigs for her basket. 'You're going to tell me that you're leaving.' It helped to keep her hands busy, but only a little. Just saying the words caused her throat to thicken. She didn't dare look at him for fear of breaking into tears. Leopold wouldn't mean to break his word—he'd kept it as best he could under the circumstances—but this had to end.

'The earldom needs me in London.' He reached to take the basket from her but she stubbornly held onto it. He wouldn't be here to carry her basket much longer. She'd best get used to doing things on her own again.

'And after that?' she said coolly. She wanted him to say he'd come back, that London would be a matter of a few weeks only, but she knew it couldn't be. Having an earldom was like having a wife; it was a prior claim made on him and they'd promised themselves to honour prior claims.

'I will need to make a tour of the estates. They've been without a guiding hand in my absence. I won't pretend this first year will be easy; there will be much to do and it will need to be done in many places.'

She tossed him a rueful smile before going back to the lavender. 'Just the first year? I don't think it gets easier. The earldom will always need you.' It would need him to manage it, to marry well, to produce an heir and see to the succession.

'Damn it, Thea. Will you look at me? The lavender can wait—and put down that basket.' He was losing patience with her. 'I want to *talk* about this.' His voice was rising and she shot him a censorious look as she put the basket down and crossed her arms.

He lowered his voice. 'Yes, I have to go to London. Yes, I have to look after estates that may not have had attention for over a year. Yes, all of that will take me—

us—from Haberstock, but I want *you* to come with me. A lot *has* changed but our plans don't need to.'

'Be reasonable. Of course our plans have to change. We did not factor being an earl into our scenarios.' She had to stand her ground here for both of them, despite the hope that flickered to life within her. He hadn't come to gently break his promises. But he needed to. Didn't he see? He needed suitable countess material in a wife and she was not that. Nor did she want to be, she told herself fiercely. The wives of peers were the most traditional of women, women who didn't challenge the system. She would have to change.

You couldn't change, not even for him, a man who swears undying devotion to you?

No. She would not give in to the voice of temptation. It would be a slippery slope towards losing her identity altogether, one that she'd worked hard to make impregnable after being so exposed by Donnatt's prank in her youth.

'Besides, we have no plans now. Our plan was to wait and see what Ferris found. We have done that.' The cottage had been a short-lived piece of paradise, the embodiment of secret hopes.

Leopold's eyes sharpened. 'That was *not* the intention behind our plans. We were going to wait so that we could commit ourselves to one another *honestly* without the fear of bigamy. We can do that now.' He paused, his eyes resting on hers. 'So, I am asking you, will you come to London with me and be my wife? Will you step into this new life with me and build it with me, just as we were going to build a life here?'

'You make it sound so simple, as if a life in Haber-

stock is the same as a life in London. You cannot conflate the two,' Thea argued. 'I cannot be your Countess.
I'm too bold, too outspoken. I want to *work*. At least
in Haberstock there is the hope of establishing a small
practice over time. A countess cannot go around delivering babies.' Even as dismal as she'd found the prospect
of trying to practise medicine in Haberstock, being a
countess was even more limiting. 'I would be a laughingstock among the idle aristocracy.'

'It seems to me that a countess can do whatever she
likes,' Leopold replied. 'You've never been one to care
what others think. Why start now?'

'While I don't give two figs for what they might
think of my pursuits, I do care what that might cost
you, and you should too. You have an earldom counting on you.' She would not do that to him, but neither
could she give up her true self simply to please. 'I can
do what I like, but others can say what *they* like. I would
be an embarrassment to you. Anne and Ferris get away
with it because they choose not to move in Society. You
can't make that choice.'

Leopold nodded, his voice stern. He was not back-
ing down. Most men would have bowed to her logic or
her sharp tongue by now and simply decided she wasn't
worth it. They would have taken the way out she'd given
them and been glad, but not Leopold. 'I *will* move in
Society, as will my wife. I will use my seat to advocate for health reform, for health care for all citizens,
even children. I would expect my wife to do the same,
to have those same values. I can think of no one finer
to have at my side for those campaigns than you. Tell

me those are not things you want, things you've not already begun fighting for.'

'They are my causes,' she acceded, 'but it's not the same. Don't you understand? I can be outspoken because no one is truly hurt by my political stance and my choice to work. My family lives in the country. No one cares what we do. But there'd be you to consider, perhaps children to consider. I cannot have *that* family embarrassed by what society might say about me. Passion has a price.' That price might very well be living her life without him. 'I am fighting for you too, Leopold. I am trying to help you see what is best.'

'I understand *that*. What I *don't* understand is why you are willing to fight for others but not for yourself.'

'I *am* fighting for myself. If I change to be your Countess, if I compromise myself now, the changing will never stop until all of what I am right now is gone, forged into someone I don't know. I can only be myself.'

'Then don't change, Thea. I want you just the way you are right now. I am not asking you to compromise anything. Come to London with me and see how it goes. Take up your post at the hospital by day if it suits you, waltz with me in the ballrooms of the ton by night. Give us a chance.' They faced each other in the garden, frustration warring with want. She could see her own feelings mirrored in his eyes.

'Come with me, Thea. Come and see the possibilities.' Then he added, 'Please. I am going to need you. I always have. I can't do this without you. If you won't come for me, come for Rawdon; he's counting on you too. You have your own invitation to Town, regardless of your association with me.'

Perhaps it was the last that persuaded her. Maybe he needed to see the reality in order to be convinced. Once people began to talk, he would understand the risk he ran in being with her. Maybe she needed to see it too, to know that they had tried and it simply wouldn't work.

'I will come to London, but I have conditions,' Thea began. 'I will stay with Ferris and Anne, I will give my talks, meet with Rawdon's people and I will pick up my work at the hospital.' To be needed was to have a sense of place, a sense of belonging. She had to establish that; she needed to know what life held for her when the experiment failed, as it surely would. Going to London merely put off the inevitable a while longer. But what was here for her in Haberstock if he was gone? No one needed her. When he left, the stone cottage would be just a cottage without him there, a shell.

She felt her world shift as they stood in the garden. Despite her best arguments, it seemed she was on a slippery slope. When had it happened that *he'd* become her home, her purpose? *He* was where she belonged. To love someone was to inherently give up a piece of one-self to them. Was this how Anne felt when she looked at Ferris? How her mother and father felt? That it didn't matter where they were as long as they were together. Perhaps that was why she'd not said the words back to him that last night in the cottage. She'd worked so hard to keep herself together. What would happen when this was over and she found herself 'homeless'? She must prepare against that day.

'And the engagement? Will you allow me to announce it tonight?' Ah, he'd noticed she'd left that out.

'Not yet, Leopold. It wouldn't be fair to you.' Once

he got to London, his world would change in ways he could not anticipate. She would not trap him. Neither would she embroil him in any scandal that might concern her and her work. He needed to be free to walk away and so did she if he would not. She could see her answer disappointed him. 'Please, Leopold. I must have that concession. Let it be enough that I will come to London. When do we leave?'

'*We* leave tomorrow, with Ferris and Anne.' It was said with grim determination, almost as if it were a challenge, daring her. He meant to do battle. For her. As much as she meant to do battle for him. But each of them had a different understanding of what that battle meant. But she would win. He would see that she was right and in time he would thank her, even if the casualties of this *guerre à deux* would be their hearts. But hearts could mend eventually; at least that was what she hoped.

'Would you like to walk down to the cottage?' Leopold asked in soft tones so reminiscent of Edward it made her heart ache.

He is Edward, you nitwit.

But not entirely. He felt like Edward, he smelled like Edward, looked like Edward, but there was already an indefinable new quality to him that was not Edward: a quality of authority which Edward had only begun to exude towards the end. There was a sense of purpose that squared his shoulders and lit his eyes. She was envious of that gleam, she supposed.

'I need to pack.' Thea made the excuse and stepped away from him. Saying goodbye to the cottage, a place she'd endowed with her fragile hopes, would break her.

The one thing she didn't need right now was to be in his arms, letting him kiss the last of her good sense from her and whispering impossibilities in her ear.

Disappointment flared in his eyes where purpose had so recently lit them. 'I'll do my best to close it up to your standards then.' He tried for a smile but her refusal had hurt him. 'Everything will be safe until we can return and enjoy it in full once more.' He did not fight fair. Even now, he was dangling that carrot of hope in front of her and refusing to acknowledge her earlier concerns.

'Edward—Leopold—' would she ever get used to his new name? '—don't. It is dangerous to pretend.'

'Don't pretend, or don't dream, Thea?' His body tensed. She thought for a moment he would reach for her to draw her close, and she would let him. His fist clenched and unclenched at his side as if it were debating the option. In the end he made no move towards her. 'Go pack your trunks, Thea.'

Thea was being stubborn. Leopold stomped about the cottage, covering furniture and sweeping the floors with an energy meant to exorcise his anger and his disappointment. All to no avail. His disappointment and indeed his perplexity ran deeper than the effort of exercise could reach. Why was it that at a time when two people should cling to each other, take strength from each other as they navigated challenges, they'd drawn into themselves instead? He'd wanted to hold her today. So many times, he'd wanted to reach for her and let his body give her the comfort his words apparently could not.

He threw a holland cover over the settee in the parlour and loosed the curtains over the window so that passers-by could not peer in and be tempted. Too bad Thea couldn't see him now, doing housework like a common footman or gentleman farmer...or like Edward, who'd worked for a living, who'd put his own horse away at night in a little barn. That reminded him, he'd have to ride out to the squire's house today and explain why he couldn't continue with the lessons.

That brought him up short. He halted in his work and leaned on the broom. He'd miss teaching that boy. He'd miss a lot about Haberstock and what might have been, but he did mean to come back, despite Thea's doubts. And he meant to come back with her as his wife. That last had not changed with the revelations of the week, nor had his desire for such an outcome diminished even as his duties and obligations grew. He was deeply disappointed he would not be able to introduce her as his fiancée tomorrow when he returned to his family, but it had been a necessary concession today, when she'd balked at accompanying him to London. He only hoped it had not been too much of a concession. She seemed as determined to prove they wouldn't suit as he was to prove the opposite. In London, he would show her what a force for good they could be together. In London, he would change her mind. He just had to get there.

Chapter Twenty-Three

Trains were a most wondrous invention. The speed at which they increased the pace of life still amazed Leopold. He, Thea and the Treshams had left Hertfordshire in the morning and by late afternoon they'd not only arrived in London but had seen Thea settled with Anne and Ferris at their home on Cheyne Walk before it was time to meet his mother. Thea even had a chance to dash off a note to Rawdon to let him know she had arrived in Town and she and Anne were already planning their outings with Tresham's mobile health clinics for the week.

'Thea, we really must go now.' Leopold laughed as the spirited conversation between the sisters lagged for a moment.

'Get used to it.' Tresham slapped him on the back in commiseration. 'There's nothing like the Peverett women when they get an idea in their heads.'

Thea looked over at him, one of the few glances she'd spared him since yesterday. 'Are you sure you wouldn't rather go alone? A reunion should be private, especially given the circumstances. Your family won't want an interloper.'

She was trying to demur and he would have none of it. 'Absolutely not. I want you there with me. You are the woman who saved my life and much more,' he said firmly, offering his arm so that there was no way out for her except by a direct insulting refusal she had no grounds for. He was paying her a compliment and a profound honour.

Thea gave a tight smile and took his arm. 'Very well, if you're sure.' He was sure. He couldn't imagine facing this moment without her beside him.

He saw her settled into a cab and gave the driver the address, his own nerves and excitement growing apace as he took his seat across from her. He was going home at last.

He reached for Thea's hand. 'Thank you for this. You made today possible for me.' He could hear the emotion in his voice. 'My family is as important to me as your family is to you. You will love them and they will adore you.'

She smiled, the first real smile he'd had from her since they'd curled up on the glider under the quilt. 'Tell me about them, Leopold. Are they as stubborn as you are?'

'Perhaps more.' He laughed. 'Leonie is the youngest; she's eighteen and this will be her first Season if my being missing hasn't interrupted anything for her. Juliette is twenty and is always redecorating some section of the Town house, and Janet is twenty-four and married. She married the year before my father passed away.' It was the last time they'd all been together. What a happy day that had been. 'There's Arthur, my little brother, he's fifteen and won't be up to Town so you won't meet him this time, but he's an adorable scamp, always into his horses.' He leaned forward to look out of the window. 'Ah, here we are.'

Thea met his gaze with a smile and squeezed his hand, saying in soft, heartfelt tones, 'The Earl of Wychavon is home at last.' His own heart swelled at the words because the woman who uttered them understood absolutely what it meant to be home, to have family waiting to wrap their arms about him. He did not think it was possible to love her more than he did in that moment.

'Thank you, Thea.' He raised her hand to his lips and pressed a kiss to her gloved knuckles before he opened the door and handed her down.

Wychavon House sat on Curzon Street, a tall three-storey townhouse painted white with sharp black shutters for contrast with long lace curtains draping the windows in perfect symmetry, the very epitome of discreet wealth and status. The perfect home for an earl. When he was in Town, this was where he'd spend his time from now on. Thea was not intimidated by the house; she'd been to Anne's in-laws before and to other fine homes during her visits to London, but she was struck afresh by what it represented—all the things she didn't know about Leopold. She'd known Edward as well as Edward had known himself. But Leopold was a stranger with a stranger's memories that she was not part of.

Leopold raised the brass lion's head knocker and flashed her one last private smile before the butler opened the door. 'The Earl of Wychavon and Miss Thea

Peverett to see the Dowager Countess of Wychavon, if you please, Peters,' he said with grave authority but Thea could see a smile twitching at his lips at the sight of the old retainer, a man, who from his obvious years, had seen a few generations of Swanns.

Peters did his best to answer with the same formality, but Thea did not miss the shine in his eyes or the pride in his voice as he said, 'Please do come in. I will announce you.'

The Earl of Wychavon was liked, Thea noted. But that was no surprise to her. Edward had charmed an MP and a vicar with nothing more than his personality.

Leopold ushered Thea inside and they followed Peters down a corridor bearing spotless white wainscoting, past walls hung with paintings she recognised as the works of Reynolds and Turner, past polished consoles bearing cut crystal vases filled with spring flowers. The butler led them to the morning room at the back of the house across from the garden and knocked on the door. 'My lady, you have guests. The Earl of Wychavon to see you,' he announced proudly. 'And Miss Thea Peverett.'

'Thank you, Peters.' The dowager's crisp tones answered the butler and that was the last of the formalities for quite some time. The butler discreetly shut the door behind him as Leopold was rushed by a gaggle of dark blonde females exclaiming over their brother all at once. There were tears too, as he embraced them each in turn. It was a beautiful reunion, Thea thought, watching from a few paces away, giving them all space to assure themselves that their beloved son and brother was home and hale.

'Oh, my dear boy, we thought you were lost for ever,'

his mother said at last, wiping at her eyes with a lace handkerchief. 'When the news about Inkerman came and we knew that Cathcart was lost and no one could find you, I feared the worst.'

'I am here, Mother, all thanks to the efforts of Miss Peverett, whom I think we've neglected sorely.' Leopold laughed and held out his hand, beckoning for her to join them. 'May I introduce Miss Thea Peverett of Miss Nightingale's nursing corps to you all? She is the reason I survived.' His hand was at her elbow as he made the introductions. 'This is my mother, Lady Wychavon, and my sister, Miss Juliette Swann, and my other sister, Miss Leonie. This is Lady Hardwick, my sister, Janet, and her husband, Lord Hardwick.'

Thea made a curtsy. 'I am so pleased to meet all of you.' She was pleased to meet them, she realised. More than once she'd wiped away a happy tear, watching the Swanns reunite. This was what she'd brought him home for, to find his place and his people. Watching him with his family was like fitting a key to a lock. He completed them and they completed him the way a final piece fitted into a puzzle to finish the shape. It was what she'd promised herself she'd do. Her work here was successful. It was also finished—a reminder that she needed to prepare herself to walk away. There was other work waiting for her, work that was not finished. She would find new purpose and new direction in that work. Her mysterious soldier was home.

'Miss Peverett? I feel that I know you,' Lady Hardwick said as they all took seats. 'Your name sounds familiar.'

Thea took a place beside Leopold on the yellow silk

settee with a shake of her head. 'I don't believe so, Lady Hardwick. I've been in the Crimea for several months and before that I worked at the Harley Street hospital for ill gentlewomen. I had no time to be out in Society.' It was best to be honest from the start. She did not intend to hide her life from them. She worked. She *liked* to work. She did it by choice. 'I was at the Duchess of Cowden's benefit ball for the hospital the year before last, so it's possible we may have crossed paths there.' But she did not recall the lovely Lady Hardwick with her applesauce-and-cinnamon hair.

Lady Hardwick shot a quick glance at her husband, a secret smile in her eyes. 'We were not in Town for the Little Season that year.' They would have been newly-weds by Thea's quick calculations based on what Leopold had shared in the carriage. Lady Hardwick cocked her head. 'Still, I feel I know your name.' She snapped her fingers. 'I know where I've heard it! You wrote a piece for *The Times* on the Sanitary Movement recently.'

'Yes, I did,' Thea affirmed as an enormous tea tray was brought in and the business of filling cups and plates deferred any further discussion. She hoped that would be the end of the subject, but Leopold didn't leave it alone.

'Miss Peverett has appointments in Town with Mr Rawdon, an MP from her home borough in Hertford-shire, to promote the health care offered to the soldiers in the Crimea.'

'You're a politician too, Miss Peverett? How admirable,' Lady Hardwick offered between sips of tea, but Thea noted she eschewed eating anything. She was definitely expecting and in the early months if smells and food were affecting her.

'How like Leo to be rescued by a famous nurse!' Juliette exclaimed with a toss of her blonde curls. Brother, you must tell us everything!'

Leo. Thea's heart squeezed. He had a nickname. How easily they fell to using it, as if he'd never been gone, as if he had never missed a moment of their lives. But, of course, he'd never been Edward to them.

Leopold favoured his family with a smile and gave them a sanitised version of his experience that spared them a true glimpse of the agony he'd suffered. 'Truly, Leo, you couldn't remember a single thing? Not even your own name?' Leonie was wide-eyed with amazement.

'No, I could not, but Miss Peverett never gave up. She kept searching, she kept sifting through my dreams looking for clues to follow, to help me find my way back, until it all clicked into place.'

The Dowager Countess leaned forward. 'Miss Peverett, we have so much to thank you for. Will you stay for supper? There is much to discuss and we must get to know you better.'

'In the meanwhile, I'll give you a tour of the gallery,' Leopold offered, implicitly accepting on her behalf as he stood. Perhaps he'd divined, not incorrectly, that she would take the chance to make her own exit. Better not to linger. It would hurt less in the long run, when she finally had to give him up.

Lady Hardwick and her husband rose too. 'We can't stay, unfortunately. Other obligations call, but I do expect to see you, brother, and Miss Peverett, at my ball next week. It will be the event of the Season, celebrating the return of the lost Earl, although I dare say the news will be all over London by tomorrow.' She shot a look towards her mother that Thea couldn't interpret. 'The news will spread, Mother. Someone somewhere knows he's been found. Someone at Whitehall, someone in the vast Tresham network. There are people who shouldn't find out in the Society pages, who should be told before then, privately.'

What people? Thea wondered. Aunts...uncles? Cousins? Extended family?

The Dowager Countess nodded. 'You're right, Janet. I'll have them to tea tomorrow, just us ladies. I think that would be the best way.' The Dowager turned hazel eyes, so like her son's, to Thea. 'Miss Peverett, it would be an honour to have you join us. I think you might lend a certain cache to the gathering. A tea is no place for a man.'

'Of course I'll be there,' Thea said, for she could hardly say anything else. The Dowager would think she was being generous by extending the invitation.

'Then all is settled.' Janet smiled and hugged Leopold. 'I am pleased beyond words to have you home safe. I want my children to know their uncle...' She blushed. 'John and I are expecting an event around Christmas, Leo. Isn't it wonderful?' She beamed, confirming Thea's suspicions. One more family member to remind Leopold where his duty lay.

'What a homecoming gift, to be an uncle,' Thea congratulated once they were alone in the gallery.

'Indeed it is.' Leopold grinned. 'It is beyond good to

see my family, to know they are well, that they've not suffered unduly in my absence. How are you bearing up?'

'I am fine,' Thea assured him. 'There's nothing to "bear". I am simply myself, Leopold, and unapologetically so. It does not matter to your family. I am just the nurse who rescued you, nothing more to them. They will fete me and offer me a few invitations in order to show their appreciation. Then they will expect you to be absorbed into your life as the Earl and for me to quietly fade away into mine.'

The Dowager was not her ally; did Leopold not see that? There'd be the tea and the ball to get through and by then it would be apparent enough that she was not countess material.

He bristled. 'You make them sound rather mercenary. It is poorly done, Thea. They're my family. You can't condemn them if you're not giving them all the facts. If they are not your immediate champions it is because they have no reason to be. If they think you are only a nurse to me, a nurse I no longer need, by the way, we can easily disabuse them of that notion if you would allow me.'

She shook her head. She could not allow it. He needed to see the lay of the land before he made such a public commitment. Only then would she permit it, although by then there would be nothing to permit. He would not want her. He would see the improbability of having such a wife as his Countess. She would not come between him and his family. It was one more reason to let him go, for his sake. He should not have to make such a choice.

'Tell me about these portraits,' she said, changing

the conversation. 'Is this you as a boy?' He'd been a handsome lad with bright eyes.

'Yes—' he laughed '—with my first pony. I was five when it was done. It was just Janet and I in those days. My other two sisters and Arthur were years away yet.'

'You would have been twelve when Arthur was born,' Thea mused.

'Yes, and away at school. He wasn't very interesting the first couple of years, but when *he* turned five, I saw to it that he had his own pony. My father had children quite late in life and, as such, his last few years were spent in declining health. He couldn't be much of a father to Arthur, not like he was to me.'

'So, you stepped in to be a brother and a father to him.' Of course he had. Here was a man who, even as Edward, a man with no memories, had a code of love and honour that ran deep, so deep that even the loss of memory couldn't dislodge it. As Edward, he'd worried about the implications of compromising her for fear of also compromising obligations he had to unseen others. As Edward, a man with no title or rank, he'd not hesitated to champion her against Clive Donnatt. She saw now where that code came from. He'd worried over his sisters and their Seasons, he'd worried over his mother's grief. He'd raised a young brother when his father could not, despite being away at university. This was a man who held the values of family as dear as she did. This was a man worthy of her love, if circumstances were different.

Of their own accord, their hands slipped into one another's grasp as they strolled past picture after picture, this one of an old relative, that one of an estate.

'Why did you join the military? It's not an heir's duty and you'd already inherited,' she asked as they came to the end of the gallery, the end of the Swann family history in pictures.

'I was not ready to be the Earl, even though I'd been the Earl in act for several years. I was the one who rode the land carrying out the business of the estates. I sat in meetings with my father and his stewards when his mind began to wander. I was twenty-five, and I felt as if I'd been the Earl since I was seventeen. In short, I was coming to resent the earldom. I understood it demanded my duty, and I had given it, but I felt it was stealing my life.' He gestured for them to sit on one of the plush cushioned square seats set in a line down the middle of the gallery and stretched his leg. He'd not brought his cane today and Thea thought he was feeling the effects of it.

'It's a bit embarrassing to confess it, Thea. Perhaps it was a moment of weakness, but I simply couldn't give any more. I'd finished university but I'd had to give up my Grand Tour due to my father's health, a chance to play the piano in Europe's great capitals, to see a bit of the world before settling down. But there was no question of that. Arthur was in need of a man's influence, Janet needed an escort for her Season, someone to play the role my father would have played in brokering a good match for her. The estates needed me. What I wanted had to wait. After seven years of it, I had to go.' He slid her a glance. 'Perhaps not unlike the reasons you had to come to London, to Harley Street?'

Thea understood that; the necessity to spread one's wings, to try and fly. 'I thought if I spent one more day in Hertfordshire, where everyone looked at me as if I were mad, I would absolutely become as mad as they believed. When Florence invited me to join her at Harley Street, I jumped at the chance.'

Leopold nodded. 'When General Cathcart invited me to join his staff as an aide, I thought it the prefect solution. Plenty of noblemen were going and aide de camps are kept out of harm's way. I could travel, have some of the adventure I'd given up, and the war looked to be a short one. If I was wrong, the earldom had Arthur in the wings. My mother didn't like the idea, but she understood the necessity for it.'

Thea laced her fingers through his with a soft laugh. 'My mother too. She was horrified at the thought of her daughters living in London on their own, but she'd raised us to be independent and she saw the necessity of letting us go.'

The late afternoon sun slanted through the long windows, turning Leopold's hair to burnished brass. His hazel gaze was thoughtful as he studied her. 'You've come full circle, Thea. You're back in London and you've accomplished so much since you were here last. You're an amazing woman.'

And he was an amazing man: committed to family, loyal to a fault. Just the sort she would have married if he wasn't an earl and all the things that made her amazing could ruin him. If she hadn't been sure of that before today, she was sure of it now.

Chapter Twenty-Four

Lady Wychavon's discreet tea was underway by the time Thea arrived the next afternoon, a good twenty minutes late. There'd been nothing for it; the meeting with Rawdon had run over and Thea had been hard pressed to gracefully extricate herself from the room full of eager women. She'd not taken time to change her gown, which would have necessitated arriving over an hour late. Her dark green carriage ensemble, which she'd left the house in that morning, would have to be smart enough for an afternoon call.

Peters met her at the door and showed her in, this time taking her upstairs to the drawing room, past more of the Wychavon opulence. The drawing room was significantly larger than the morning room. How many people had Lady Wychavon invited? Only eight, counting herself, as it turned out, and she knew four of them, those being Leopold's sisters and mother. Although it soon became clear that it wasn't the quantity that mattered here but the quality.

'My dear Miss Peverett.' The Dowager came forward to introduce her. 'You know my girls, of course.

Let me present our guests, the Marchioness of Stryde, her daughter Lady Elizabeth Towers and the Marchioness's companion, Mrs Elliott.' That explained the use of the drawing room, Thea thought. One must always impress a marchioness even if one was a countess. One had only to be in the Marchioness of Stryde's company for half a minute to know she expected and demanded the best of her surroundings.

'Miss Peverett, I am so glad to *finally* meet you. I was beginning to think you were a fiction.' The Marchioness gave an airy laugh that didn't hide the barb referring to Thea's lateness. One did not keep the Marchioness of Stryde waiting. Nor did Thea miss the sharp, dismissive perusal the Marchioness gave her ensemble.

Thea took the empty chair that had obviously been meant for her. 'I do apologise for being late, Lady Wychavon. It was not my intention, but my prior engagement ran longer than expected.' She made it clear that her apology was for her hostess and no one else. When it came to games of sharp words, she was the equal of anyone, marchionesses included. 'I was meeting with a group of ladies interested in the Crimean situation and explaining the circumstances at the Scutari Hospital where I was stationed.'

She took a teacup from Lady Wychavon and took the measure of the room over the rim of the delicate china. Had they invited her here to find her own level? Were they waiting for her to sink herself with her revelations? She was not naïve enough to think she had an ally in this room. Today, Leopold was not with her. She was on her own.

'I can't believe conditions are as bad as the papers

report.' The Marchioness raised a carefully cultivated disdaining brow. 'People will say anything for a bit of attention and once they've got it, they'll do anything to keep it, even fomenting riots with their untruths.' By 'people' the Marchioness meant Florence and others who dared to report the reality behind the military lines. That moniker included her too. She'd written an article on the subject.

'You refer to the snowball riot this past January?' Thea enquired. That riot had been pivotal in getting necessary change.

'Not a riot, Miss Peverett, an *insurrection.*' The Marchioness spat the word. 'Prime Minister Aberdeen resigned over it. Now Palmerston is demanding an account of every casualty and man in the British army.' She made it sound as if the demand were unreasonable.

It was all to the good, in Thea's opinion. 'As he should, my lady. Did you know that the usual ratio of loss is a two per cent casualty rate in battle? But the British forces have lost twenty-five per cent of the men who went to the Crimea. It is unheard of. Not even the French have lost as many men, and for no good reason.' She went on to enumerate the failings of the British army, of which there were many, from miscommunication during manoeuvres to mismanagement of supply lines that left men far afield and unsupported. 'So much loss was preventable.'

'We must always remember that our dear Wycha-von was nearly among those lost, Mama.' Lady Elizabeth spoke for the first time, laying a gentle hand on her mother's arm.

Thea did not miss the '*dear Wychavon*' or the softness with which it was said, or the slightest blush that followed the reference. What was it that Lady Hardwick had said yesterday? That there were those who needed to know before news of Leopold's return became common knowledge? These were the two who needed to know. It begged the question in her quick mind, what was the Lady Elizabeth Towers to 'dear Wychavon'?

'I, for one, Miss Peverett, am so grateful for whatever assistance you offered Wychavon, for bringing him home safe to those who love him.' She rose. 'Perhaps you'd like to take a turn around the room with me so that we might talk further?' It was the last thing Thea wanted to do. She was keenly aware of how her height and dark hair; her age and her plain carriage ensemble would look next to the dew-tinged youthfulness and sartorial beauty of Miss Elizabeth Towers. The girl was no more than twenty and she was dressed in the height of fashion in an exquisitely made afternoon gown of the finest white linen that boasted hours of embroidery at its hem. But there was nothing insincere in her tone and no grounds on which to resist the invitation.

'Thank you so much for walking with me,' Lady Elizabeth began once they were out of earshot of her mother and the Dowager Countess. 'I have a delicate question to ask, and you seem the person who would know.' Again, the rosy blush. 'It's intimate in nature, and Mother would flay me alive if she knew I was asking, but a girl needs to know these things. It's about Wychavon's injuries.' She lowered her voice to a mere whisper. 'Will he be able to…' She couldn't quite finish her sentence without blushing furiously. She tried again. 'Will he be able to…?'

Make love, make babies, make a woman feel like she's the sum of his world?

Oh, yes, he could do that. Thea debated the merits of finishing the girl's sentence for her. She was searching her vocabulary for the right delicate phrasing by which she might refer to the act Miss Elizabeth apparently could not, when Elizabeth found her tongue again. 'Dance. Will he be able to dance? To ride? He is, *was*, a lovely dancer. Every girl wanted to dance with him and he was such a bruising rider. No one ever looked half as handsome in the saddle as he did when he rode to hounds at Papa's estate.'

Oh, thank goodness she'd not finished the girl's sentence for her. 'Yes, in time he'll be able to dance and ride. He only uses a cane on occasion now as it is. He's made remarkable progress.' But his leg would probably always pain him as he aged or when the weather turned cold. That kind of wound never healed entirely.

Miss Elizabeth looked crestfallen at the news. 'He won't be able to dance at Lady Hardwick's ball.'

'He might manage a dance or two,' she offered.

'How awful that he uses a cane,' Lady Elizabeth murmured.

'I disagree. How wonderful that is all he needs, how wonderful he hasn't lost his leg altogether,' Thea corrected, bristling in Leopold's defence. 'How wonderful he's able to get out of bed when for months he could do no such thing.' She grew impatient with the pretty girl.

'And is there a scar?' she asked timidly, as if that were the worst fate imaginable. Perhaps it was to a girl who'd clearly been raised to put great value in one's looks.

'Yes, there most certainly is, a badge of bravery if

you ask me.' Thea tried to counteract her assumption that scars equated with ugliness.

Elizabeth gave her a shrewd look at odds with her dewy appearance, a reminder that debutantes had claws. 'I think you're the sort of woman who would tell me her opinion even if I didn't ask.' It was the first intelligent thing the girl had said, perhaps she ought to give her more credit.

'A wife must get used to such things, I suppose.' Elizabeth gave a quick downward cast of her eyes and another rosy blush.

A wife. The words froze Thea. Lady Elizabeth was staking her claim. She felt entitled to Leopold. How dare the girl when Leopold was hers? He'd made love to her, kissed her, whispered his fears and dreams to her. She'd seen him through illness. Every bone in her body cried out that he was hers.

Is he? Why does it matter? the voice in her head whispered. *You are giving him up anyway. Lady Elizabeth is countess material in every way that you are not.*

But it did matter because he'd made promises to her, he'd chosen her even after his memories had returned. Why would he say such things to her if he planned to marry Lady Elizabeth? But then came the rebuttal: why hadn't he told her about Elizabeth once his memories had come back?

You know the answer. Because men lie to you, because no man has ever wanted you before. Why should Leopold Swann be any different?

But he is, he is, her heart insisted, even as her stomach churned with foreboding, even as her mind said coolly, *It doesn't matter, you were going to let him go anyway. Best to let him go before he lets you go.*

'Miss Peverett? Are you well?' Lady Elizabeth asked. 'You seem pale; perhaps we should sit down?'

Sitting down only made the moil in her head worse. None of this made sense. Why would Leopold have not told her about Elizabeth? Why would he insist he loved her, that she come to London with him, if *this* waited for him? Wouldn't it have made sense to give in to her arguments and leave her in Haberstock?

It was impossible to sort through it when the conversation swirling about her was all to Lady Elizabeth Towers' advantage: Lady Elizabeth's mother and the Dowager dredging up past memories. How handsome they looked together taking the hedges at Stryde's Sussex estate, the one that bordered Wychavon's seat. What a pair they'd made at Elizabeth's birthday ball, nearly stopping the dancing with the way they'd waltzed together, so mesmerising, so graceful, everyone had wanted to stare. They praised Elizabeth's skill with the needle and with the piano, how wondrous she and Leopold were when they performed a duet. It was the last that was a dagger in Thea's heart. She'd performed duets with Leopold. That was her memory; he'd been her champion that night. How awful to discover he'd made that memory with someone else first.

Talk turned to the Hardwick ball. 'Madame Gustave has made the most divine creation for Elizabeth,' the Marchioness said with pride, describing a gown that had cost a small fortune. 'When Leopold sees her in it… Well, it will be a divine moment.'

'Miss Peverett, do you have a gown for the Hardwick ball?' The Dowager enquired. 'I need to take Juliette and Leonie for their fittings. I would be more than happy to ask my modiste to find something for you.'

The Dowager was a cool piece of work, Thea thought. She'd not once done or said anything that would be taken amiss. No one could accuse her of sounding the wolves to chase off this interloper—her. She'd let the Marchioness and Miss Elizabeth do the work for her. Thea thought of her dark blue gown, the one she'd worn almost two years ago to the Duchess of Cowden's charity ball. She'd brought it to London just in case.

'I have a dress that will suit, although your offer is very kind.' The last was a lie. There was nothing kind about it. It was likely another ploy to remind her of her place. Her gown would be too plain for their tastes but it suited her perfectly. This was what she'd feared, this pressure to change, not that a fancy ball gown would make her acceptable to them, but it was a start—a start down a slippery slope of changes.

She set down her teacup. 'This has been an interesting afternoon, ladies, but I must take my leave.' Before she broke down and admitted to a broken heart, before she admitted to having been taken in again. Lady Elizabeth was meant to be Leopold's.

Thea managed to escape from the room, but she got no farther than the foyer before Leopold walked through the door, his face lighting up at the sight of her. 'Thea, what luck to find you still here. I wanted to hear about your...' he began, his smile freezing as he registered her stormy countenance. 'Thea, what's happened? You look ready to hurl thunderbolts. Not at me, I hope?'

'That depends,' she said in a tone that belied her true

feelings. 'Do you have an understanding with Lady Elizabeth Towers?' She speared him with her gaze, searching his eyes for any clues, not sure what she wanted to find: validation that he had lied to her? That he, like other men, had treated love as a game? Or that he'd told her the truth, that he loved her, that he chose her, which would pit him against Society and others that he loved. Neither was a good choice.

'No, of course not, no promises were made.' He put a steadying hand on her arm and glanced about the corridor, hazarding a look upstairs towards the drawing room. 'Might we talk about this somewhere private?' His tones were low, his eyes sincere. 'Just for a moment, please, Thea, in the garden.'

They walked silently to the back of the house and let themselves into the garden. 'This is becoming a bad habit, of holding difficult conversations in gardens,' Thea said, thinking back to the garden at Haberstock Hall. Had it only been a few days ago they'd been in Hertfordshire? Only a week since his memories had returned and Edward had disappeared? Edward seemed a lifetime ago already and yet her heart still ached for him.

'Does it take so little to doubt me?' He faced her, his arms crossed over his chest. 'One afternoon with an ambitious marchioness and you are willing to take her word over mine?' he asked quietly, but there was no mistaking the steel that underlay his words.

'No, of course not,' Thea began, He'd backed her to the wall with his words, just as he had pinned Donnatt at supper. Back then, she'd never imagined that sharp insight would be turned in her direction. But back then she'd never had reason to doubt him.

'Then why did you? The Marchioness of Stryde has been eyeing the earldom for her daughter before Elizabeth was even out in Society. She likes the adjoining estates and her husband likes our coffers. Wychavon won't be draining her dowry to cover debts. The marquessate of Stryde may have its eyes on the earldom, but I do not have my sights set on Stryde.' He paused, making sure he had her whole attention. 'Thea, my sights are set on you.'

'Your mother's are not,' Thea answered with a stern whisper. 'She sat in that drawing room and ensured I compared myself to the pristine Elizabeth at every turn, and that when I made the comparison I came up lacking.' She could barely control her voice.

'And did you? Come up lacking?' Leopold pressed.

'No, because the things that are important to your mother and the Marchioness are not important to me. I work. I've returned to my position at the Harley Street hospital as of this morning. They cannot fathom such a thing. I have a political cause that I interact with in a practical manner while they throw a charity ball.' She was nearly shaking, overcome with the emotion she'd bottled in the drawing room. Her greatest concerns were coming to life and it had only taken a few days. 'This is exactly what I feared would happen. That people would ask for compromises, implicitly, but compromises, nonetheless. That who I am would not be well received. Worst of all, you are being put in a position where you will have to choose between me and your family. I will *not* do that to you.' If he chose her, he would be fighting that battle the rest of his life with Society, with his family. There would be no peace for him.

It seemed to Thea that a shadow had crossed the sun, that the garden was darker than it had been a few moments ago. Her heart certainly was. This was how and where it would end between her and Leopold. She had to free him before the situation intensified, before other relationships were harmed in a misguided effort to fight for them.

'Do I not get a say? Do you and my mother and the Marchioness of Stryde get to decide for me?'

'Offering counsel is not "deciding for you",' Thea replied sharply. 'It's helping you to see the situation clearly from all angles.'

His hazel eyes flashed with a streak of temper. 'If it were up to me, I would have you against the fence in a moment's notice. I would kiss you senseless and never let you leave my arms. I've wanted to hold you, kiss you, make love to you so many times since that night at the May fair, but every step I make towards you, towards our life together, you step back.'

'Do not make this my fault.' Thea bristled. 'I'm not the Earl with a countess-in-waiting sitting in my drawing room. I am what I've always been. I'm not the one who changed.'

'I did not change, Thea, only my name. I need you to move past that.' His voice was quiet, tired almost as if the fight was leaving him at last. There was hurt in his eyes where anger had flashed so recently.

'I can't, Leopold. I can't move past it and neither should you. What you are now cannot be ignored.' She swallowed hard. Leaving him was far more difficult than her logic had told her it would be. Leaving him was the rational decision. She'd even convinced herself it was the emotional decision too. If she truly loved him, she would do what was best for him: set him free to pursue the kind of wife he needed. It would be best for her too. She was setting herself free to pursue the things she'd convinced herself mattered the most to her.

But all that was forgotten when he stood before her, saying such wondrous things. *'If it were up to me, I would have you against the fence...'*

'Goodbye, Leopold.' She had only the resolve left for those two words. The time for argument, the time for reasoning, for hoping they'd mutually decide to part ways had passed.

She turned and left the garden without a backward glance. He might think her cold, but if he could have seen her face, he would never have let her leave the garden. She would go home and grieve and then she'd go to work, burying memories of Leopold beneath Rawdon's committees, the hospital, the Movement, the joy of holding her nephew and being with family and a hundred other things until the ache went away. She was sure this was for the best.

Chapter Twenty-Five

He should not have let her leave the garden. That had been a tactical error on his part. Leo turned the note over in his hand, staring at the unbroken seal. Thea had returned it to him unopened—the second one in three days. He'd thought to give her space, time to sort out her emotions and her priorities. Now, reality was settling in. Perhaps she had sorted through her emotions and priorities and he'd been the one sorted out, relegated to the pile of things Thea Peverett could live without.

But he could not live without her. Three days away from her had been enough to show him that. He found himself listening for her step in the hall and the sound of her voice. He found himself turning to ask her a question or expecting to find her in the garden as if they were still at Haberstock Hall. There was work to be done, ledgers to be reviewed and he could concentrate on none of it. He spent his days in the music room at the piano, lost in the music, lost in the memories. He'd gone from being a man with too few memories to being a man with too many, all of them of her: the piano at

Haberstock, the day he'd remembered how to play, the night he'd played the duet with her.

There were other memories too. He had hundreds to pick from: the first day he'd come downstairs and seen her in the green dress, market day and chocolates under the tree, trailing behind her in the cottage as she told him what she'd done that day, making love to her on John Anderson's big carved bed, making love to her on the picnic blanket outside of Hoddesdon, making love to her in the cottage barn…making love to her with his body, his words, his touch, his hopes, and in those memories she'd made love to him with the same: her body, her words, her touch, her hopes. And now she'd left him, taking those hopes with her and declaring he'd changed.

His hands crashed on the keys in a loud, discordant cacophony. That was just an excuse, a convenient distraction from something else he was having a difficult time facing. He'd been so focused on choosing her, he'd not stopped to consider whether or not she'd choose him. Whether he'd been Edward or Leopold, her resistance had always been there, hadn't it? She'd resisted the idea of a surgery at the cottage, she'd resisted coming to London for him. She'd only relented on the grounds of having her own invitation from Rawdon and her own purpose in coming. Dammit, how had he not seen this before? Thea had told him point blank she didn't want to marry and in his arrogance, he'd thought she meant she didn't want to marry in general, but perhaps she'd want to marry him, the 'right' man for her. He banged his fist on the piano keys. Dammit, dammit, dammit.

He'd been so blind. He'd pushed and he'd pushed, and in doing so he'd pushed her away.

'Darling, is everything all right?' His mother stood in the doorway, concern etched on her features, the day's news sheets in her hand. She'd come straight from her morning correspondence. His banging had worried her. She glanced at the unopened note on the music rack of the piano. 'Miss Peverett has returned your note?' His note, his heart, but not his affections. He'd not discussed the tea with his mother; there'd seemed no point until he and Thea resolved things between them. In truth, he was wondering how much of the blame could be assigned to the tea? Perhaps not as much as he'd like. Thea's resistance had been there long before tea with the Marchioness. The tea had merely brought matters to a head.

Returning unopened notes was more than merely ignoring someone; it was a cut direct delivered by mail.

'Miss Peverett disdains my company.' How had it happened so fast? One day they were facing the world together, making promises, and the next she'd simply said goodbye and walked out of his garden.

His mother sat in a chair near the piano, perhaps sensing that this would be a longer conversation. She settled the newspapers beside her. 'She was never meant to stay, son. It was bound to happen. I am sure that it leaves something of a gap for you. You've lived in one another's pockets for months now in ways I can only imagine. You must feel that you owe her something. She saved your life, she brought you home, she helped restore your memories by reaching out to others when you could not. We are all grateful to her and always will be, but that's not a reason to think she'll be with you every day.' Only she would be, Leopold thought. If not physically, she'd be in his heart, in his mind, in his every waking thought and every night-time dream.

'She is part of me.' Leo tried to put it into words.

'She is part of your past. She's a nurse; she's perhaps more aware of how these attachments form than you are. She's probably been through this before with other patients. She understands. She's a smart woman, son. If she's chosen to separate immediately and completely, it's because she knows it's for the best. She understands that you reached out to her at a time when you were alone, and you begged her to stay. And she stayed, because that's her job. Her job was done the moment you set foot in Wychavon House.'

It was more than a job. He knew it in his bones.

He wanted to yell, *We made love three times—three glorious times! I fed her chocolates from my hand, she threw a pie at a man who meant to humiliate me, we championed one another. That is not a job!*

But how did he explain that to his mother in reasonable terms? How did he explain it to that part of himself who had posed the rather cynical question: would she have chosen him? So instead he said, 'Elizabeth was at the tea. I thought it would just be you, the Marchioness and the girls.'

His mother waved a hand to dismiss the concern as inconsequential. 'How could I not invite Elizabeth? She goes where her mother goes and she deserved to know you'd returned.'

'Thea deserved to be warned about that. I believe Elizabeth confided some rather shocking things to Thea, things that Elizabeth had no right to claim. There is nothing binding between us, although Elizabeth led Thea to believe there was.' Of course that was Elizabeth's fault, not his mother's.

'Elizabeth is young; she will make mistakes, but she will learn.'

'As someone else's wife, not my own. Let us be clear about that. No matter what happened with Thea, I am not marrying Lady Elizabeth Towers. This is not a case of either or.'

His mother's brow furrowed for a moment as she processed the statement. 'Ah, I was right then. I did think there was something more between you and Miss Peverett. The way you sat together, so close, so comfortable in one another's presence. Did you think to marry *her*? It would not have suited. Society would not have tolerated the match.'

'Would you tolerate it?' He refused to talk about it in the past tense. This was not over.

His mother held out the newspapers. 'When I heard the piano noise I thought you'd seen these. Have you? Society has not even officially met her yet and they are being unkind.'

Leopold took the papers, the pages already folded back. The first was a column. He scanned and read.

Rumour has it that the missing Earl of Wychavon has been returned to his rightful place, mostly recovered from severe wounds sustained in the Crimea, thanks to the care of one Miss P, a nurse known for her outspoken views on health care and in whose home he spent two months recu-

*perating before venturing to London, his dutiful
nurse by his side.*

*How lucky for her to have such an illustrious
patient. It will, no doubt, protect what is left of
her reputation.*

The next paper was less polite, insinuating that Thea
was fortune-hunting, hoping to use his sense of gratitude to snare herself a husband at long last. The third
was a political cartoon featuring a rabid Thea foaming
at the mouth as she spouted the credos of the Sanitary
Movement, a leash around her neck being held by Florence Nightingale.

'Who published this?' He looked up, his jaw tight.
'I will buy up every copy—this is trash!' There was
more being implied in the cartoon than simply mocking a political movement.

'You can't buy them all up for ever.' His mother took
back the papers and folded them carefully beside her.
'Do you think this won't happen again?'

No, he didn't think that. With Thea, it would be a
regular occurrence if she decided to live a public political life, a life which women were not encouraged to
pursue, although Rawdon seemed to have no compunc-
tion about joining forces with her, nor she with him.
Did she prefer a man like Rawdon to him? The thought
gnawed at him.

'Who shared this information?' After he bought out
the printer's copies of the cartoon, he'd go after who
had ever imparted such lurid speculation about him
and Thea. He did not fool himself; most of the specu-

lation had been directed towards Thea, painting him as a misguided victim.

'Anyone could have access to that information,' his mother argued. 'Stryde, anyone who might have run into Hardwick at his clubs and passed the information on. You know how information travels in this society.'

Yes, he did. None of it accurate, the message reshaping itself each time it was told, until speculation layered upon speculation. He did not think Hardwick would be so indiscreet. But he did think Stryde would see it done, perhaps goaded to it by his wife in an attempt to solidify the alliance they coveted.

'You did not defend Thea at the tea. Why? I've never known you to be manipulative or unkind.'

'I did not know for sure there was a reason to defend her. If she was just your nurse, it was not worth angering the Marchioness. If Miss Peverett was more than your nurse, I wanted to see her mettle. Who was driving this relationship? Both of you? Or was she using you? Taking advantage of your gratitude, perhaps? I will not tolerate my son being misled by such a woman. But Miss Peverett can handle herself; she didn't need me, I assure you.' There was a gleam of appreciation in his mother's eye as she said the last.

'And yet she left here, left *me*, under a cloud.' The sight of her in the garden was imprinted on his mind. She'd not wanted to leave him. She'd felt she had to. Because she cared for him. A woman who didn't care, who wanted to be free of entanglements would not have argued with him, would have simply walked away, uncaring if he saw reason or not. Thea was not a selfish woman. She'd not wanted to hurt him; she'd argued because she wanted him to see reason, to accept the decision so that perhaps he'd agree, so that the hurt would sting less with understanding. Even in her pain, Thea had been trying to save him. Hope flickered.

'If she is your choice, it will be a difficult road always, unless she chooses to conform, and I suspect she won't. Unlike so many women, she has a mind of her own.' His mother gave a smile. 'But I know a little something about that. I have three headstrong daughters of my own, and a son too stubborn to die. We are your family, Leo, and we will support you and your choice, no matter how difficult.'

'Thank you, Mother.' He rose. 'If you'll excuse me, I have my marching orders now, I believe.' For the first time since Thea had left him in the garden, he felt focused, full of purpose.

He had dragons to slay. First the printers, then the club, and finally the Harley Street hospital to determine, once and for all, if Thea would choose him, instead of her fears. It wasn't the title she had to get past, it was herself.

Thea couldn't get past the first page of the report she was drafting, a numerical accounting of supplies used in Scutari, purchased from Florence's personal funds. She had the numbers in her journals; she needed only to translate those numbers into a report and analyse them and show the importance of those accounts. But tonight the effort was beyond her. She told herself it was because it was the end of a very long day, the end of a series of long days. She'd worked three twelve-hour shifts in the last three days, looking over the hospital's ledgers and updating patient records and writing a long letter to Florence to let her know the state of things. There was no need beyond personal desire to have assigned herself so much work, but it was the only cure she knew.

Thea put her pen aside and rolled her shoulders. She did not regret what she'd said in the garden. It had been not a moment too soon. The papers had wasted no time noting her presence at Leopold's side and speculating on it. Her work had caught the printer's attention too, or, rather, someone had whispered in a printer's ear about her meetings and the earlier article she'd written. Leopold would be glad she was gone. He must have thanked her foresight. The moment he'd opened the papers this morning. He would know now that it was for the best. She just wished it didn't hurt so much. She wished she didn't think about him even when she was supposed to be thinking about something else.

'Miss Peverett—' one of the young nurses interrupted, breathless, her colour high as if she'd been running '—there's a man here, and he's hurt.'

Thea was in motion at once, rushing past the nurse, asking questions as she ran towards the front of the building. 'How hurt? Is he bleeding? Gunshot? Knife wound?' Perhaps it had happened in the street; goodness knew, London was rife with crime. Why else would a man show up at a hospital for women?

'I don't think so, ma'am.' The nurse struggled to keep up with her long strides. 'I think it's his hand, but it was bloody.' A cut most likely then.

'Fetch me hot water and bandages, and ice if we have any. We'll treat him in the front parlour.' Where his presence might go unremarked by the patients and less likely to cause a disturbance if he didn't get past the foyer.

Going around the last corner, Thea came to an abrupt stop. This wasn't just any man; this was Leopold Swann, standing in the entrance, his cravat undone, his shirt open at the throat, his hair messed, his right hand bloody and cradled by his left, a thick sheaf of papers nearly the size of a quire tucked beneath his left arm. He had the beginnings of a black eye too, which the nurse had forgotten to mention.

'Leopold, what has happened?' She had him by the elbow, guiding him to the front parlour, her concern stripping away all else, her feelings flooding to the fore at the sight of him hurt. Someone brought the hot water and supplies.

He sat down heavily on the settee. 'I brought you a present.' He reached for the papers tucked beneath his arm. She took them, recognising the lurid cartoon that had come out that morning and gave him a quizzical look. It was an odd present and there must be hundreds of them here. 'I bought them all—all that I could.'

'Did the printer punch you?' Thea hid her trembling hands in the papers as the realisation swamped her. He'd bought out a print run. Why would he do such a thing? But she knew why. Because Leopold wouldn't give up on her, on them, even when he should. What was she going to do with him? She couldn't leave him if he wouldn't be left.

He gave a raspy laugh. 'No, the printer made money. Men don't punch men bearing pound notes.'

'Then what happened?' She dabbed a warm rag on

the cut on his swollen hand, his beautiful piano-playing hand. He should be more careful.

'I punched the Marquess of Stryde at the club earlier this evening.' He shrugged. 'I'm sorry, Thea. There will be a bit of a scandal. It's already making the rounds. It will be in the papers tomorrow.'

'And he hit you back?' Thea surmised, rinsing the rag.

'In my defence, he looks worse, and it was indeed the best brawl the club has seen in ages.' Leopold chuckled as she carefully wound long strips of bandage around his hand. 'I don't think the papers will have anything else to top it for a few days, not until my sister's ball at any rate, and then I'll be back in the news again, returned Earl and all that.'

Thea sat back on her heels and studied him in silence. 'What am I to do with you, Leo?' She didn't pretend not to recognise what he had done. He was her champion, once more deflecting attention away from her so that she might find her feet. 'You can't buy out all the printers and punch all the men who will say things about me.' Although the thought of what he'd done today warmed her in dangerous ways. She could not let herself be moved. 'It will happen again, Leo,' she said softly. 'The world is not kind to women who speak their mind.'

'But I am. Perhaps that's all that matters, Thea.' He held up his hand and studied the bandages with a smile. 'I've been miserable these past three days. I'm no good without you, Thea. I kept torturing myself, thinking that I had chosen you but you had not chosen me, that you wouldn't choose me. That you loved freedom more than me, that I was just an experience you were looking to acquire.' He paused with a frown. 'But I couldn't quite get myself to believe it. The way you made love with your whole soul. No woman makes love like that without meaning it.' He reached out his good hand and stroked her cheek, his touch warm against her skin. How she'd missed his touch. Part of her started to melt; this was not good. She needed to be stronger than this.

'You kept saying it was the earldom you resisted, but that wasn't it. You weren't resisting me—you were defending yourself.' He held her gaze. 'You have to open the gates of your castle, Thea. You have to get past yourself, give yourself permission to love me.'

'I do love you, Leopold. Too much to ruin you.'

He saw her too clearly; all her resources were stripped away. He understood every ploy, every obstacle and he rendered them to nothing more than smokescreens.

'Tell me you haven't been miserable since you walked out of the garden.'

'It's not that simple, Leo.'

'It is. I want to marry you. I want you to be my unconventional Countess. I want you to educate people about sanitation and germs, I want you to lead the fight for our soldiers, I want you to come to work here at the hospital as much as you'd like. I want you to rewrite the rules of what a countess can and should do, or perhaps I just want you to remind people of what countesses were meant to do all along, and that is to take care of their people.' He gave her a sheepish grin. 'Most of all, I want you to love me, and I want to love you to the fullest of my abilities. I don't give a damn about anything else; tell me you don't either.' He leaned into her then, pressing a soft kiss to her mouth that had her melting when she ought to have been thinking about who might walk in, who might see. 'Will you choose me, Thea? We make each other happy. We make each other whole.'

He would not ask again; his determined hazel eyes said as much. Every word he'd uttered had been entirely serious. There would be no second chance. He was right about all of it. She had to let go of her defences in order to really let him in.

'Are you sure you're willing to spend your life fighting the Clive Donnatts of the world?' She felt those defences crumbling. She bent her forehead to his and they were cocooned in a world of their own.

'Yes, if I need to, although I have it on good authority you throw a mean pie. Between your pies and my punches, we should fare pretty well.' He was kissing her again. 'But I need the words, Thea. I need to hear you say it.'

'Yes,' she whispered beneath his mouth.

Yes to him, yes to her, yes to a life together...a life she'd once thought was beyond her.

Epilogue

Lady Hardwick's ball would be the talk of the Season for more than one reason. Not only did she host the newly returned Earl of Wychavon, whose survival story had quickly supplanted the reports of his fisticuffs with the Marquess of Stryde in Society's short attention span, but she could also claim her ball as Wychavon's engagement fete, when he announced to Society his betrothal, right before the supper waltz, to the woman who'd saved him, Miss Thea Peverett. It would be a short engagement. The Earl of Wychavon had made it clear that he had a special licence in his pocket even as the engagement was announced.

'The gossips will have something to say about your haste,' Thea commented as Leo led her to the floor for the supper dance. He had not danced all night, but he'd insisted on having one dance with his betrothed.

He winked as he pulled her to him. 'If I don't dance with you now, it will be too late. You won't be my betrothed for long.' By the weekend, it would be a fait accompli, done in a private ceremony among family.

'I can hardly wait for the wedding, though, because it means the wedding night won't be far behind.' They would honeymoon in Haberstock in their cottage with the blue shutters for the remainder of the summer before moving on to tour his estates in the autumn.

The music began and he moved her into a slow waltz. She did not care if it was slower than the other couples around them, or that it might be slightly off the tempo. It was what they could manage and she was grateful for it. She knew how close it had been to him never waltzing again.

'This is a miracle,' she whispered up to him, 'to be dancing with you, to be marrying you.'

'We are going to change the world, Thea. You've already changed mine.' He stole a kiss.

'And you've changed mine,' she whispered. 'That's how we'll do it, one life at a time.' His hands slipped to her waist and he drew her close. She breathed in the scent of him and twined her arms about his neck, not caring that they'd broken protocol. They'd break so much more than that before they were through. Society would need to get used to it. 'Everyone talks about how I saved you, but I know better. You didn't just change my life, you saved it, every bit as much as I saved yours.'

'I think partnerships work best that way, Thea.' He laughed, resting his chin on her head. 'I'd say let's go home, but I am already there.'

'Me too.' She raised her head to meet his gaze. Once she'd figured out home was a person, the rest was easy.

* * * * *